PRAISE FOR TRISHA DAS

'Will leave the readers in splits and is a perfect read.'

Times of India

'Das seamlessly weaves issues affecting contemporary life, giving fiction the perfect depth of reality. A saucy amuse-bouche.'

ELLE

'Das writes with great wit and imagination.'

Hindustan Times

'One of the modern writers to consider who are questioning, portraying, and contributing a significant amount to the conversation about who is a strong woman and what can be construed as woman power.'

Jaya Bhattacharji

The Grand Samara

ALSO BY TRISHA DAS

Ms Draupadi Kuru: After the Pandavas
The Misters Kuru: A Return to Mahabharata
Kama's Last Sutra
The Mahabharata Re-imagined
The Art of the Television Interview
How to Write a Documentary Script

The Grand Samara

Trisha Das

BLOOMSBURY
NEW DELHI • LONDON • OXFORD • NEW YORK • SYDNEY

BLOOMSBURY INDIA
Bloomsbury Publishing India Pvt. Ltd
Second Floor, LSC Building No. 4, DDA Complex, Pocket C – 6 & 7,
Vasant Kunj, New Delhi, 110070

BLOOMSBURY, BLOOMSBURY INDIA and the Diana logo
are trademarks of Bloomsbury Publishing Plc

First published in the United States of America as *Never Meant to Stay*
by Amazon Crossing, Seattle 2023
First published in India 2024
This edition published 2024
This edition is made possible under a licence arrangement originating
with Amazon Publishing, www.apub.com.

ISBN: PB: 978-93-61318-25-2; eBook: 978-93-61319-97-6
2 4 6 8 10 9 7 5 3 1

Typeset in Bembo Std by Manipal Technologies Limited
Printed and bound in India by Replika Press Pvt. Ltd

For sale in the Indian Subcontinent only

FSC
www.fsc.org
MIX
Paper | Supporting responsible forestry
FSC™ C016779

To find out more about our authors and books visit www.bloomsbury.com and sign up for our newsletters

To Ma and Naniji: for being my army,
for being my home

CHAPTER 1

'Would you like a Bhetkilini? Or a Negrui?' the bartender asked with an expression no less serious than a nurse asking if she was allergic to penicillin.

Samara Mansingh frowned and focused really hard on his mouth, as if that would make sense of the question. 'What are those?'

The bartender flipped his Viking braid over one shoulder and pointed to a blackboard menu adorned with illustrations of fish. 'They're cocktails,' he replied. 'The bride's late grandmother was Bengali, so today's signature cocktails are named after her favourite Bengali fish: bhetki and rui. And before you ask'—he rolled his eyes—'there's no fish, fish scales, fish sauce, or fish oil in the drinks.'

Despite her frustration with this particular event she was photographing in South Delhi, Samara had to smile. 'How many times have you been asked that today?'

The bartender's eye roll became a full-on snort. 'Every second guest has asked if the drinks are vegetarian or vegan. One guy actually *wanted* fish in his drink. Oh, and about a dozen people asked if the gin in the Negrui is organic.' He shook his head. 'These weddings are out of control, man.'

Samara had to agree with him—some of these weddings *were* out of control. Case in point was today's assignment, a pre-wedding photo shoot for the immediate family and friends of the bride and groom. The hosts had made an occasion out of it, a poolside 'Photo Shoot Party' on the rooftop of a five-star hotel. As though the gorgeous pool and expansive view weren't enough, the surrounding gardens were littered with giant movie-set-like props: an elaborately decorated gazebo, enormous letters spelling out the bride's and groom's names, a massive pomander pit that was at least four feet deep, a mechanical rodeo bull, and even a huge statue of Ganesha, complete with an altar for prayer. Samara was one of two on-site photographers, along with a drone-photography team, a videography team, an art director, wedding planners, and a passel of hair and makeup artists.

All this was just for the family and friends. The couple had already had a separate photo shoot with a celebrity photographer. Samara hadn't been hired for that one.

'I'll just have water, please,' she told the bartender after taking a deep breath. The event had started late, which was pretty standard—absolutely nothing started on time in Delhi—but then it had progressed at a painfully slow pace. Two hours in, many of the guests were drunk, and getting them to pose for photos was an exercise in endurance. Samara took the camera strap off her stiff neck and sipped the ice water the bartender handed her.

Her phone buzzed in her pocket, and she scooped it out. It was her best friend, Maya, calling from New York.

The second she took the call, Maya's plaintive voice blasted into her ear, *'Come back!'*

Samara laughed. 'What happened?'

Maya launched into what was now a well-worn tirade. 'I'm in roommate purgatory! Neel's stopped washing his dishes, and Sylvia Prat—possibly the most depressing name ever, by the way—keeps leaving her leather and fur thongs soaking in the bathroom sink. I don't get it. What kind of person spends thousands of dollars to have it all lasered off, only to wear fur on top?'

Samara couldn't help another laugh. Her bestie was such a writer.

'I'm serious, Sammy,' Maya whined. 'When are you coming back?'

Absently stroking her camera on the bar counter, Samara exhaled.

It was a good question, one for which she didn't have an answer. Yet. 'I don't know, babe.' She'd been camping with her father at his ministry-issued apartment in Delhi for a year now, making the rounds as a high-end wedding photographer after completing her degree in photography at New York University. 'I've applied for more jobs in the city than I can count, but . . . nothing so far. Well, at least nothing that'll pay the bills. There are unpaid internships aplenty. Besides,' she continued, 'you won't believe how much money I'm making photographing weddings here. It's only November, not even halfway through wedding season, and not only have I already been to Mauritius, Sri Lanka, Thailand, and Dubai, but I got paid in US dollars!'

Silence greeted her exuberant words, the line crackling uncomfortably for a few moments. Then, Maya asked in an accusing voice, 'Why does it sound like you're having fun shooting big fat Indian weddings? You should be miserable, waiting to come back so we can live together, like college.'

'I *do* want to come back,' replied Samara. 'I miss you, miss New York, miss having a social life. Dad's been really busy, and I literally know no one in Delhi. But,' she said, her voice becoming an apologetic murmur, 'Indian weddings aren't as bad as you—'

'I *knew* it.' Maya let out a dramatic moan. 'I can feel you getting sucked in, Sammy. Fight it! I need you. You're the yang to my yin. The sweet to my snarky, the Li'l Ms. Fix-It to my Cat Lady. Come home!'.

Samara let out a sigh. The idea of 'home' was important to Maya, who'd grown up in the comfortable predictability of a suburban nuclear family. For Samara, however, home had always been wherever in the world her diplomat father, Dilip Mansingh, had been relocated by the Indian Foreign Service. She'd lived on five of the seven continents by the time she was eighteen. The only constant had been her dad, and suffice it to say, he wasn't the most involved single parent on the block. Samara had been brought up by a somewhat arbitrary multitude of day care providers, teachers, neighbours, embassy staff, and parents of friends.

Along with the shadowy void left by a mother who'd died before Samara had gotten a chance to know her.

She cleared her throat and focused on comforting Maya. 'I'm coming back, babe. Hang in there. We've got plenty of time to take Manhattan together.'

'You're sure?'

'Yes!'

'Fine. Hurry up!' Maya huffed. 'All right, I've got to go fish out bushy underwear from the sink with tweezers so I can brush my teeth. Love you!'

'Love you too!'

Samara ended the call and grabbed her camera, slinging the strap around her neck again. Truth be told, she *was* having fun—at least part of the time. There were perks beyond the free travel, luxury hotels, and chunky payouts. She turned and scanned the mingling crowd, her eyes zeroing in on one person.

Hot Designated Driver.

At least, that's what Samara was calling him. He was the only thing making this shoot bearable. While the groom's other friends were behaving like toddlers on a sugar high, Mr HDD stood back, nursing a single malt and a panty-melting smirk as he watched their inebriated antics. He was tall, with a stubbly beard, strong, broad shoulders, and arms to match.

Samara was a sucker for stubbly beards. There was something about running your fingers over—

'I'm dying. That shrew is *literally* sucking the life force from my body.'

Ferzin, a member of the wedding-planning team, came and stood next to Samara and ordered a Diet Coke with a grimace. 'She wants me to add more pomanders to the pomander pond. There are literally a million flowers in there! We had twenty people working for three days and nights to fill that thing, and now she wants *more*?'

'Hmm,' replied Samara, still checking out HDD, who was currently talking one of the groom's sherwani-clad friends out of jumping into the pool. He was gesticulating with his free hand, and Samara couldn't help but notice his long, shapely fingers.

Maybe he was an artist. 'Did you hear what I said?'

She sighed. Ferzin was well known for her constant griping and misuse of the word *literally*, so Samara knew better than to encourage her. 'Uh-huh. Think of how much you'll charge her per extra . . . pomander.' She didn't need to ask why the flower balls in the flower-ball pit had been given a fancy name. Wedding planners would call a pencil *noir graphite encased in a cedar plume* if it meant they could charge more for it.

'Literally *no* amount of money is worth the hassle. Plus, it would take hours to make fresh ones!'

Oh God, no. She couldn't let that happen. The guests would be throwing up by then. 'Tell her I'll photoshop more pomanders into the photos later,' said Samara.

'Fine,' huffed Ferzin before downing her drink and flouncing off. Samara saw her walk up to the bride's mother, put on a syrupy smile, and try to reassure her that the photographer would digitally expand an already-pond-size tank of flower globs so that her precious daughter's pre-wedding photos could be even more #beautiful. After a few harrowing seconds, the bride's mother relented, and Samara heaved a sigh of relief—the remainder of the shoot wouldn't be stalled. In fact, if things moved smoothly from here on, she might even make it home for dinner.

Which brought her to the next setup she was photographing: the bride and her friends 'frolicking and celebrating springtime in the colourful pomander pond,' according to the very unironic brief. Samara put her water down and focused on the task ahead. It took half an hour for the bride and her fifteen friends to be rounded up, herded, and assisted—one by one—into the flower pit. Then it took another half an hour for them to restore their outfits, hair, and makeup because, *surprise*, when you pile a million fresh-flower bundles together and then try to wade through them, it gets a bit messy.

Finally, they were ready. Samara climbed onto a high stepladder positioned next to the pit and shouted instructions while snapping photos. The women laughed and threw the flower balls at each other, raining petals on everyone and everything. Against the backdrop of the city skyline, the spectacular burst of floral colour, their shimmery outfits, and their happy faces made for stunning photos that Samara was sure both the bride and her mother would love.

As long as, in the words of the aforementioned brief, 'no one looked fat.'

With her mind so fixated on her task, Samara didn't notice the rowdy voices of the groom's friends coming closer. Sudden shouts broke her concentration. She looked down and saw a drunk groomsman standing right next to her ladder, vigorously shaking and then popping open a magnum of champagne. Before anyone could stop him, he began spraying the women in the pit. Meticulously contoured faces were startled by the smack of gushing bubbly, hair was drenched, outfits were ruined, and screams pierced the air.

'Nooo!' howled the bride's mother, lifting her sari and running full tilt at the rogue groomsman. She crashed into him, karate-chopping the bottle out of his hand like she was Jackie Chan disarming a Hong Kong mafia boss. Unfortunately, the man lost his balance and collided with Samara's ladder. Hard.

Suddenly, she was falling. The camera flew out of her hand as Samara plunged headfirst into the pomander pond. She opened her mouth to scream, but it was instantaneously filled with petals upon impact. There were flowers everywhere, pressing against her face, in her nose, around her head and upper body.

She couldn't breathe.

Samara began to struggle, kicking out her arms and legs, trying to swim through the mass to right herself. She needed to stand up, but every time she moved, her body sank deeper into the pit. The flower balls were like quicksand, eating up anything that wiggled into the spaces between them. Samara started to panic. She couldn't hold her breath for much longer.

An arm clamped around her waist with a viselike grip and heaved her upward. Her back slammed into a hard chest, while the rest of her lay twisted in the flowers. With sputtering gasps, Samara coughed out the petals in her mouth and nose, yet their overpowering floral scent and probably a gazillion pollen bits remained, making her sneeze uncontrollably in between coughs.

'It's okay. You're okay,' murmured a deep voice in her ear as the arm around her held her steady. A gentle hand began picking petals off her face.

The sneezing fit passed, and Samara tried to calm her racing heart by taking deep breaths. She leaned back against the wall of warmth behind her and closed her eyes, her heartbeat slowing as the panic gradually abated. *God, that was scary.* Flower-ball pits were officially the worst idea ever.

'Good. Now, put your legs down and try to find your footing,' the voice said in her ear.

She opened her eyes and followed its instructions. It was easy to stand up now that she wasn't upside down. She turned her head to thank her rescuer, and her hard-won breath hitched.

It was him.

HDD's dark-brown eyes gazed down at her. They looked concerned but also tender and unguarded, pools of smoky quartz that would be much better to drown in than flowers.

There was a frown line in between his brows, and Samara distractedly wondered if it would still be there when he slept. His beard was slightly more than stubble up close, and his lips were exhaling softly on her cheek, making tingles of awareness shudder through her. He was so snug, so solid, wrapped around her in an embrace that felt so . . .

. . . safe.

'You okay?' he asked, his brow turning downward and making her pulse speed up again. *Why* are *frowning men so sexy?* she wondered. *Do they feel the same way when women smile?*

Samara couldn't help it. She smiled at him. 'Uh-huh.'

'You feel strong enough to stand on your own?'

No. She wanted to stay in his arms, to slide hers around his neck and ignore the shrill voices and utter chaos around them. But what was the point? She probably looked like a forest-fresh Mowgli covered in flower juices right now. Hardly someone he'd find attractive.

She sighed and nodded. This was a workday, and as much as she'd like to gaze into HDD's handsome face and maybe share a Bhetkilini with him in a dark corner, she needed to fire up her camera and—

Oh God. *'My camera!'* she shrieked.

She dived back into the floral death trap and began rummaging wildly for her camera. 'No, no, no, no . . . Don't you dare die on me!' she called out to it. That hunk of plastic, metal, and glass wasn't just an expensive possession—it was an extension of her. A loyal friend and business partner.

The only constant in her life.

'Calm down,' came HDD's voice as he pulled her back up again. 'It's over there.' He pointed a few feet away to where her camera lay safely atop the mass of flowers. It had obviously fared better than Samara had. She hurried towards it.

'Don't,' he warned. 'If you move the balls around it, the camera will sink like you did. We'll fish it out with a stick once you're safely outside. Okay?' He spoke to her as if she were incapable of rationality. A tone which, if she weren't actually hysterical, she would have resented.

'Okay,' she replied. Then she remembered that this man had probably just saved her from death—or least a trip to the hospital. She turned and blinked up at him. 'Thank you for rescuing me.'

He smirked, and Samara felt a zinging in her nether regions. 'No problem,' he said softly while guiding her to the side of the pit. Once there, he lifted her out as though she weighed nothing. While she stood off to the side and mentally chastised herself for being turned on by what was essentially patriarchy-reinforcing behaviour, HDD fished out her camera with the help of a light stand and handed it back to her.

Then he winked and walked off.

Which was just as well because all hell had broken loose with the wedding party.

The bride and her friends were now screaming at the groom's friends, some of whom insisted that it was all in good fun and proceeded to spray each other with more champagne to demonstrate how one didn't have to be uptight about it. The hapless groom, far from sober himself, was playing peacemaker, while the bride's mother barked instructions at the staff, the makeup-and-hair crew, and the wedding-planning team. She bustled up to Samara and held out an envelope that obviously contained a wad of cash. 'Here, take this for your trouble. We'll resume after we get everything cleaned.' She handed it to Samara and hurried away. No apology, no asking if she was all right, no suggestion to go take a break to clean up or calm her nerves. Just cash.

Samara shook her head and gave a humourless chuckle. What was she expecting? This was Delhi. Money spoke louder than words in this town.

Most days, it positively screamed.

'Here.' Viking bartender shoved a glass into her hand. 'Drink this.'

She held it up and stared at the clear liquid inside. 'What is it?'

'The only thing that's going to get us through the rest of this train wreck—tequila.'

She squeezed the glass tightly for a moment before shaking her head and handing it back to him. 'I can't. I'm still working.'

Her phone, miraculously still in her pocket, buzzed again. After fishing it out with trembling fingers, Samara saw that it was her father calling. Alarm chilled her insides for the second time in less than ten minutes. Her father *never* called her. She always called him.

'Daddy?' she squeaked as she pressed the phone to her ear. 'Daddy, are you okay?'

Dilip Mansingh's brusque voice replied 'I'm fine' before giving someone instructions about a press release.

She released her breath with a soft groan. 'Why are you calling?'

He sounded distracted, as usual. 'I wanted to talk to you about my transfer.'

'Ok-ay.' Samara closed her eyes and waited, hoping he'd been reassigned to the ministry in Delhi. Probably not. Delhi-based positions in the Indian Foreign Service were rare and highly sought after.

'I'm going to Nigeria.'

'Nigeria?'

'Nigeria,' he replied with finality. 'I have to pay my dues if I want to go all the way, pumpkin. Anyway, I leave in a month, so we'll have to give up the apartment.'

Samara's shoulders slumped, her camera suddenly weighing a ton.

This was how it always went, every two years.

Before she could say anything, he continued in a tentative voice, 'Now, obviously we have to decide what this means for you. You could come with me and find a job there, in Lagos. At least we would be together.'

Samara cleared her throat. 'Not this time, Daddy. I've signed a bunch of contracts for the next few months. I'll stay on in Delhi until the wedding season is over in March so I can earn enough to return to New York and keep applying for jobs.'

'But where will you stay after I've left?'

'I'll rent a place.'

'No.' His tone was firm. 'It's not safe to live by yourself in Delhi. Are you sure you won't come with me?'

With a small huff, she replied, 'Delhi is as safe or unsafe as New York, and I've been navigating it just fine for over a year. Besides, millions of single women live alone in Indian cities, Daddy. I'm perfectly capable—'

'Samara,' he interrupted, 'I know you're used to getting your way, but don't fight me on this. I'll make arrangements for you to stay on, if you're sure that's what you want.'

She opened her mouth to argue but quickly realised there was no point. Rarely did Dilip Mansingh exercise his parental authority, but when he did, there was no changing his mind. 'I'm sure.'

'Good. I have a place in mind. Let's discuss it tonight at home.' There was that word again: *home.* For one more month.

'Fine,' replied Samara, but he'd already hung up. It was just like her father to drop a bombshell and then act as if it weren't a big deal. As if he hadn't just uprooted her life for the millionth time without the smallest semblance of empathy.

One of these days, she was going to allow herself to get upset about it. But not today. Not while she still had this shoot to get through.

She bared her teeth at the bartender, grabbed the tequila glass from his hand, and lifted it in the air. 'Bottoms up.'

She tossed it down her throat.

CHAPTER 2

The day after attending his friend's utterly chaotic wedding photo shoot, where he'd saved a pint-size photographer from drowning in a tank of flowers, Sharav Khanna sat at the head of his family's elaborately laid out dining table, frowning at his dinner. On a gold-rimmed Noritake plate was a delectable combination of some of his favourite foods: butter chicken, palak paneer, batter-fried okra, sautéed broccoli with red peppers, street-style dal, and a crisp salad. On a matching side plate sat a hot, fluffy roti, just waiting for him to tear it open and scoop up some gravy.

Sharav, however, barely registered the food. Beside him, his mother, Jyoti, and his younger sister, Diya, were engaged in what could only be described as the most unproductive argument of all time.

'But he's *such* a nice boy, and you've known him since you were children! The Malhotras will love you like a daughter, Diya. What girl could ask for more?'

'This girl! *I* ask for more!'

'He's intelligent, kind, and polite. Well educated. He's a *banker*!'

'What about *my* career?'

'What career? You've been sitting at home for two years. You're already twenty-three!'

'I'm a jewellery designer!'

Jyoti exhaled with a groan. 'Mr Mehra only had that amethyst set made for his showroom as a favour to our family because your grandmother was one of his first patrons.

Besides, you can always design your own wedding jewellery. Won't that be fun?'

Diya threw her arms into the air, her cheeks flushed with anger. The unruly mass of dark-brown curls at the top of her head, barely held together in a topknot, wobbled precariously. 'I'm not getting married to Yash Malhotra just so I can design my wedding jewellery!'

'But he's *such* a nice boy!'

Sharav felt a responsibility to intervene, even though it was the last thing he wanted to do. Eventually his mother would look to him to sort out the issue anyway, just like she did with everything else. Six years ago, when his father died of cancer, Sharav had become not only the head of his father's extensive industrial machinery manufacturing business but also the de facto head of the family.

It was a heavy load to carry on the best of days.

He said to Diya in a mild voice, 'There's no harm in considering Yash Malhotra.'

Diya swivelled her head and glared at him. 'Don't *you* start!'

'That's no way to talk to your elder brother!' objected Jyoti.

'He's only six years older than me! Why does *he* get to decide my future?'

Jyoti threw up her hands. 'Nobody's decided anything, child! All we're asking is that you give poor Yash a chance. He's *such*—'

'Ma,' interrupted Sharav in a firm voice, 'can we talk about Yash later? I'm starving and the food's getting cold.' This wasn't the first, or even the tenth, time the women in his family had argued about Yash Malhotra in the last month, and it certainly wouldn't be the last. It could wait till after dinner.

His mother huffed but let it go, thankfully. Sharav finally broke off a piece of his roti, dipped it in butter-chicken gravy, and began eating. As the familiar flavours of home danced on his tongue, his mood began to lift. Maybe, just maybe, this evening could be salvaged after all.

'Oh, I forgot to tell you,' mumbled Jyoti as she chewed on a chunk of paneer. 'I invited Dilip Uncle's daughter to stay with us for a few months.'

Sharav balked, his dinner turning to dust in his mouth. *'What?'*

A sliver of uncertainty flashed across her face before she replied, 'Well, Dilip called this morning. He's been transferred out of Delhi . . . to Niger or Nigeria, or was it Algeria? I can't remember, and you know how Dilip is, always in a hurry to get off the phone. Anyway.' She smiled. 'His daughter, Samara, is all grown up and living right here in Delhi! Imagine that. How time flies!' Her voice grew wistful. 'Your father only knew Samara as a child. He loved her like his own, you know. Even offered to take her in after her mother died. Said Dilip had no business carting a toddler around the world on his own. Dilip refused, of course.' She shook her head. 'Opposites they were—Rajeev and Dilip. But thick as thieves. Anyway, Samara's moving in next month. Won't that be exciting?'

Sharav had little memory of Dilip Uncle's daughter, given that he hadn't seen her since she was a short preteen with shiny braces, untidy hair, and an annoying all-over-the-place accent. 'Does she have to stay here? Can't they make other arrangements for her?'

Jyoti's upbeat smile was a little forced now. 'I did mention that things were'—she glanced quickly at Diya—'tricky right now, but Dilip doesn't want Samara to live alone after he leaves. I could hardly refuse to help, could I?'

Sharav fought off a wave of irritation. Normally, he wouldn't have minded a houseguest—even a grown version of preteen Samara. However, this was a *really* bad time for the Khannas to be inviting anyone to live with them. With Diya's unexpectedly virulent reaction to the Malhotra marriage proposal and his own recently arranged engagement still finding its feet, Samara would be privy to all their family problems if she lived here. Things that were private and certainly none of her business. 'Maybe we can put her up in the company guesthouse. There's twenty-four-hour security and an in-house cook. She won't be alone. This isn't a good time for us to be hosting anyone here, Ma.'

Before she could respond, their cook, Biba, stepped into the dining room with a plate of fresh rotis and loudly mumbled in a mix of Hindi and Punjabi, 'When is it ever a good time in this house?' She began dropping the rotis into a small, cloth-lined basket at the centre of the dining table with a look of disapproval on her face.

'Not now, Biba,' said Sharav in a stern voice.

'Don't you use that tone with me, young man,' snapped Biba. 'Let's not forget who changed your nappies and wiped your nose when you used to run around this house with your pee pee hanging out.' She glared at Diya with a pointed look. 'Yash Malhotra is a good boy. Much better than some scoundrel with a fancy car and bad attitude.'

Their mother looked confused. 'What scoundrel? Have we received another proposal? Sharav, has someone spoken to you? Is it the Bhatt boy?'

Sharav scooped up a spoonful of dal with a long-suffering look on his face. 'Nobody has spoken to me about any scoundrels.'

Diya shot Biba a warning glare. 'I am old enough to make my own decisions.'

Biba grumbled, 'Obviously not.' She was just starting to leave the room when the door opened and one of the main reasons for Sharav's apprehension—dressed in ripped Gucci jeans, a cropped sweater, and stiletto boots—walked in. His fiancée sauntered into the dining area and flashed a coy smile at Sharav. Then she noticed Biba glowering at her and recoiled slightly.

'Scoundrels *and* shrews,' muttered Biba as she brushed past the newcomer and exited the room, shutting the door behind her with an aggressive thump.

'Nonita,' said Sharav with a tight smile. 'Come and join us.' He pointed to an empty seat at the table.

Ignoring it, Nonita walked up to Sharav and waited until he rose to greet her. Nonita's tall, willowy frame, high cheekbones, and sleek, glossy hair perfectly matched Sharav's athletic build and strong jaw. More than a few people had told them they made a strikingly attractive couple.

She gave him a firm hug that was more decorous than affectionate. Sharav responded by patting her on the back and awkwardly side-eyeing his mother. Nonita then walked over to Jyoti and swooped down to touch her feet in a somewhat theatrical show of filial respect. 'Good evening, Mummy,' she declared.

His mother patted Nonita's shoulder with a strained smile. 'Good to see you, Nonita. No need to touch my feet every time we meet. Come, sit and have dinner!'

Nonita sat at the table and looked around. 'So, what were you talking about?'

There was a tense silence before Sharav sighed and said, 'We were discussing Diya considering Yash Malhotra for a potential match.'

'Sharav!' exclaimed Diya.

'Well, she would find out eventually, Diya,' he replied, irritated. 'She's going to live here in the future.'

Nodding and casting another smile at Sharav, Nonita replied, 'That's right. When Sharav and I get married, I'll be your elder sister, so I should know what's going on.' She patted Diya's hand and added, 'Your brother knows what's best for you, Diya. Trust him.'

Diya looked back at her with barely disguised hostility. 'I can make up my own mind about this, thank you.'

Nonita giggled and winked at Sharav. 'Don't worry. Diya and I will have a girls' chat later.' She glanced around the dining table again and asked, 'So where is Dhruv today? Doesn't your baby brother eat his meals here anymore?'

A dry voice answered from the door, 'Yes, he does.' Dhruv walked in with his phone in his hand as usual, shoulders hunched over his lanky body. He ignored Nonita, nodded at Sharav and Diya, and bent down to kiss his mother on her cheek. 'Hi, Ma.'

Jyoti caught his chin and squeezed. 'My darling baby. Come, sit. You must be hungry. Biba!'

'Coming, coming.' Biba hurried in with two place settings for Nonita and Dhruv and proceeded to lay them out on the table. Dhruv tapped her wrist affectionately as she put his cutlery in front of him, and they shared a warm smile. She said, 'I'll get you a fresh roti, child,' and then rushed out.

'Only Dhruv gets fresh rotis from Biba, it seems,' announced Nonita with a laugh as she began to serve herself. She meticulously scraped the buttery gravy off two small pieces of chicken before putting them on her plate and helping herself to a generous portion of salad. Then she looked over at Diya's plate, which was filled with a little of everything, and overtly glanced over Diya's non-model-size body. 'You should try to avoid carbs at night.'

Diya pushed her chair out, scraping it on the Italian marble floor with an ear-piercing screech. 'I've *had* it with you all!' she cried before running from the room. The door slammed behind her.

There was a moment of stunned silence before Dhruv reached over for the butter chicken, helped himself to four large pieces, and then tipped the serving bowl so that the thick gravy pooled generously on his plate. He smiled at Nonita the entire time.

Sharav groaned inwardly. While Nonita's comment about carbs had been a little insensitive, she'd been trying to help in her own way. His siblings overreacting and taunting her was hardly a good start to a lifelong relationship. Whereas Diya would move away after her marriage, Sharav hoped that Dhruv would continue to live at home after his. At least until he had children and they ran out of space.

Then they could make an offer on a neighbouring house.

Biba rushed into the room and put a piping-hot roti in front of Dhruv. She looked at his plate and exclaimed,

'No vegetables *again*? After gently smacking the back of his head in doting reprimand, she served him salad and broccoli herself. Dhruv grumbled while Biba's sharp eyes homed in on Diya's empty seat. 'Where's Diya? She hasn't eaten.'

No one answered her. Biba cast disapproving eyes at them all before picking up Diya's plate and leaving.

They ate in silence for a few moments before Nonita asked Sharav, 'Did you have a good day?'

Sharav nodded and continued eating, finally making a dent in his dinner. 'Mm-hmm.'

'What about you, Dhruv?' she asked.

'Fine,' he mumbled through a mouthful of food.

'Still into music?'

Dhruv nodded.

Putting a minuscule bite of chicken in her mouth, Nonita giggled again. 'Ever since you joined that silly band of yours, I feel like I hardly get to see you anymore.'

Dhruv stretched his lips in the smallest semblance of a smile. 'That's strange. Ever since you got engaged to my brother, I feel like I get to see *a lot* of you.'

'Dhruv,' rumbled Sharav, casting a warning glance at his younger brother.

Clearly buoyed by her fiancé's support, Nonita continued, 'How's college?' Then she attempted a teasing tone. 'I hope you're not cutting too many classes?'

'You know what?' Dhruv put his spoon down with a little more force than necessary. 'I'm not hungry anymore.' He got up and walked out of the room, ignoring the sharp 'Dhruv!' emitted by his brother and the plaintive 'But you've hardly eaten!' from his mother.

His fading footsteps could be heard stomping up the staircase while Biba lamented loudly from the kitchen, 'Can't even eat a meal in peace anymore!'

Sharav had had just about enough. All he wanted at the end of a long, hectic day of trying to put out a hundred fires at work was a quiet, uncomplicated dinner with his family.

A couple of hours when nobody wanted anything from him and he didn't feel like the weight of the world rested on his shoulders. Was that too much to ask?

He looked over at his mother, who was anxiously glancing between him and Nonita, trying to decide what to say to defuse the situation. 'Ma,' he said in a strained voice, 'this is why I don't want Samara Mansingh to stay with us.'

'What's this?' Nonita immediately perked up. 'Who's coming to stay?' Sharav's reply was abrupt and didn't invite further questioning, 'A family friend's daughter.' He turned to his mother. 'Can we put them off?'

Jyoti sighed. 'Dilip was your father's closest friend—practically a brother. Besides, Samara is a lovely young woman.'

'How do you know? We haven't seen her since she was a child.'

'People don't change that much. Besides, she has no one else in Delhi, son. Your father would have taken her in. In fact, he wanted to take her in when she was a baby! Had Dilip agreed, she would have grown up beside you, Diya, and Dhruv. We must honour your father's wishes.'

If there was anything more influential than Sharav in the Khanna household, it was the memory of his father. You couldn't argue with a ghost.

Biba chose that moment to walk in with fresh rotis, which she thwacked down on the table while muttering furiously to herself, 'Six years since he passed . . . barely recognise this place . . . tomb with strangers . . . last thing he would have . . . but who cares about my opinion? I'm just the cook, right?' She gave Sharav a pointed glare before stalking off with Dhruv's plate.

There was only so much a man could take. 'You know what?' Sharav said as he stood up. 'Since storming off seems to be the only way to get some respite this evening, I'm going to eat my dinner in Dad's study.'

'No, no,' pleaded Jyoti. 'Please stay and eat with us, son.' Her eyes brimmed with tears she was too embarrassed to shed in front of Nonita.

Sharav's chest felt tight, clenched by the pressure in the room, but he couldn't bear to see his mother cry. 'All right.' He sat back down and began to eat as calmly as possible, even though his insides were writhing.

Down the table, Nonita picked at her salad and looked at the empty seats with disdain, while Jyoti just looked defeated.

Then, with a sigh and a thin smile, his mother held up a serving dish towards Nonita. 'Broccoli? It's from the garden.'

CHAPTER 3

Samara ran a slightly nervous eye over the bungalow from inside her parked rental car. It was a fairly conventional structure—a massive, two-storey residence with a generous veranda, a four-car driveway to the side, and outdoor lawn seating. There was nothing that distinguished it from every other long-standing, multigenerational house in Panchsheel Park, a posh, gated Delhi community.

Except its garden.

The word *lush* could never have encompassed the sprawling cornucopia that fronted the house. Multicoloured bougainvillea erupted in walls of lovingly entwined stems; mature rosebushes with translucent petals that virtually glowed under the glint of a gentle winter sun; plump geraniums, hibiscus, dahlias, and snapdragons displayed artfully amid ferns and foliage to look like uncut bouquets; soaring tibouchina trees competed with flowering creepers to reach the upstairs front balcony, while underneath, a carpet of dewy grass backgrounded the flamboyant canvas.

It was obviously the lifelong work of a very devoted artist.

Which Samara remembered Jyoti Aunty to be, even though she hadn't seen her since she was in primary school and couldn't exactly recall what she looked like. Her memories of the Khanna family were vague, jumbled in with all the other families from her early years, but this garden was unforgettable.

She grabbed her backpack, stepped out of the car, and walked towards the gate. Standing outside it on the street was a neighbourhood vegetable-seller, his mobile cart stacked with fresh vegetables and fruit, and a craggy woman, who could have been anywhere between forty and seventy, with a shawl knotted tightly around her waist. She was shouting at the vegetable-seller.

'You call this fresh? Looks like a shrivelled worm!' The woman held up a limp bitter gourd and brandished it like a weapon.

The man stepped behind his cart with an apologetic look on his face. 'Sister, this is how they're coming these days. The season hasn't started yet.'

The woman dismissed his words with a scornful grunt. 'Rubbish! The ones in the market look fine, and they're twenty rupees cheaper per kilo.' Despite that, she piled at least two handfuls of bitter gourds into a basket and handed it to him with the air of a queen bestowing a pot of gold to a beggar.

With a look of relief, the vegetable-seller quickly weighed the produce and tallied the total cost. He wrote the price down and then handed his notepad over for the woman to inspect.

Samara, standing a little distance behind them, watched the woman snatch the pen from his hand and begin changing the numbers on the notepad.

The man objected in a harried voice, 'Sister, you can't expect wholesale prices. I am bringing these vegetables to your doorstep . . .'

'None of that home-shopping-premium nonsense! I know exactly how much you charge the Bhatts' maid, Sonal, because of her pretty face. Now, give me the free chillies and coriander.' The woman began to load her own basket with the produce she'd purchased.

As he grabbed a bunch of leafy coriander and placed it in her basket, the seller continued to plead, 'You live in such a big house, and I'm a poor man. I have to make my living somehow.'

But his words fell on deaf ears. The woman briskly handed him the money and lifted her basket from his cart.

The man stared at his meagre profit with a sullen face. Then, as the woman turned away from him, he leaned over and deliberately shouted near her ear, '*Vegetables! Fresh vegetables!*'

The woman started with a little shriek, and her basket went flying into the air. Overpriced tomatoes and onions, limp bitter gourds, and free chillies and coriander tumbled out onto the road, along with heads of garlic, cauliflower, and cabbage. A clump of greens and a litter of carrots thumped to the ground after them.

The vegetable-seller grinned as he pushed his cart away. 'Sorry, sister!' he called out in glee.

'Just wait till tomorrow! I'm going to tell Sonal about you!' shouted the woman after him. Then she looked around at the produce she'd dropped, muttering loudly, 'Not that she cares. Got her eye on the boss's son, that one. I swear, if this fool didn't have the best vegetables, I'd send him packing in a heartbeat.' She crouched down to fish two carrots out of a pothole and yelped, clutching her back with a pained expression.

Samara rushed forward to help. 'Are you all right?' She bent next to the woman and put an arm around her shoulders to offer support. 'Do you need me to lift you up?'

The woman shrugged off Samara's arm in disgust. 'Don't crowd me, girl. I'm healthy as a horse.' She glanced up at Samara's face. 'Just like Sonal. All you pretty girls are the same. Think the world owes you something just because you smile at them. Now, help me collect my vegetables.'

Samara didn't dare smile. 'Yes, ma'am,' she replied with a solemn nod and began picking up the strewn produce from the street and putting it into the woman's basket.

The roar of two motorcycles sounded in the distance, rapidly getting louder with each second. The woman, still crouching and holding her back, called out in a frantic voice, 'My coriander! Get my coriander!'

Samara turned to see a bunch of coriander lying bang in the middle of the road, where it could easily be run over.

As she started walking towards it, however, the motorcycles came into sight, speeding down the road like they were racing each other. The riders were whooping and driving recklessly and would be upon them in a moment. She hesitated.

When the woman realised Samara wasn't going to heroically rescue the fallen coriander, she leapt up and scurried towards it.

Gasping, Samara quickly pulled the woman back, twisting her away from the road with great difficulty just as the motorcycles whizzed past in a noisy blur. They turned to see the fate of the precious herbs.

Crushed into the gravel, completely ruined.

After letting go of the woman, Samara rushed towards it and picked up a bunch of dirty, droopy stems. Handing them over, along with the refilled basket, she said, 'I'm sorry. But I couldn't let you risk your life.'

The woman ran a surly but considering eye over Samara, taking in her long wavy hair with cobalt-blue tips, her oversize NYU hoodie, and her towering blue suede boots, which she wore to compensate for the fact that she was only a couple of inches taller than five feet. Finally, she said, 'You owe me for the coriander.'

Samara knew full well that the bunch had been free, along with the chillies, but coriander was obviously *really* important to this person, so she said 'Of course' and withdrew her wallet from her backpack. She handed over a hundred-rupee note with a tentative smile.

The woman nodded and stuffed the money into her blouse. Then she turned and walked right through the gate for the Khanna house.

Samara slapped her forehead as recognition suddenly struck her. 'Biba! You're Biba, aren't you?'

Startled and suspicious, Biba looked back over her shoulder. 'What's it to you, girl?'

'I'm Samara Mansingh. We met years ago, when I was here with my father.'

Biba's eyes flared as she scrutinised Samara's face. With an irritated grunt, she reached into her blouse and withdrew the money. 'Why didn't you say so in the first place?' Grabbing Samara's hand, she pressed the note back into it. Then she sighed and said, 'Follow me, girl.'

A hero's welcome, it was not. Still, Samara slung her backpack over her shoulder and followed Biba into the gate.

A stout, middle-aged woman in a billowing kaftan and massive sun hat walked out of the front door with a preoccupied look on her face. 'Is the gardener here yet?' she asked Biba. Then she saw Samara walking behind her and sucked in a loud gasp. 'Samara?'

With a grin, Samara replied, 'Hi, Jyoti Aunty.'

A small squeal came out of Jyoti's mouth as she enveloped Samara in a tight hug and rocked her sideways as if she were a baby who needed soothing. She stepped back to take a good look, touching Samara's face and hair as she did. 'I can't believe what a beautiful young lady you've become! Why, you look just like your mother! She would be so proud.' Not knowing how to react to the idea of her late mother being proud simply because she looked like her, Samara smiled back and said, 'Thank you for inviting me to stay with you, Aunty. I hope this isn't inconvenient. My father can be a bit of a bully sometimes.'

'Not at all! We're so happy to have you stay, child. Come, come inside.' Jyoti led her into the living room and sat her down on a plush cream-coloured sofa after shooing away a young maid who was in the process of sweeping an enormous Kashmiri silk carpet with a hard stick broom. The air was thick with dislocated dust, but Jyoti didn't seem to notice as she bellowed towards the hallway door, *'Biba!'*

Samara jumped and then grinned as the maid rolled her eyes at Jyoti's back and walked away, the broom dragging on the floor behind her.

'What?' came Biba's hoarse bark from somewhere inside the house. Jyoti took a deep breath, readying her lungs. 'Bring *nimbu pani*! And *biscuits*!'

Much as she loved nimbu pani, Samara protested, 'Please don't wait on me, Aunty. I'll help myself if I need anything.'

Jyoti turned to face her. 'Nonsense! You've just driven halfway across Delhi. You must be starving.' She smiled again as she glanced through the bay windows towards the garden. 'Isn't it a lovely winter's day?'

'It is.'

'Lovely day,' Jyoti continued as though she hadn't spoken. 'A bit unseasonably hot, but that's better for the garden, you know. I was telling the kids that spring came in winter this year! Can you believe it?'

Samara nodded. 'Yes, global warming.'

Jyoti hummed. 'I'm planting zinnias. Just in case.'

Samara didn't know how to respond to that. Luckily, she didn't have to because Biba suddenly strode into the living room carrying a tray laden with nimbu pani, biscuits, nuts, sweetmeats, and savoury fritters. She began arranging plates, glasses, and cutlery on the large coffee table next to the sofa.

Samara, in awe of how quickly Biba had mustered up this elaborate spread, uttered, 'Wow. This looks amazing.'

'You must try the gajak!' exclaimed Jyoti, pointing to squares of sesame seeds and jaggery arranged on a platter as she poured the nimbu pani into glasses. 'Biba makes it in time for the harvest in Punjab.' She turned to Biba. 'Bring some of that lovely pink guava we had yesterday. And those oranges that Amita Kapoor sent from her orchard. Oh, and maybe some paneer pakoras. You kids are so big on protein these days,' she said, winking at Samara.

Biba nodded blithely and left.

Masking her amusement at the thought of eating paneer pakoras for protein with a discreet cough, Samara simply mumbled 'Thank you' as she chewed on a piece of gajak and watched Jyoti switch on gold-accented lamps that had been distributed around the luxurious living room.

'Sit back and relax, child. I can't believe how long it's been since we've seen you,' Jyoti said as she settled into the sofa.

After placing her backpack on the floor, Samara tried to lean back but was hindered by an assortment of plump cushions in various sizes, shapes, and shades of gold. Old gold, rose gold, light gold, dark gold, beige gold, white gold, and—of course—gold gold. 'Yes, it's been a while. I was studying in New York and didn't get a chance to visit India much. I was so sorry to hear about Uncle's passing.'

Jyoti nodded and sat down on the other end of the sofa. 'He had been sick for a long time, but you'd never know it. Rajeev was always so full of life.' She sighed, misty-eyed. 'Of course, you know what it's like to lose a family member. You must miss your mother terribly.'

Samara shrugged with taut shoulders. 'She died when I was so young—I don't remember much about her.' It was the easiest way to answer the question without inviting further questioning.

Most people would have nodded politely before changing the subject, but clearly not Jyoti. Instead, she blinked for a shocked moment before her expression turned distressed, 'Oh, you *poor* girl, growing up without any memory of your mother. Dilip did his best, of course, but he's a man. Every girl needs her mom!'

Before Samara could respond, Jyoti continued in a voice full of conviction, 'Well, now you have me. Consider yourself a daughter of this house, child.' She laid a hand on her heart and leaned forward. 'Whatever you need, just ask.'

'Thank—'

'This is your home for as long as you like.' Jyoti was on a roll now. 'I can't even imagine how difficult it's been for you, growing up with a father as busy as yours and all that nonstop travelling around to God-knows-where. Children need roots, a family. But then, life isn't always fair, is it?' She sighed again. 'We all have our burdens to carry, child.' She patted Samara's hand, her eyes welling up with unshed tears. 'You'll be okay. Eventually. You must believe that.'

Samara guessed that Jyoti wasn't talking about her anymore, so she placed her other hand upon the woman's and squeezed. 'I will. And I'll make myself at home, Aunty. Don't worry.'

'Good, good.' Jyoti smiled, blinking away the tears and the moment. 'Now, Dilip tells me you studied photography in college?'

'Yes, I have a BFA in photography. I'm currently freelancing, doing portraits and candid photography at weddings as part of larger teams, but I've applied for a few photographer positions in New York.'

Jyoti smiled warmly. 'Good, good. And what about boys?'

'Boys?'

'To marry, of course. You must be meeting a lot of eligible bachelors at weddings!' Jyoti had that hungry look on her face that all married women got when trying to extract romance-related information from single women.

This wasn't the first—or even the fiftieth—time someone had mentioned marriage to Samara in the last year, despite the fact that she was barely twenty-five. Delhi was full of well-meaning aunties and not-so-well-meaning busybodies. Complete strangers felt it was their moral duty to advise her on marriage. It was a national preoccupation.

She smiled and gave her stock answer. 'Well, it's been a busy year. And given that I'm usually working at the weddings I attend, I don't get a lot of time to socialise. The only man I really interact with is the groom.'

Jyoti shook her head. 'Oh no, no, that would be wrong.'

'Interacting with the groom?'

'No, well—not *interacting*, but you know . . .' Jyoti cleared her throat and put an awkward smile on her face. 'Anyway, I would love to see your photos sometime.'

Samara felt her insides warming even as she barely managed to contain a chuckle at Jyoti's discomfiture. 'I'd love to show them to you, Aunty,' she said as she looked out of the window. 'In fact, I would love to take a few photos of your garden while I'm here. It's beautiful!'

That, of course, seemed to make Jyoti's day. All awkwardness forgotten, she launched into details about her garden while Samara sat back, sipped on nimbu pani, and watched in wonder as Biba laid out an elaborate spread of snacks in front of her. She dug in and enjoyed both the food and Jyoti's enthusiasm. Growing up, she'd been the recipient of many people's generosity, and it had taught her not only to appreciate the sentiment but also return it. Jyoti clearly needed someone who would listen to her. *Really* listen, not just pretend to do so while thinking about something else. So Samara would be that person. For the moment.

Until she left for New York.

A few minutes later, a young woman walked in, focused on her phone. The light from its screen illuminated a round face strewn with freckles, bow lips, and doe eyes, making her look younger than she probably was, given her voluptuousness. A messy bun made from enough hair for two women was on top of her head.

'Diya! Come meet Samara,' called Jyoti in a cheerful voice.

Diya glanced up from her phone with a troubled look that was replaced by a mannered smile when she saw Samara. 'Oh, hi, Samara. It's been a while.'

'Hi. Wow, you've grown up!' Samara stood, and the two women shared a brief, loose hug. 'Lovely to see you again.' She looked down at the oversize pendant hanging over Diya's T-shirt. It was an artfully mangled knot of silver-coloured metal and cowrie shells. 'This is gorgeous. Where did you get it?'

Diya's smile turned friendly as she replied, 'I made it.'

'No way! That's so cool. Do you design jewellery professionally?'

Her eyes widened, as though surprised by the sincerity in Samara's question. 'Yes,' she replied with conviction in her gaze. 'I *do* design professionally.'

'Great. I can't wait to see your pieces.' Samara looked between mother and daughter. 'I've obviously come to a house full of artists. Aunty with her garden, you with jewellery, and Biba with her food!'

Diya giggled even as she shrugged in an attempt at modesty. 'I don't know about artists. Dhruv plays the bass guitar and sings, so yeah, I guess each of us has our thing.' Then her face clouded over. 'Well, everyone except Sharav.'

'How is Sharav?' All Samara remembered of him was a tall, gangly teenager who hardly came out of his room.

'He's fine, I guess,' replied Diya with another shrug. 'You'll meet him at dinner. If he bothers to come home.'

'Diya!' protested Jyoti. 'Your brother works very hard for this family. He deserves our respect and gratitude.' She turned to Samara. 'Sharav keeps very busy, you know. He runs his father's business, so he doesn't have much time to do other things.' She got another wistful look on her face. 'Although, when he was around twelve, he was quite the chef. Always talking about recipes with Biba, helping her bake cakes and cookies. Now any free time he gets, he's either playing tennis or holed up in his father's study. And there's Nonita, of course.'

'Nonita?'

Her jaw tight, Diya replied in a sullen voice, 'His fiancée.'

Jyoti kept quiet. Her fingers absently fiddled with the tassels on a gold cushion.

It was fairly obvious that things were complicated on the Sharav front, so Samara changed the subject. 'Anyway, my suitcase is in the car. I better go get it.'

Both Diya and Jyoti got up and went outside to watch Samara remove a single suitcase from the trunk of her hatchback, exclaiming how incredible it was that all Samara's belongings fit into one suitcase when neither of them could even go on holiday without at least two or three.

On the way inside, they were interrupted by a piercing whistle from the gate.

Jyoti jumped, her face and demeanour instantly lighting up. 'The gardener is here!' She waved towards the house, already distracted.

'Diya will see you up to your room, child. Settle in and make yourself at home.' She tramped off purposefully into the garden.

Diya rolled her eyes. 'She'll be gone for hours.' She began to lead Samara towards the hallway, but her phone started vibrating in her hand. After looking at the screen, she got a preoccupied look on her face. 'Sorry, I need to take this.'

'No problem,' replied Samara. 'Just tell me where to go, and I'll find my way.'

Diya waved her hand in much the same way her mother had a minute ago. 'Upstairs. It's the second one on the left. You can't miss it. I'll be up to help you soon.' With that, she picked up the call and darted down the corridor and into a room, shutting the door firmly behind her.

Samara shook her head with a wry smile. She'd expected a halfway house and had instead landed in a minefield full of furtive calls, surly cooks, unpopular fiancées, men of mystery, and one lonely widow.

It was going to be an interesting couple of months.

CHAPTER 4

Well, this is a bit of a conundrum.

As it turned out, 'upstairs' wasn't just a straightforward hallway that led directly to the second room on the left. The staircase led to an open great room of sorts, with a large sectional sofa pointed towards a TV that covered most of the wall. In one corner was a bar counter with a glass front. The decor here was more casual than the living room, but it had a forgotten air about it, as if it had once buzzed with activity and now was just part of the route downstairs. Both the counter and the shelves in the bar cabinet were empty, the tables had no personal items on them, and the TV remotes were positioned in a neat line on the arm of the perfectly fluffed sofa with its perfectly fluffed cushions. No one had sat there in a while.

That, however, wasn't Samara's current concern. The great room had not one but two corridors leading off from it. Diya had said 'second one on the left.' Had she meant the second door on the left side of the *left* corridor? Because there were doors on both sides.

She wondered if she should go back downstairs and ask Diya, but she didn't want to interrupt what was obviously an important phone call. Then again, she didn't really want to go around randomly opening doors and snooping either.

'Second on the left . . .' she repeated to herself. She walked towards the second door on the left side and opened it.

A storeroom stared back at her.

Okay, maybe not. Samara sighed. Maybe Diya had meant the second *room*, not the second *door*. Storerooms don't count as rooms, right? She looked ahead, saw another door on the left, and rolled her suitcase towards it.

The door led to a bedroom that was impeccably turned out. Crisp navy-blue bedding covered the king-size bed, which featured a large headboard made of grainy walnut wood. It was flanked by matching bedside tables and ash-grey stone lamps. On the side was a dresser with a modest mirror, and a sofa and coffee table were in the corner. No lotions, hair products, or brushes littered the dresser, no clothes had been carelessly slung on the back of the sofa, and no slippers lay upturned under the bed. Not a single photo frame or personal item. Not even a book.

This must be it. Samara entered and sat on the bed with a puff, kicking off her heels. It had been a hectic morning. Her father had insisted on leaving for the airport on his own and, after much arguing and randomly throwing things into suitcases, had shoved her out the door and into her car. All their belongings had been sent ahead to the Indian High Commission in Nigeria, and their apartment had looked like a disaster zone for the last few days. Samara knew that he probably wouldn't even unpack most of their stuff when he got to his new posting. He'd see no point in it. 'We're just going to move again in two years,' he'd said to her countless times in the past. It was always Samara who strived to make every one of their new dwellings feel like home.

She shook her head. Then she fished out her phone, dialled her father, and waited for his brusque 'Yes, Samara?'

'This is your first move without me. You're going to mess it up,' she grumbled.

He chuckled. 'We'll both survive. Are you settled in?'

'I'm going to start unpacking now. Are you on your way to the airport?'

'Yes.'

'Don't forget to—'

'Samara,' he interrupted firmly, 'I know what to do. I'll be fine. Will call when I arrive.'

She knew he wouldn't, but that was fine. She'd calculate his arrival time, factor in the time difference, and call him instead. He knew that too. 'I love you, Daddy.'

'Love you too, pumpkin. Don't worry about me. Now, go manage the Khannas for a change.' He hung up.

She stared at her phone, fighting the twinge of sadness borne from the knowledge that her father was moving on with his life without her. That it obviously wasn't as big a deal to him as it was to her. He loved her—of course he did. He just wasn't a demonstrative person. But Dilip Mansingh was all she had in this world, and trying to pin down a rolling stone was a fruitless job.

She wondered if her mother had tried and failed too.

Closing her eyes, Samara decided to do what she always did in moments when the void threatened to consume her. She called Maya.

'Sammy!' Maya's voice slurred into the phone. 'I love you, Sammy!' A heavy bass thronged rhythmically in the background, along with the chatter of a noisy nightclub.

Samara smiled. 'Where are you?'

'At the Warehouse? Or the Workhouse? *What's this place called?* screamed Maya into the background.

Samara held the phone away from her ear.

'Wheelhouse! It's the Wheelhouse, Sammy! I'm here with the girls. We miss you!' sang Maya in a high-pitched voice. 'It's got wheels *everywhere*! *Wheeee . . .*' The call got cut off.

So much for that.

With a deep, shuddering breath, Samara tried to channel her thoughts, focus on the future. Weddings, travel arrangements, job applications, taking photos of the garden, maybe some of Diya's jewellery pieces. Resolve to have a cup of tea with Jyoti every day. Buy a *big* bunch of coriander for Biba.

Have a shower. In her experience, hot showers were an excellent cure for low spirits and bad moods.

Minutes later, her suitcase and backpack had virtually exploded all over the bed, and the floor was playing host to a variety of biodegradable plastic bags that had been divested of their cargo and were now drifting along with the breeze from the open window. Most were torn and speckled with holes, reused so many times during her travels that they were little more than wrappers.

Samara carried two of them, still full of toiletries, into the bathroom and dumped them on the gleaming black granite counter. She put another one, full of makeup and personal-care products, on the dresser. A small pile of books made its way to the bedside table, along with a photo frame containing a picture of her and her dad. A few smaller photo frames she placed on the dresser. Finally, she flung three shoe bags across the room to a spot near the door.

There. She was unpacked.

Leaving her empty suitcase open on the bed, she walked into the bathroom, pulling off her clothing on the way. The shower was fancy, with black-and-silver mosaic tiles, a rain-shower overhead, and a handheld nozzle with multiple speeds and settings. The expensive shower gel and shampoo she found there smelled fresh and citrusy, so she didn't bother using her own. As the hot water sluiced over her skin, she felt a bit of her melancholy wash away. Life was good, and the next phase was just another adventure waiting to be had.

She wrapped a towel around her hair, turban-style, and another one around her body and then came out, a blast of steamy air following her into the much colder bedroom. As she rummaged around the piles of clothing on the bed, the door opened.

A tall, broad-shouldered man walked in, his handsome face a mask of irritation. He drew up short and looked around the room, clearly stupefied, before his eyes fell on Samara, dressed only in a towel.

'Aaaaaah!' he screamed and hurried out, slamming the door behind him.

Samara frowned. She hadn't gotten a long-enough look, but he seemed very familiar. And not in a *I met you a decade ago, how you've grown* kind of way. She stared at the door in confusion.

Outside the door, Sharav scowled and looked around. He was definitely in the right house. On the other side of this door, underneath that godforsaken heap of paraphernalia, was the usually immaculate room he'd occupied for the last twenty-nine years. What on earth was a woman doing in there?

Anger overtaking his embarrassment, he knocked forcefully on the door. Upon hearing a singsong 'Come in,' he threw the door open once more and marched inside. The woman was still standing next to his bed, looking, for all intents and purposes, like she owned the place. Her eyes widened with recognition as she took him in. 'Oh my God. You're HDD!'

'You're naked!' he sputtered, gesturing at the scrap of towel that barely covered her breasts and bottom.

Her breasts and bottom . . .

He shook his head hard enough to give himself whiplash. Focusing on her heart-shaped face, he said, 'This is *my* room.'

She turned towards him fully and tilted her head, her surprised expression turning full lips into a wry smile. 'You don't recognise me.'

Too frazzled to try to figure out what she meant, he repeated 'This is *my* room!' and pointed to the floor, as if that would somehow underscore his point.

The woman's smile turned into a smirk. '*Okay.* I guess I got the wrong room, then. Nice rain shower,' she added, pointing a thumb back towards the bathroom.

Sharav frowned. 'Who *are* you?' He knew her face, but he couldn't place it. That smile. Those iridescent, impish eyes . . . he'd seen them before. They'd gazed up at him . . .

Covered in flowers.

He sucked in a breath. 'You're the photographer! The one that almost drowned in that ridiculous flower ditch.'

'That's me, Death by Dahlias.' She moved closer, and he took a step back, almost as though he was expecting an attack, despite the fact that the top of her head barely reached his shoulders. Or maybe not. It was difficult to tell with that towel-turban thing on top. As she drew near, he smelled his shampoo and shower gel on her, saw water droplets dripping down from her smooth shoulders into her cleavage, and felt a sharp tug of desire. He quickly tamped it down as she looked up and stretched out her hand. 'Samara,' she said. 'Dilip Mansingh's daughter. You must be Sharav.'

Ignoring her hand, he clutched his forehead. 'I am.'

Samara withdrew it and chuckled, her eyes dancing with humour. 'Shucks, I wish I'd known then. Oh well.' She tried to catch his eye, but he kept looking beyond her. So she stepped into his line of vision and waved a hand over her head to draw his eyes down. 'Hi! Nice to see you again. Thanks for inviting me to stay.'

Sharav had done no such thing—but he couldn't tell her that, obviously. Instead, he focused on the towel directly above her head and snapped, 'Could you put some clothes on, please?'

'I was planning to when you barged in.'

'This is my room!'

Samara laughed, and all the blood rushed out of Sharav's head and straight into his trousers, which suddenly began to feel way too tight.

He ground his teeth together. 'The guest room is on the opposite side of the corridor.'

'Got it. I'm sorry for the mix-up. Would you like me to go there now?' She spoke as if he were a child in the middle of a tantrum, only fuelling his anger.

'Yes!'

'Okay,' she murmured as she walked back towards the bed and picked up a pile of clothes. 'Do you want your towels back too?'

His gaze flew to meet hers. 'What?'

She laughed again. 'Finally got you to look at me. Relax, I'm going.' Reaching up, Samara unwound the towel from her head, and damp locks of long, blue-tipped hair fell around her shoulders. She walked past him and dropped the towel into his hands. 'Can I give you the other one later?' Without waiting for an answer, she left the room, shutting the door behind her.

Sharav stared down at the wet, wrinkled towel in his hand. Then he looked up. His room appeared tossed, like a tornado had swept through.

Which was, from what he'd seen of her so far, exactly what Samara Mansingh promised to be.

He threw the towel on the floor in frustration.

CHAPTER 5

Samara glanced around the dining table as she scooped a spoonful of chicken-corn soup from her bowl and blew on it softly before putting it in her mouth. The soup was hearty and delicious and perfect for the cool evening that had followed a distinctly unwintry day. Laid out on the table before her was an Indo-Chinese feast—glistening chilli chicken and dragon prawns, spicy Szechwan paneer and cauliflower Manchurian, stir-fried greens in a garlic sauce, egg-fried rice, and mixed-vegetable Hakka noodles. It was all homemade, even the accompanying chilli-garlic sauce. This, despite the fact that Biba had served up samosas at teatime.

'Biba is an incredible cook!' Samara exclaimed, eating another spoonful with gusto. 'Is this fabulous spread just a regular dinner or in my honour?'

For a few moments, the only answer she got was the clinking of cutlery. Then Jyoti cleared her throat with a distracted smile and replied, 'Just a normal dinner, child. The greens are from the garden,' she added as an afterthought before casting a nervous glance around the table.

She had good reason to look worried. Sharav glared at the prawns on his plate as he impaled them with his fork and chewed far more forcefully than required. Diya pushed a spoon around in her soup bowl with a sullen face. And Dhruv, whom Samara had met only when he'd rushed in late for dinner, scrolled through his phone with his free hand as he ate. None of them spoke or even looked at each other. The strain in the air was sliceable.

Samara took a deep breath and tried to lighten the mood. 'You know, most days, my dad and I eat cereal for dinner. As a kid, I had my own special mix: Frosties, Coco Pops, Froot Loops, and Bran Flakes—only so we could pretend it was healthy.' She laughed as she put her empty soup bowl aside and served herself some noodles.

'Oh, you poor child,' said Jyoti, looking for all the world like she wanted to put Samara on her lap and sing her a lullaby.

'No, no.' Samara quickly shook her head. 'Don't feel bad for me, Aunty. I *love* cereal! But this is better, obviously.' She deposited some rice on top of the noodles on her plate, poured a generous dollop of chilli-garlic sauce on top, and mixed it into an untidy mélange of colours and textures. After taking a big bite, she mumbled 'Yummy!' with a full mouth and a smile.

Across the table, Sharav stabbed at his food even more forcefully than before.

She put a piece of chicken dripping with gravy into her mouth. It was tender and spicy, with a hint of sweet. 'Oh my God, *so* good!'

His fork clanked loudly as it hit the dish instead of the food.

Pushing a fat prawn past her lips, Samara closed her eyes as layers of flavour burst forth on her tongue. *'Mmmmmm.'*

A baby onion went flying off his plate.

Jyoti looked over at Sharav, seeming confused by his sudden inability to control his cutlery. Then she asked in a placating voice, 'How was work today, son?'

His voice was a growl. 'Fine.'

'I signed the papers and left them in Daddy's study, on the desk.'

'Thanks.'

'You need me to sign anything else?'

Sharav shook his head.

Jyoti waited for him to say something, but when he carried on eating, she sighed and went back to her own meal.

Samara felt a surge of sympathy for her. She straightened her shoulders. 'So anyone got interesting plans for the weekend?' she asked.

Diya shrugged. 'Not really.'

Dhruv didn't look up from his phone.

She tried again. 'Sharav?'

He frowned and replied without looking up. 'I'm going to the office.'

Jyoti's head popped up. 'But tomorrow is Saturday!'

'So?'

'So . . .' Jyoti gave him a meaningful look. 'We've got *guests* coming in the morning, remember?'

Sharav's irritated frown turned into one of confusion. 'Who?'

A brief moment of silence, and then Jyoti replied, 'The Malhotras.'

Diya erupted out of her chair with a loud *'What?'*

Startled, Samara jumped in her seat, and Dhruv groaned, proving he'd been listening to the conversation after all. Jyoti eyeballed her daughter warily. 'Now, child—'

'I *told* you, I won't marry him!'

'Just listen—'

But Diya was quickly becoming hysterical. 'No, *you* listen!' she shouted. 'I don't care if he's nice, I don't care if he's a banker, and I certainly don't care about his parents! This is *my* decision, not yours. I'm not a *child* anymore!'

Sharav exploded. 'Then stop behaving like one!'

Everyone whipped their heads around to look at Sharav in shock, including Diya. His lips were pressed together and his jaw was clenched, as if he were struggling to control his outburst. Finally, he said in a softer, but no less firm, voice, 'If you want to be treated like an adult, you have to first start behaving like one. You keep talking about your career. Well, you can decide to become a jewellery designer, but it doesn't count if you do absolutely nothing about it. It's been almost two years since you graduated college, Diya, and what do you have to show for it? A handful of necklaces and one design that Mom's jeweller bought from you as a favour.'

He shook his head. 'All you do is hang around the house, glued to your phone, having hysterics every time you're asked to actually move forward with your life. That is not adult behaviour.'

Tears began running down Diya's cheeks, and she let out a loud wail. 'You don't understand. Not everyone can be as heartless as you!'

Sharav let out a bitter laugh. 'Trust me, I have feelings, just like you. But unlike *you*, I don't have the time to feel sorry for myself day in and day out.' He ran his hand through his hair in frustration. 'Look, no one is forcing you to marry Yash. But this is important to Mom, so you will respect her enough to meet with him and his family properly. It's the least you can do.'

Before a weeping Diya could respond, Dhruv spoke without looking up from his phone. 'FYI, the running-out-of-the-dining-room-and-slamming-the-door thing is getting old. Loses impact if you do it every day.'

Diya rounded on him. 'Shut up, Dhruv!'

He shrugged. 'I'm just saying.'

'Don't! Keep your trap shut!'

'Why don't you show me how?'

'Enough, both of you!' Sharav's voice bounced off the walls. 'Diya, sit down and finish your dinner—and, Dhruv, put that bloody phone away! We're going to stay here and eat our dinner like a family even if it kills us! *Got it?*'

After a suspended moment when everyone stared at Sharav in alarm, Dhruv switched off his phone and put it away. His expression stayed mutinous as he began to shovel food into his mouth. Diya sat down in her chair, sobs racking her body.

Torn and totally bereft of any context for the family drama unfolding before her, Samara continued to eat quietly, trying to make herself as unobtrusive as possible.

Soon, tears started streaming down Jyoti's face too.

'Ma, please,' Sharav whispered.

'Sorry,' croaked Jyoti as she hurriedly wiped her wet cheeks. 'Sorry, son. I know my crying upsets you.'

He sighed. 'Let's just eat, okay?'

'Yes,' Jyoti replied in a wobbly voice and then picked up her spoon. She cast an embarrassed smile at Samara. 'I'm sorry for all the confusion.'

Samara immediately shook her head. 'Please don't apologise, Aunty. You said I'm part of the family now, right?'

Jyoti nodded. 'Of course. I know you understand that parents must try to do what is best for their kids, even if it seems harsh at the time. I hope you'll stay to meet the Malhotras?'

Diya covered her face with her hands and continued to sniff harder, as if realising that this meeting was actually going to happen, no matter how many tears she shed over it.

Insides churning with confusion, Samara nodded and replied, 'I will, Aunty. Can I help with anything?'

Jyoti cast a plaintive glance at her daughter. 'Maybe you could stay with Diya—to support her.'

Samara wasn't entirely sure Diya would welcome her support, given that she was making a big deal out of what seemed to be a simple meetup. She was hardly being dragged to an altar of any sort. Arranged meetings between prospective couples were routine in this part of the world—like blind dates but with families instead of individuals. Only the most backward and tyrannical of parents forced their children into marriages. The Khannas, at least from what Samara remembered, were fairly progressive. Maybe there was something deeper at play that she couldn't put her finger on.

'I'd love to.'

Sharav cleared his throat and added, 'I'll ask Nonita to come and help also.'

Jyoti hesitated, eyes darting towards Diya, but then she replied, 'Of course.'

Diya now began to full on blubber. Her mother leaned over and stroked her back and hair. 'Don't worry, child,' crooned Jyoti. 'Everything will be better tomorrow.'

Samara fervently hoped it would be.

CHAPTER 6

It wasn't.

Not even close.

'I'm not meeting him!' were the first words Samara heard when she opened her eyes the next morning. Diya had screamed them from the other end of the house, and there was little doubt that people on the road would have heard her.

Diya wasn't the only one screaming. Completing what quickly became a shrill symphony were the neighbourhood vegetable-seller, who pushed his cart and shouted *'Vegetables! Fresh vegetables!'* from outside the gate, and Biba, who shouted *'Go away!'* at the seller from inside the gate.

'Leave me alone!'

'Diya, come out!' That was Jyoti's plaintive cry.

'Vegetables!' 'I won't!'

'I said, go away!'

'Someone wake up Sharav!' 'Fresh vegetables!'

'Shaaa-rav!'

'Vege-ta-bles!'

Biba's voice chimed in for a roaring crescendo. *'Go sell your limp gourds to Sonal, you rascal!'*

Finally, the climax—doors banging, gates rattling, glass smashing, loud wails, and cries of *'I hate you!'*—crashed over the entire street.

Samara sighed. 'Good morning,' she mumbled to herself before rolling from bed and fishing out her best jeans and a bright lemon-coloured knit top from the cupboard.

Yellow was a happy colour, and she'd need all the happiness she could get today.

An hour later, Samara marched down the stairs in her trusty blue suede boots, ready for battle.

In the living room, seated around the Khannas, were the Malhotras, a middle-aged couple with a young man who must have been the same age as Samara. Both Mrs Malhotra and Jyoti were dressed in embroidered designer tunics with cashmere shawls, and Mr Malhotra wore a tweed jacket and matching hat, which were probably better suited for shooting ducks in the English countryside than eating paneer pakoras in Delhi. Their son, Yash, looked a little like an overgrown schoolchild, with his neatly combed hair, collared shirt, and chinos that were at least two sizes too big for him. *Perfectly pleasant looking, if a little geeky,* thought Samara.

Her gaze crossed the room to where Sharav sat in a stylish bomber jacket, while a sullen Diya wore torn jeans and a faded grey sweatshirt, her hair piled on top of her head as usual and not a scrap of makeup on her face. Samara held back a chuckle. Diya was obviously trying to make a point, and everyone else was pretending not to notice. Except Yash, who kept casting surreptitious, longing glances at her.

'Samara!' Jyoti exclaimed as she walked in. 'Come meet our dear friends.' She turned to Mrs Malhotra. 'Samara is Dilip Mansingh's daughter. She's staying with us for a little while.'

Mrs Malhotra smiled benevolently at Samara and murmured, 'Pretty.' As though that were all that needed to be acknowledged.

Mr Malhotra, who had previously looked a little bored, now perked up. 'Ah, yes, Dilip Mansingh. How is your father these days?'

'He's fine, thank you, Uncle,' Samara replied as she sank into a plush armchair.

'Still galivanting all over the world?' Mr Malhotra laughed as if he'd made a joke. 'Where is he posted now?'

'Nigeria.'

'Really?' He shook his head as though troubled, but his eyes shone with self-satisfaction. 'He'll have his hands full. Terrible, terrible situation over there. But I won't bore the ladies with politics.' He laughed to himself again and gestured towards Yash. 'This is my son. Works for YBS Bank.'

Samara smiled and gave him a small wave. 'Hi!'

Yash nodded, looking a little embarrassed that his father had introduced him by his job instead of his name. 'Hi. I'm Yash.'

His mother cast a coy glance at Diya. 'It's a Swiss bank, you know. Have you been to Switzerland yet, Diya?'

Mutiny battled manners on Diya's face for a tense moment.

Manners won. 'No, Aunty.'

'Oh, it's beautiful! Yash took us there last year. It was a work trip for him, you know, but he made time for us. Even took his father skiing!' She laughed as if the thought of Mr Malhotra skiing were the funniest thing in the world. 'My favourite place was Interlaken. The scenery was just breathtaking!' Mrs Malhotra gave Jyoti a conspiratorial smirk. 'Perfect for a honeymoon.'

Her words hung in the air, the guests eager for a response while the hosts waited, with no small amount of dread, for Diya to react. Fortuitously, Diya was probably wiped out after her morning outburst and contented herself with silently pressing her lips together and staring at the floor.

Jyoti sighed in relief. 'Rajeev and I went to Switzerland many years ago. We left the kids behind with Mummy and Papa. They were too young to enjoy it anyway. Although Sharav went last year. Right, son?' She looked at Sharav expectantly.

Sharav nodded. 'There was a conference in Zurich. I didn't get any time to see the sights, though.'

Mr Malhotra nodded with an authoritative expression. 'Work trips are like that. I myself travelled the world without seeing any of the sights!' Again, that laugh. 'How is the business doing?'

'Coming along,' Sharav responded. He didn't elaborate.

Mr Malhotra leaned forward and said, 'Well, if you ever need any advice or help, you can call me. After all, I ran a successful business for over thirty years before I sold it!'

Before Sharav could reply, Jyoti piped up. 'Oh, Sharav is doing very well. So young he was when he had to take over the business. As though building industrial machinery wasn't difficult enough, now he's expanding into AI!' She gave Sharav an appreciative smile. 'Our saviour. Best son, best big brother, and soon-to-be best husband. Rajeev would be so proud!'

Sharav gave his mother and their guests a tight smile.

'Oh yes!' said Mrs Malhotra. 'I heard about your engagement, Sharav. Congratulations.' In a teasing voice, she added, 'Of course, we weren't invited.'

Jyoti quickly replied, giving Mrs Malhotra an apologetic smile, 'Oh no, it wasn't a proper engagement, just a betrothal! A *very* small ceremony with the two immediate families. Only because the girl's parents insisted we make it formal if the couple were going to be seen together.' She leaned forward and squeezed Mrs Malhotra's hand. 'I'll need your help for the *actual* engagement and the wedding, of course. We wouldn't be able to do it without you!'

That seemed to mollify Mrs Malhotra, who smiled and asked, 'Who is the girl?'

'Her family is originally from Ludhiana. The father is in textiles, and the girl has an MBA. She's very attractive. Tall,' Jyoti added. 'The marriage proposal was brought to us through one of Rajeev's cousins, who is their family friend.'

'Is the girl working?'

'I think she's doing some modelling but nothing full time.'

Mrs Malhotra nodded with a sage expression. 'Good. She'll have time for family, then.'

Jyoti looked at the floor. 'Hmm.'

Turning to Sharav, Mrs Malhotra asked, 'So when is the wedding?'

Sharav shrugged. 'We're getting to know each other for a little while before we set the date, Aunty.'

That prompted another signature laugh from Mr Malhotra. 'All these newfangled ideas. In my day, we just got married and got to know each other on the honeymoon!' He gave Sharav a wink that made everyone in the room cringe. Diya stared at him with open distaste.

Yash frowned at his father, finally goaded into uttering his fourth word of the day. 'Dad!'

'Sorry, sorry.' Mr Malhotra winked at Jyoti next. 'Kids these days think that we were never young.' He turned to Samara. 'We are Punjabis,' he stated, as though she weren't already aware of the fact. 'We say it like it is. We're loud, shiny, and love our drink, but we wouldn't change a thing. *Pun-jaa-bii!*' He rally-cried the last word with a raised fist, peering around as if expecting a cheer, maybe a spontaneous bhangra dance.

Awkward silence greeted him.

Jyoti attempted to turn her discomfiture into a smile but didn't quite succeed. She turned to Mrs Malhotra and gestured at her neck. 'Very pretty necklace.'

Mrs Malhotra fingered the long string of uncut rubies with a diamond pendant that perfectly matched her tunic. 'Oh, this. It's from Mehra and Sons. They've got some lovely designs these days.'

Jyoti's face broke into a relieved smile. 'Yes. Diya has been designing jewellery for them too. Mr Mehra was very impressed with her work.'

'Really?' Mrs Malhotra turned to Diya. 'So talented! You must show me your latest designs.'

Diya's expression thawed just a tiny bit. 'Actually, there is a platinum set in the Mehra and Sons showroom right now. With amethysts.'

'Well, then, I must go over and see it!' Mrs Malhotra declared before looking over at her son. 'You must come with me, Yash. Maybe we can buy it. For later.' Her coy expression was back.

Diya looked away, and Yash squirmed in his seat. Jyoti and Sharav both looked thoroughly uncomfortable, while Mr Malhotra looked bored again.

Samara held back a sigh. What a mess.

Instinctively, despite her father and friends *constantly* telling her to stay out of other people's business, Samara wanted to intervene. She couldn't help it. Growing up in a different empty house every couple of years with an absent father and virtually no extended family, she could easily have self-destructed as a child. It had been the intervention of other people—neighbours who'd taken her into their homes and fed her dinner, teachers who'd stayed late at school to keep her company, friends who'd invited her home for the holidays, and embassy staff who'd watched out for her—that had ensured Samara developed into a relatively productive member of society. In return, Samara had become involved in their lives and didn't hesitate to act when she felt a situation needed remedying.

She stared at the faces around her, their bored or belligerent expressions almost challenging her to take them on. To do the right thing.

That decided it. She would intervene. 'The garden!' Samara exclaimed.

All eyes turned towards her.

'The garden is looking lovely!' Samara pivoted to Diya. 'Let's go outside and soak up some sun for a bit, shall we?'

Diya nodded, obviously eager to get away from possibly the most awkward gathering ever. 'Great idea.' She got up.

Samara stood and looked around. 'Anyone else want to come outside?'

Mrs Malhotra, clearly sensing an opportunity, waved at her son. 'Yash, why don't you go with the girls? Keep them company.'

Obviously not the outright reprieve that Diya had likely been anticipating, but to her credit, she held her tongue and exited the living room. Yash and Samara followed behind her. As she passed Sharav, Samara gave him a pointed look. He grimaced before sighing and getting up. 'I'll join them.'

'Wonderful.' Jyoti looked pleased. The Malhotras were probably much easier to deal with without Diya sitting across the room glaring at her. 'The lawn chairs were cleaned this morning, so make yourselves comfortable. I'll tell Biba to bring some drinks.'

Outside, Samara ushered them to the freshly cleaned chairs, which were perfectly situated for basking in the winter sun amid the garden's colours and smells. *Next up, conversation that doesn't immediately offend anyone,* she thought. 'So how long have you all known each other?' she asked with an encouraging smile.

Silence for a moment, and then Yash replied, 'Since we were kids.'

'Our parents were friends,' Diya added.

'*Are* friends,' corrected Sharav.

'What?'

'Our parents are still friends.'

'Oh. Right.'

Silence.

Samara tried again. 'What did you guys usually do when you hung out as kids?'

'Watch TV.'

'Played, I guess.'

'There were other kids too.'

Crickets.

Literally, because they were in a garden.

Just then, a ray of golden sunlight hit the top of Diya's head, making the lighter strands of her hair shimmer, and Samara had an idea. 'This light is perfect for outdoor photography,' she declared. 'Let me get my camera, and I'll take some photos. It'll be fun.'

'But I'm not dressed for photos,' Diya objected with a frown.

'Don't worry about that.' Samara chuckled as she stood. 'I could give you a full face of makeup and a new outfit with the kind of filters I have for my clients. Trust me.' She winked before rushing off to her room.

She made quick work of unpacking her DSLR camera from her backpack and setting it up. On the way back out, she stuck her head in the doorway of the kitchen, where Biba was busy squeezing lemons into a large jar of ice and water. 'Hi, Biba! Is that nimbu pani for the garden?'

Biba replied in a terse voice, 'Yes.'

'Great.' She entered and peered around. 'What else are you bringing out? Anything interesting?'

'Why?'

'Yash and Diya are struggling out there,' replied Samara. 'I thought maybe you could serve up something . . . romantic.' She thought hard and snapped her fingers. 'Like strawberries and chocolate!'

'I don't have strawberries.' A troubled look creased Biba's forehead as she glanced over her shoulder. 'They aren't talking at all?'

'No. It's like no-man's-land out there.'

That made Biba pause midtask and think for a few moments. Then she said, 'In my village, we used to give young couples ginger. It heats the blood. Makes the'—she waved a quick hand in front of her pelvis—'wake up.'

Samara nodded. 'An aphrodisiac! That's a great idea, but how will you get them to eat ginger?'

'I can add it to the nimbu pani,' replied Biba with a resolute grimace, as if she couldn't bear the thought of compromising her recipe but understood that sometimes sacrifices had to be made for the greater good. 'Leave it to me.'

'Can I help?'

'No,' Biba blustered. 'You'll only get in the way.'

Barely holding back a grin, Samara made her way back to the garden. She ran into Dhruv, who came in through the gate with a guitar bag strapped to his back, his face focused on his phone and earphones in his ears, completely unaware that there was a tense little party of three sitting in the garden beyond.

'Hi!' She waved in his line of sight.

Dhruv looked up like he was surprised that someone had spoken to him. 'Hi.' He took one earphone out, held it exactly three inches away from his ear, and tilted his head. The universal stance for *I don't really want to talk, but I'm being polite, so hurry up and state your business.*

Samara planted herself directly in front of him, blocking his path so he couldn't get past without doing a circle around her. 'Beautiful morning. You been busy?'

Dhruv reluctantly put his phone in his pocket. 'Yeah.'

'Stuff to do today?'

'Band practice.'

She smiled. 'What do you play?'

Dhruv gave her a small, tentative smile in return. 'I play bass guitar. And do vocals.'

'Wow! What kind of music?'

'Rock covers, mostly. A bit of soft metal. We only got together recently, so we're still trying to figure out our sound.'

'Do you guys perform locally?'

'Not yet. Our lead guitarist is trying to book us some gigs, but it's not been easy.'

'Oh? Where's he looking?'

Dhruv scratched the back of his head and looked down. 'Bars, festivals. Whatever's available for amateurs.'

Normally, Samara would have followed up with 'Can I help?' or asked about attending a rehearsal so she could watch them perform, but he clearly didn't want to share information. Instead, she said, 'That's great! I can't wait to meet your bandmates.'

'Yeah.' He began to look longingly behind her, at an escape route to the kitchen.

She decided to let him off the hook. 'Well, I'll see you later.' She stepped out of his way.

Dhruv rewarded her with another smile. 'Yeah, bye.' He walked past, retrieving his phone and unlocking the screen as he went.

Samara watched his departing back for a moment. Then she held up her camera to her eye, switched it on, and called out, 'Dhruv!'

He turned around, and she rapidly clicked a few photos of him. Looking surprised and slightly confused, Dhruv offered her a halfhearted wave and then hurried into the house.

She brought her camera down with a soft laugh. As ebullient as Jyoti was, her kids were ridiculously unforthcoming. Three sulky peas in a prickly pod.

She looked over at the garden. Sharav and Yash were conversing in stilted bursts, while Diya sat cross legged in her chair and stared at the flowers, the street, the house, and basically anything that wasn't the two men sitting in front of her.

Samara sighed. Time to go shell some peas.

CHAPTER 7

'Say cheese!'

They turned their heads towards Samara, who clicked her camera rapidly in their faces.

'Brilliant,' she declared with a laugh. 'All three of you looked like I had a gun in my hand instead of a camera!'

A gun would've put me out of my misery, at least, thought Sharav. The last twenty-four hours had left him feeling positively harassed, from encountering Samara in a towel and having to tidy his upended room in an aroused state to the yelling match with Diya over dinner and *again* this morning to this fiasco of a meetup.

He couldn't wait to get to the office. Signing papers for payroll processing and annual audits was a vacation compared to this.

Samara walked over to Yash. Pointing her lens to the side, she said, 'You have an excellent profile. Turn your head a little . . . no, the other way. That's it. Stay like that for a moment. Smile!' She clicked the shutter in quick succession from a few different angles. Then she looked at the photo on her LCD screen and crooned 'Hel-lo, handsome!' with a goofy grin, making Yash shake his head and laugh.

Sharav rolled his eyes. Trust her to be a flirt too.

Next, Samara turned to Diya and crouched next to her chair. 'Diya, your hair in the sunlight . . . it looks stunning! Are those natural highlights?'

The spontaneous compliment seemed to fluster Diya a bit, and Sharav wondered whether she'd purposely kept her hair unkempt and, to that end, unattractive. 'Er, yes.'

The camera clicked. 'Beautiful. Now, look towards the house—quick!' Diya didn't have time to think about what was happening, so she simply did what she was told. The camera clicked a few more times. 'Now, down at the grass. Perfect!'

Samara kept up a flow of instructions and compliments for a few seconds before finally looking at Sharav, camera already focusing on his face. 'Your turn.'

He squashed the small twinge of anticipation her sole attention on him generated and firmly replaced it with disdain. He shook his head. 'Thanks, but I don't like having my photograph taken.'

Ignoring his words, Samara frowned at the area behind him. 'This background is wrong. The other side of the garden would be a better backdrop.'

'Are you listening to me?'

'No,' replied Samara with a firm smile. 'I'm not giving you the chance to be a spoilsport this morning.' She looked over her shoulder. 'I think those flower bushes over there would be a good contrast to your jacket. Come with me.'

The woman was impossible! Sharav crossed his arms and kept sitting, challenging her to try and make him move. He saw her eyes flicker towards his biceps and almost smiled. She liked his arms, did she? He flexed and sat up a little straighter, feeling a rush of pure male satisfaction when she cleared her throat and looked away.

Then she had to go and ruin it by giving him a stern, meaningful look over the tops of Yash's and Diya's heads, as if to imply that if he wanted those two to talk, he shouldn't be so bloody obstinate.

Sharav was used to being the one in charge. The manager, not the managed. So it was particularly infuriating to realise that Samara might have a good point. Yash and Diya needed to connect, and their presence was hardly conducive to a romantic conversation.

'Fine,' said Sharav in a gruff voice as he stood up and followed Samara to the other end of the garden.

Once out of hearing range, he looked down at the pushy woman in front of him and reiterated, 'I still don't want my picture taken.'

Samara huffed. 'You are such a grouch. Is it just me, or are you like this with other people too?'

'Other people aren't constantly giving me instructions.'

Samara winked at him and said, 'I feel so special.'

Sharav clutched his forehead, holding back a rude retort. Samara had arrived less than twenty-four hours ago, and already they were bickering like siblings. No, not like siblings—he didn't feel the least bit brotherly towards her. Like an old married couple. Not that he'd ever marry her. Obviously. He was marrying Nonita.

No-ni-ta. He chanted her name a few times in his head, as though that would prevent him from imagining Samara in a towel every time he looked at her. Smelling of his shower gel and shampoo, water dripping down her body. Last night, he'd had a very inappropriate dream about the two of them and stayed awake, awash with guilt, for much of the night afterward. By morning, he'd justified it with the fact that he hadn't been with a woman in a while. His relationship with Nonita was an arranged match, set up by their families. He was expected to show respectful restraint. It was how these things were done, and Sharav had no problem keeping it PG with his fiancée.

The very thought of Samara, on the other hand, seemed to divest him of his self-control.

They reached an alcove on one side of the garden where a fence of tall, flowering hedges enclosed a small, somewhat secluded nook. In it, surrounded by floral abundance, sat a pink sandstone bench that had been lovingly carved with a Rajasthani lattice design. Next to it was a matching birdbath that held a hanging bird feeder in the shape of—of all things—a gilded bird cage. The bath had fresh water in it, and the feeder was full, ready for an avian feast.

Samara bent down and peered at its contents. Her eyes widened as she murmured, 'Your mom feeds birds quinoa, cranberries, chia seeds, and . . . are those chopped-up . . . *almonds*?'

Despite his irritation, Sharav cracked a small smile. 'She does. Along with the usual birdseed and grains.'

'Wow. It's like a five-star restaurant for birds!'

'Not so much a five-star restaurant as a health-food one. Mom did a lot of research about bird diets, and she came up with her own mix that's apparently like a protein shake for fowl.'

Samara glanced up at him with a wry look. 'No paneer pakoras for the pigeons, huh?'

That made him laugh. 'No. She tried worms once, but they made the mixture soggy.'

'I can imagine. Wiggly too.'

'They were dead, and dried. Still, the worms decomposed faster than the rest . . .' He saw her face scrunch up in distaste, and he shook his head with another laugh. 'Sorry. Mom talked about nothing else for months, so we're all very familiar with the intricacies of bird food.'

Just then, a small bird flew down and sat on the side of the birdbath, flicking its head towards the two humans for a few moments before proceeding to drink water. It was soon joined by another identical bird.

'Are those sunbirds?' whispered Samara, looking at the iridescent-purple patches on their backs.

Sharav shrugged slightly and whispered back, 'No idea. Mom only talked about the food.'

That made her laugh, which, unfortunately, spooked the two birds into taking flight. For a moment, they stood in silence, soaking in the sounds of the garden and their own momentary truce.

Then Samara went and ruined it by pointing her camera at the scene and clicking a few shots. She turned to him. 'Can you sit on the bench? It'll make a beautiful frame.'

'On a pink bench surrounded by pink flowers? No chance.'

'Oh, come on! Be a sport.'

'When big fat pigs fly.'

She huffed. 'Fine. Look up at the tree and stand still.'

After glowering at her for a brief moment, Sharav looked at the tree with a little grunt of defeat. The sooner he complied, the sooner they would be done.

A minute of studious photography later, Samara looked over her shoulder at Diya and Yash. 'You know he has no shot with her, right?' *Click.*

'Why not?' *Click.* He frowned. Another *click*.

'She's already made up her mind about him, for whatever reason. Maybe she just doesn't want to get married right now. Focus on her career.'

Sharav shook his head. 'If Diya was serious about her career, she would have done something about it. Taken a course, made some calls, looked for job opportunities. She's done none of that. The least she can do is consider a match. Besides, marriage doesn't mean the end of a career.'

'Maybe she wants to choose her own husband, not have a family-approved one foisted on her.'

'Nobody is *foisting* him on her! It's a cup of tea, not an engagement.'

Samara positioned a branch in front of her viewfinder with Sharav in the background before clicking and replying, 'Yeah, but she's known him from when he was a gawky, pimply teenager. Not exactly a sound foundation for attraction.'

'Nonsense. It's not like he's going through puberty right now. Plus, he's from a good family, well educated, professionally successful. Kind and principled. She'd be lucky to end up with a man like him.'

That made Samara laugh. 'Okay, Uncle.'

'I'm serious.' Sharav tried to tamp down his rising irritation as he turned towards her and held up a hand to stop the photo-taking. 'This means a lot to my mother, and all she's asking is for Diya to keep an open mind, so I hope you won't undermine that while you're here. Besides'—he frowned at her bright-yellow blouse and blue boots—'attraction is overrated.' Looking away, he added, 'Shared values, common goals, and similar backgrounds make a better foundation for a relationship.'

Samara shot him a piercing look before asking in a soft voice, 'Is that how you feel about your own fiancée?'

He started. 'We're talking about Diya.'

'We're talking about relationships.'

Shifting his weight, he shrugged and replied, 'Nonita and I share those things, yes. We want that for Diya too.'

'Does Diya want those things?'

'She should.'

'Maybe she doesn't. Maybe'—Samara waved an arm over her head and twirled—'Diya wants to be swept off her feet, have the breath taken out of her by a smouldering glance, break into goose bumps at the mere brush of a sleeve,' she declared with a wistful sigh. She walked up to Sharav and gently tapped her finger against the back of his hand. 'Feel her insides fire up and then melt at the smallest of touches. Wouldn't you ever want to experience that?'

Something had definitely fired up inside Sharav at the touch of her finger, and the safest thing to do was call it anger. Anger was convenient and justifiable. He shoved his hands into his jacket pockets, rounded in on her space, and growled through gritted teeth, 'Please don't spout such drivel in front of Diya while you're here. We're not in some romance film!'

Samara blinked. 'What's wrong with romantic films?'

'Nothing. They're movies. This is real life.'

She peered up at him with a small shake of her head. 'I think you should watch a few of those movies. The ones with songs and dancing and chiffon saris flying in the wind. Uncoil those wound-up nerves and relax a little.'

He lost it. '*Why* are you so difficult?'

'Why are *you* so difficult?'

Sharav's hands clenched inside his pockets as he looked down at her taunting face and very tempting neck, framed by those ridiculous blue tips of her hair. He was going to strangle her.

And then kiss her.

'Hello?'

He jumped back a step just as Nonita strode into the alcove. She had a wary look on her face, which was obviously the result of seeing her fiancé having what must have looked like a secretive argument in close quarters with a strange woman.

His stomach sank.

Samara turned to look and beheld Nonita, attired in a knit bodycon dress, in all her flawless glory. 'Wow.' She frowned and glanced between Sharav, Nonita, and the garden surrounding them. '*Are* we in a romance film?'

With a suspicious look on her face, Nonita eyed Samara from the tips of her toes to the top of her head. Then she pasted on a polite expression and asked, 'Have we met?'

Adopting a similar look, Samara said, 'I'm Samara.'

'Nonita. I'm his fiancée.' Nonita glanced at Sharav. 'What were you two doing?'

Sharav cleared his throat and put an arm around her shoulders, squeezing her for a second and then withdrawing in what must have been the most awkward side-hug of all time. 'Nothing. Samara is taking photos of the family and the garden.' He waved a hand at the camera, like that explained everything.

'I see. It looked like you were arguing.'

'No.' Sharav avoided Samara's eye. 'Just . . . er, trying to figure out the best background for the photos.' It wasn't a lie, technically. They *had* been arguing about the bench. Still, his heart was beating uncomfortably fast.

Samara lifted a wry brow. 'Yes, Sharav is very particular about backgrounds. Wants them *just right* or else he freaks out.'

Nonita cast Sharav a surprised glance. 'I didn't know you were interested in photography.'

'I'm not. I'm just helping Samara.'

'Right,' added Samara with an eye roll. 'I'm a professional photographer with a degree in photography, but I really needed Sharav's advice on backgrounds. Anyway'—she turned to Nonita—'I'd love to take some photos of you. And of the two of you together.'

A dismissive snicker left Nonita's lips. 'I'm usually paid to pose for photos.'

'Oh, are you a model?' Samara shook her head with a smile. 'What am I saying? Of course you are. You're gorgeous!'

That statement had the immediate effect of wiping off Nonita's stand-offishness and replacing it with a smile. 'Thanks. I do some modelling in my spare time, but mostly I do product endorsements on social media.'

'That's great. What kinds of products?'

Nonita waved a vague hand. 'The usual. Makeup, clothes, shoes. Hair and skin.'

Samara looked impressed. 'You must have a ton of followers. What's your social media handle?' She reached into her jeans for her phone.

Now it was Nonita's turn to clear her throat and avoid the question. 'I'm still building my following—but yeah, it's growing fast. Getting lots of calls for content creation . . . anyway . . .' She turned to Sharav, tightening her hold on his arm. 'Should we take some couples photos?' she asked with forced cheer.

'Sure.'

She tugged on his arm. 'Come. There's a nice bench over there. Next to the birdbath.'

Sharav wanted to pull away more than anything, but his guilt-ridden conscience stopped him. He'd been inappropriate, both in thought and action, and his fiancée deserved better. He allowed Nonita to pull him into the alcove and sit him down.

Samara gave Sharav a wicked grin. 'I just love pretty, pink benches surrounded by pretty, pink flowers.' She pointed up at the sky. 'Hey, what's that big fat thing flying around?'

He glared back at her through hooded eyes.

Nonita craned her neck upward. 'I don't see anything.'

CHAPTER 8

It's way too cold to be wearing flip-flops, Diya thought absently, staring at her feet. Her toenails were probably turning blue under the nail polish.

Which was, coincidentally, also blue.

She sighed and began to twirl and retwirl a stray lock of her hair until a few knotted strands inadvertently got yanked out of her scalp. Wincing, she rubbed the spot.

'Are you okay?' Yash looked at her with a concerned expression. He had a deep voice, which seemed a little at odds with his clean-cut, fresh-faced appearance.

Diya nodded at her feet, not wanting to engage in conversation or encourage his interest in any way. Her predicament wasn't Yash's fault—she knew that. There was nothing wrong with him, per se. Growing up, he had been nice to her, always respectful. Studious, sensible, and a favourite of the aunties who liked to point out the well-behaved children to ones who stepped out of line. Never the centre of attention but never timid either. Yash had just been around, a part of the scenery of her childhood and adolescence.

Now they wanted her to marry him.

The foot she was staring at started twitching nervously. She *had* to convince Yash to refuse the match. Her mother wouldn't listen to her objections, but she'd have no choice if Yash was the one to say no. The only problem was, Yash kept smiling at her.

It was unsettling.

'Diya.'

She frowned. 'Hmm?'

'What's wrong?'

'Nothing.' Not nothing. Everything! But how could Diya tell him without it getting back to her mother? And Sharav. Tears stung her eyes. Sharav had yelled at her last night for the very first time in her life. His disappointment and disapproval had rankled much more than her mother's. She had to tread lightly.

'You've never ignored me before,' Yash prodded in a low voice as he leaned forward with a little gleam in his eyes. 'In fact, I can't remember a time when you ever stopped talking.'

Diya huffed. 'I didn't talk to you that much. It's not like we were the best of friends!'

'No, but we were able to have conversations.'

'Fine.' She looked up at him. 'Talk.'

He sat back and smiled again, as if Diya hadn't just been outright rude. What was *wrong* with the man? Then he asked, 'So designing jewellery for showrooms, huh?'

'Yes.'

'How's it going?'

'Fine.'

'Are you enjoying it?'

She shrugged. 'I don't know.'

Shifting in his chair a little, Yash took a deep breath. 'Okay. Then how about movies? Seen any good ones lately?'

'No.'

'Read any good books?'

'No.'

'Sharav mentioned you went to Comic-Con last month. How was it?'

'Fine.'

Yash pressed his lips together and took a good look at a now hunched Diya, who had begun pulling threads out of the sleeve of her sweatshirt. 'Look, Diya, I don't want to make you uncomfortable—'

'Nimbu pani!'

Biba suddenly materialised out of nowhere and thumped down a tray, laden with drinks and an array of snacks, on the table between them. She unloaded it in a brisk manner. When finished, she picked up the empty tray, tucked it under her arm . . .

. . . and waited.

When neither Yash nor Diya made any move to serve themselves, Biba glared at them both in turn. Then she huffed, put the tray down, and poured nimbu pani into two glasses. Placing one glass each in front of them, she grunted, 'Drink.'

Confused, Diya frowned up at Biba. 'We'll help ourselves.'

'No,' Biba replied. 'Drink.' She kept standing with her feet planted and arms crossed, like a tiny sumo wrestler.

Wilting under her fierce scowl, the seated pair took tentative sips of their drinks and immediately choked. It was heavily sweetened and pungent with the bitter twang of raw ginger.

'More,' instructed Biba in a firm voice.

Yash cast her a baffled look as he took another small sip with watering eyes.

Diya rapidly blinked and sipped at the same time. 'What's in this—'

'Drink *more*!'

They quickly gulped down the remainder of their glasses. Yash finished his first and gagged with a fist in front of his mouth, as though to punch down the liquid should it dare to come back up his oesophagus.

Biba spun around and walked off.

Despite the piercing aftertaste of ginger in her own mouth, Diya felt the need to defend the woman who'd been a second mother to her since she was a baby. 'Biba's normally a great cook.'

Yash smiled. 'I know. It's been a while, but I've eaten here before, remember?'

She nodded.

'So . . .' He cleared his throat and poured water for the both of them. 'What's different about today? Why am I suddenly making you uncomfortable?'

'You're not!'

'Yes, I am. Tell me.'

She kept quiet.

He tried again. 'Is it because our parents have been doing some heavy-duty hinting lately? I know mine have.'

Diya pressed her teeth together to try and bite down the bitter retort at the tip of her tongue. She failed. 'I don't want to marry you!'

Yash started and leaned back.

Shaking her head, she tried to make up for her rude outburst. 'I didn't mean I don't want to marry *you*. I just meant I don't want to get married. Right now. To *anyone*.' She took a shuddering breath. 'I'm sorry.'

After looking at her obvious distress for a short moment, Yash nodded slowly and replied, 'Okay, that's absolutely fine. It's a bit early to start talking about marriage anyway. I was thinking more like a cup of coffee, away from the families. If you're up for it—no pressure.'

That surprised Diya. Her mother had made it sound like it was a done deal. 'Oh, uh . . . I actually don't want to get involved with anyone right now either.'

'Then why did you agree to meet up like this?'

'I didn't. Mom insisted.' She looked up to see a sympathetic look on Yash's face and couldn't help but burst out, 'And Sharav yelled at me!'

His eyes widened. 'Oh my God, I'm so sorry. I had no idea you were being forced.' He began to get up. 'I'll tell my parents—'

'No!'

He froze halfway between sitting and standing, his butt hovering over the chair. Sharav, Nonita, and Samara looked over at them from the other end of the garden with matching frowns.

'Sit down.' Diya eyed his chair.

Despite the confusion in his eyes, Yash gave Diya a calm nod and sat back down. Crossing his arms over his chest, he said, 'Okay, talk to me. What's going on?'

'You can't tell your parents that I don't want to get married.'

'Why not?'

'Because then they'll tell my mom!'

'So? Isn't that something Jyoti Aunty should know before she goes around trying to set you up?'

Diya shook her head and exhaled in frustration. 'I *have* told her. She doesn't understand.'

He gave her a compassionate look and said, 'I'm sorry to hear that. Can I help in any way?'

'Yes. Tell your parents that you're not interested in me. That way my mom has no choice.'

'I can't do that.'

'Why not?'

Yash gave a small shrug. 'Because I *am* interested in you.'

The brief camaraderie that they'd shared in the previous moments immediately evaporated. Diya began to fidget in her chair. Her voice dipped to a whisper as she said, 'I'm sorry.'

Yash merely looked at her quietly for a few moments. Then he exhaled and stood up. 'Fine. I'll tell my parents I'm not interested.'

She looked up at him in surprise. 'You will?'

He nodded. 'Yeah.'

Unsure how to react, Diya hesitated for a moment before giving him a tiny, tentative smile. 'Thanks, Yash.'

He didn't smile back. 'All the best, Diya. I'll see you around.' He began to make his way back to the house.

Diya watched his retreating form and felt a pang of shame. Yash had been nothing but gracious and composed, and she had behaved like a complete shrew.

She sighed. Had circumstances been different, maybe she would have had that coffee with him, seen where things went now that she knew he wasn't planning to show up at her door on a horse with five hundred of his closest relatives dancing around him, as her mother had made her believe.

Anyway, she'd made her choice. It would work out in the end.

It had to.

CHAPTER 9

They were quite a pair—full and luscious. Two perky globes that would spill generously from even the largest of hands. Ripe, fragrant . . .

. . . and bright green.

Samara looked down at the two bunches of fresh coriander in her hands and took a deep breath. This had gone on long enough. For the last week, Biba had either completely ignored her or glared at her in passing like the evil mother-in-law in a B-grade soap opera.

So in between rushing around for the next wedding she was photographing, Samara had found time to have a chat with the vegetable-seller and pay him a substantial fee to find the two biggest and best bunches of coriander available in Delhi. Bunches that even the most fastidious of cooks would be delighted to possess.

This morning, he had finally delivered.

She entered the kitchen with trepidation, watching Biba carefully as she bustled about, in perfect harmony with her space. The pressure cooker sounded its whistle periodically, and a large pot of milk boiled on the hob while she stirred a delicious-smelling something in a wok, stopping occasionally to chop vegetables on the side. Every now and then, Biba would add a little oil, water, or spice to a vessel, wash a bowl, or put away clean dishes. It was seamless, graceful. Almost like a dance performance.

Aside from the constant grumbling.

'Hi, Biba,' Samara said in a cheery voice. She held up her peace offering for inspection as Biba turned to look at her. 'I brought you some coriander.'

Biba ran a critical eye over the bunches in Samara's hands. It was obvious she approved, because the next words out of her mouth were 'Where did you get those?'

'The vegetable-seller.'

Biba frowned, inexplicably outraged. '*Our* vegetable-seller? The one who comes to *our* gate?'

Confused, Samara replied, 'Yes.'

Furious, Biba barked, 'That lying cheat! He sells you and Sonal all the good produce and I get the leftovers? Wait till I see him tomorrow.'

Uh-oh. Samara shook her head hurriedly. 'No! These were a special order. It took him *days* to find these. I knew you were very particular, and I wanted the very best coriander for you. I've rejected many, *many* bunches and only brought you the best ones. I promise. Please don't reprimand him for something that's not his fault.'

That seemed to appease Biba a little. She stopped scowling and merely stared at the bunches of coriander as if it was their fault instead.

'Biba,' Samara said in a placatory voice, 'I know we started out on the wrong foot, but I would really like to change that. Even though I'll only be here for a short while, I hope that we can be friends. I'm *really* sorry for not saving your coriander from the motorcycles and even sorrier for messing up the refreshments at the garden party last week.' She shook her head. 'I thought something romantic might loosen them up. It was a bad idea.'

Biba humphed. 'It was a *terrible* idea.'

'So terrible!' Samara tried not to smile. She certainly didn't mention that Biba was the one who'd added raw ginger to the nimbu pani and pushed Diya and Yash to drink it. 'Not only did it not work, but it ruined the drinks you made. I know how much pride you take in your cooking. You are really the best cook I've ever met. How you put together such lavish spreads at the drop of a hat is beyond me!'

Again, Biba humphed, but this time it was gentler. 'You're just trying to butter me up, girl.'

'No, I mean it,' Samara replied. She really did. 'I would love to learn a couple of things from you before I leave. Since I'm going to go back to cooking for myself soon.'

Biba shook her head, but there was no heat in her words anymore. 'I don't share my recipes.' She took the coriander bunches and nodded in thanks. It was as much of a concession as Samara was going to get.

Samara grinned. She leaned back against the counter. 'Understood. How about I share some of mine?'

Biba looked intrigued. 'What kind of recipes?'

'I make a killer breakfast taco and green smoothie. Should I show you?'

There was that frown again. 'I'm making parathas and egg masala for breakfast. With fresh pickle. And lassi.' She pointed at a container of homemade yogurt sitting next to the blender, which she would flavour with sugar and blend into a frothy shake to combat the heat from the chillies in the pickle.

'Have you made the parathas and eggs yet?'

Biba gestured towards a bowl of dough covered with a wet cloth and a tray of raw eggs still in their shells.

Dusting her hands off, Samara grinned. 'How about we use the same ingredients to make breakfast tacos and a green smoothie instead?'

A considering moment and then Biba nodded. 'Fine. Show me.'

Samara spent the next half hour under the older woman's critical eye. She fire-roasted tomatoes for salsa, which Biba called 'burning perfectly good tomatoes,' and used the dough to make wheat tortillas, which Biba labelled 'flat rotis no self-respecting Punjabi would ever make.' After scrambling eggs with copious amounts of cheese, broiling potatoes and chicken, tossing a salad, and refrying beans, Samara finally presented her version of breakfast tacos to an unimpressed Biba.

'Try one,' she insisted, assembling a sample. 'Next time, we'll add some avocado and Mexican spices for extra flavour. We can even get the original corn-masa flour for the dough and use black beans instead of kidney beans.'

Eyeing the small half-folded tortilla stuffed with all the fillings they had cooked separately, Biba said, 'So much work for a tiny roll that isn't even rolled up properly. How am I supposed to eat it?'

'You lift it up like a boat, with the folded side at the bottom so nothing falls out.'

Biba frowned. 'Why can't you just make it bigger and roll it up properly?'

'Because then it'll become a burrito. *This*'—Samara pointed at the plate—'is a taco.'

'What's the difference?'

'Tacos are smaller. Burritos usually have rice in them too.'

'People eat rice wrapped inside a roti?'

'Yes. It's very popular!'

Shaking her head in disdain, Biba muttered to herself while gingerly picking up a taco and taking a bite. Her expression said she was determined to hate it, but then her eyes lit up and she gave a grunt of approval.

Samara beamed. 'Now for the smoothie. I'm going to need spinach, lettuce, carrots, peanut butter, tofu, yogurt, banana, apple, berries—'

Waving her hand, Biba interrupted, 'Hold on, girl. What are you going to do with so many ingredients?'

'I'm going to blend them all together, and then we'll drink it.'

If Biba was troubled before, she was positively horror-struck now. 'You can't be serious.'

Laughing, Samara chirped, 'Trust me, you'll love it!'

And she did. Well, not *love* it, but she did give Samara another grunt at the end. Along with a curt 'This is acceptable' when she looked at the platter of tacos and jug of smoothie, which she proceeded to take to the dining room for breakfast.

Samara, meanwhile, began hurriedly cleaning up the mess she'd made in the kitchen, not wanting to lose whatever brownie points she'd just racked up with Biba over spilled peels and pips.

'So you *do* know how to tidy up,' came Sharav's caustic voice from the kitchen door. 'I had wondered, after digging my bed out from under your stuff.'

Without turning around, Samara replied, in an injured tone that she hoped gave no indication of her sudden breathlessness, 'Good morning to you too.'

After a moment of contrite silence, Sharav responded, 'I'm sorry, that was rude of me.'

'Just kidding. Your bedroom looks like it belongs to an android. Like Spock and R2-D2 got married, and the bed is a charging dock.' She glanced over her shoulder and immediately regretted it. Sharav leaned against the door, looking mouthwateringly good in a fitted henley and jeans.

He huffed. 'Different franchises. And technically, Spock was half-human, so he wouldn't need charging.'

'Like you.' She smirked at him.

Sharav rolled his eyes, a small lift of his lips indicating that he had taken the hit in good humour. 'I'll be in the dining room, recharging.'

'Enjoy! I made tacos,' she told his retreating back.

'Funny, that's what my bed looked like with your stuff on it,' he called over his shoulder.

Har har. Now she was picturing his bed as she cleaned the countertop, wondering which side he slept on or if he slept in the centre, spread-eagled. If he shuffled, kicked, or snored. Or if he lay on his back, arms folded on his chest.

Like Dracula.

Great, now she was imagining Sharav sucking on her neck. In bed. While she made moany noises. He would be focused on his task, that sexy frown line lost in her hair while his lips teased the sensitive spot beneath her ear. Maybe he'd make noises too.

What would Sharav's sucking-neck noises sound like?

An animalistic growl? Or those grunts men made in the gym when they wanted to bring attention to the fact that they were lifting heavy things? No, she bet his would sound like a breathy rumble from his throat—something he tried to hold back but couldn't.

Oh God, she had to stop.

Just as Samara was about to throw the kitchen towel across the room, she was startled out of her thoughts by the deep thrum of a bass guitar. It came from the garage, farther up the driveway, outside the kitchen entrance. Curious, she washed her hands and made her way towards the sound.

Inside the garage, sitting in the midst of boxes, old furniture, piles of suitcases, storage trunks, and more layers of dust than on the street outside, was Dhruv. He was perched on a sturdy end table, a guitar in his hand and a bass amp at his side. His expression seemed focused yet contemplative as he tuned his strings with complete disregard for his less-than-ideal surroundings.

Not wanting to disturb him, Samara paused at the door and watched. Once he was done tuning, Dhruv started playing chords, his concentration never wavering. He was a talented musician, Samara noted as he effortlessly combined the melody with slides and bends. His head and arms moved with the rhythm, as if he felt the music as much as he made it.

Stepping inside the garage quietly, Samara sat down on a dusty trunk and listened to Dhruv play. After a few moments, Dhruv finally noticed her and abruptly stopped, conceding an awkward smile that spoke of his embarrassment at being watched.

'You're very good,' Samara said in a soft voice, not wanting to spook him.

Dhruv nodded. 'Thanks.'

'Which song was that?'

He shrugged. 'Just something I'm working on.'

'You write and compose as well?'

'Just for myself right now. As I said, the band only does covers.' He looked away.

He's like a skittish horse, thought Samara. *Reluctant to give even an inch.* 'Will you play something for me?'

He shook his head. 'This is a bass guitar, so you won't really enjoy it without the other instruments and vocals.'

'You do vocals, too, right?'

Another shrug and he cleared his throat, looking even more uncomfortable. 'I'm still practising. Nothing's ready yet. Anyway, isn't it almost time for breakfast?'

'Almost.' She'd come this far and wasn't going to give up yet. 'How about I sing and you accompany me?'

That made Dhruv sit up and look at her. 'You sing?'

She laughed. 'Badly, but I love doing it. Do you know how to play "Stand By Me" by Ben King?'

Dhruv laughed. *Finally!* 'That's like beginner-level stuff.'

'So you play and I'll sing.' Samara stood and walked closer, picking up a screwdriver that was lying on top of a broken table on the way. This was her chance to break the ice between them, and she was going to take it. She held it up under her face like a microphone and said with all the air of a pop star who was about to go onstage and perform, 'Ready.'

Chuckling at the comical sight, Dhruv found the song key on his guitar. Then he began to play.

Samara warbled the lyrics tunelessly in time with his notes, waving her arms and shimmying her hips for histrionic effect. At the end of the first verse, she all but yowled 'Staaaaand by meeee' into the room, making Dhruv wince like she'd scraped her nails against a blackboard.

'Stop! Please stop.' Dhruv could barely get the words out he was laughing so hard. He leaned over his guitar, his shoulders shaking, as she stopped her performance and glanced at him.

'What?' she asked.

He wiped his eyes. 'You weren't kidding when you said you were bad.'

Samara grinned down at him. 'I wasn't. But it's a high, right? Do you get this feeling when you sing?'

'Absolutely.' Dhruv nodded and returned her smile. 'That's why I do it. I could give you pointers, if you like.'

'I would love that. Maybe after breakfast, if you're free?'

His face fell. 'I can't. I have to go scouting for a practice space for the band. We've been rehearsing at the drummer's apartment until recently, but she just got a roommate, so we need to come up with a new place.'

The penny dropped. Samara knew exactly what she needed to do. She bit back a grin and asked, 'Oh? What kind of space do you need?'

'Just someplace big enough for our equipment and where no one minds a bit of noise. Nothing fancy.'

'How about here?'

He frowned. 'Where?'

'Here, in the garage. It's separate from the house, so the noise won't be a bother. We can move all this stuff into another room or just throw most of it away, really.' She walked around the garage, pointing and waving. 'You could set up your drums here and your guitars here and have plenty of space to sit and relax. The kitchen is right next door with refreshments, and the best part is, it's free!'

Dhruv shook his head with a wry smile. 'I don't think my family will share your enthusiasm.'

'How do you know? You haven't asked yet.'

'They won't.'

'Don't be defeatist. Look around.' Samara twirled to illustrate her point. 'This place just needs a good cleaning and it'll be perfect!' Before Dhruv could object again, she stuck her head out of the garage door and caught the eye of the gardener, who was mixing fertiliser in the driveway. Smiling, she asked him to find Jyoti and bring her to the garage, quickly.

Then she went back in and faced a slightly dazed Dhruv. 'Look, I know you're probably going to be angry that I'm interfering in your business, and I can live with that. But I think that if you ask, your family will surprise you. Either way, I'm going to start clearing out this place. It's a dump.'

She opened the garage doors all the way, flooding the interior with daylight. In the previously dim lighting, the place had looked dusty and decrepit. Now it looked positively grisly. A menagerie of spiderwebs hung in the air, and assorted insect nests were nestled in every crevice. It was like a lost temple in the rain forest that had been reclaimed by the jungle and its creatures.

'Okay,' Samara breathed out as she and Dhruv stood in the driveway, staring inside. 'First, we cull the wildlife. Then we move out the outdated stuff. Finally, we clean. I suggest you call your bandmates to help.'

'Samara? Dhruv?' The kitchen door opened, and Jyoti came out with Biba and Diya in tow. 'What happened?' They stopped in the driveway and looked inside. All three recoiled.

'Nothing, Aunty,' replied Samara. 'Dhruv wanted to ask you something.' She looked up at Dhruv and nodded, confidence and reassurance in her eyes.

Shifting his weight and with a reluctant expression at first, Dhruv finally sighed and asked in a subdued tone, 'Ma, my band is looking for a regular space to practise our music. Samara suggested the garage.'

Of all things, his mother clearly hadn't been expecting this. 'Oh, er . . .'

Before she could reply, Samara cut in. 'Aunty, the garage would be perfect for them. We could clear out and clean up the place this weekend, and Dhruv's friends will help.'

Still looking a bit dazed, Jyoti asked, 'But where will you put all this?' She waved a weak hand at the interior, wincing.

Samara wasn't going to back down. This was too important. 'Most of the furniture is old and broken, so we can dispose of that. What is in these suitcases and trunks?'

Jyoti frowned. 'Well, the suitcases have mostly old clothes, I think. Some belonged to Mummy and Papa—Rajeev's parents—so I'm not sure what's in them. We packed away Rajeev's clothes as well. I think a couple of the trunks have things from my wedding . . . Oh, there's a lovely Wedgwood dinner set in there! My mother bought it when I was still in school and saved it for my trousseau.'

'Have you ever used it?'

'Oh, no, I was saving it for Diya's trousseau.'

At this point, Diya piped up. 'I don't want it.'

'Oh, but it's a lovely set,' promised Jyoti. 'White with little pink flowers on it. Very charming. You can use it for dinner parties!'

Diya rolled her eyes and gestured to her torn jeans, oversize crop top, and leather and silver bracelets. 'Mom, do I look like someone who likes plates with little pink flowers on them?'

Jyoti was undeterred. 'Tastes change, child. Your husband might like it. Besides, a Wedgwood dinner set will last you a lifetime!'

'Mo—'

'Aunty,' interrupted Samara, 'I suggest we go through everything and sort it out. The furniture, clothes in the suitcases—are you planning to use them, or can they be donated?'

Jyoti sighed. 'Well, it's been six years since Rajeev passed and even more since his parents did. I already set aside the heirlooms. So, yes, I suppose they can.'

'Great!' Samara turned to Dhruv. 'You've got yourself a band space!'

Dhruv looked at Jyoti for confirmation, a hopeful spark in his eyes. 'Is that okay, Ma?'

That spark must have done Jyoti in. 'Yes, son. Of course.' She patted his cheek almost gratefully. 'Anything for my baby.'

Dhruv burst into a smile and gave his mother an impromptu hug. 'Thanks, Ma!' He turned to Samara. 'Thanks for your help.'

She grinned. 'Don't thank me yet. You still have to give me singing lessons. Now, let's go have a big Mexican breakfast and then get started on the cleanup!'

'"Mexican breakfast"?' Jyoti turned to Biba.

'She made takors. It means *hot-water bottle* in Punjabi.' Biba spun around and marched back to the kitchen.

Jyoti frowned. 'We're having hot water for breakfast?'

CHAPTER 10

The phone rang and rang but went unanswered.

Samara exhaled. Her father, now ensconced at the Indian High Commission in Nigeria, should have wrapped up his workday by now, but he was obviously working late. Dilip usually turned the ringer off on his personal phone and checked it only once he left the office. He was remarkably old-fashioned that way.

Which meant Samara would go another day without speaking to him. It had already been ten.

She leaned back against the headboard of her bed. Normally, her father ignoring her calls wouldn't upset her. He ignored everybody's calls. Samara was used to being the one who pushed him to stay in touch, was used to being alone in her need for regular connection. As a child, she'd made her peace with her father's reticence. Learned to adjust, go with the flow, and stay positive.

Recently, however, it had begun to grate on her. Perhaps it had something to do with the fact that she was living with a family. Samara knew her stint with the Khannas wouldn't last long, and she'd soon be on her way to New York, but it felt . . . nice.

To belong, even temporarily.

It felt really good, in fact.

As if to underscore that point, a gentle knock came at her door.

She smiled and said, 'Come in.'

A cheerful Jyoti walked into the room. 'How are you, child? Still working, so late?' She pointed at Samara's laptop, which lay open next to her on the bed.

Samara shook her head. 'No, just checking my emails, Aunty.'

Seating herself on the edge of the mattress, Jyoti asked, 'I hope you're not too tired after that marathon cleaning session today!'

They had made some great progress on the garage. Dhruv's bandmates and friends had pitched in and held an impromptu garage sale at the front gate. Neighbourhood vendors, staff from other houses, and random passersby had taken almost everything away to reuse or repurpose. 'Oh, I don't tire easily,' Samara assured her. 'Weeklong weddings require stamina!'

Jyoti laughed. 'They do, don't they?' She gave Samara an affectionate pat on the cheek. 'I'm very happy you came to stay with us, child. And I wanted to thank you for what you did for Dhruv. He's so happy and excited!' She laughed before turning pensive. 'It's rare to see him like that these days.'

'Not at all. I should be thanking you, Aunty, for letting me stay and being so welcoming.'

'Nonsense! I've said it before, and I'll keep saying it: this is your home, and you are a member of the family.' Jyoti rose and held out her arms. 'Now, come give me a hug.'

Overwhelmed, Samara silently got up and hugged Jyoti, who held her in a brief but tight embrace and murmured, 'Thank you for today. Sleep well.'

Choking back a lump in her throat, she whispered, 'Good night, Aunty.'

After Jyoti left, it took Samara a few moments to collect herself.

Then she sat back on her bed and dialled Maya.

Her best friend picked up on the second ring and whispered, 'My editor is doing the rounds. Hang on!'

Samara set her phone on speaker and waited. Maya worked as an editorial assistant in a publishing house, a job she loved primarily because she didn't have to pay to read books anymore.

Maya returned a minute later. 'She's stressed. One of our authors is having a meltdown because his name on the cover isn't bigger than the title. What's up?'

Samara hadn't planned on a diatribe. In fact, she'd just been calling to check in. But what came out of her mouth was 'You know what's really great? Having someone ask you what you ate for lunch when you get home after a long day at work. It's an inane question, asking which food you ingested seven or eight hours ago, but it shows involvement, you know? Like that person cares enough that the dullest minutia of your life is consistently important to them.'

'Uh-huh . . .' Maya replied cautiously.

'You know what else is great? Someone who answers your calls!'

'Hey. I always pick up your calls!'

Samara huffed. 'Not you—my dad. He never picks up, he never calls back. I mean, is it too much to ask that a father speak to his only child once a week? To check if she's alive?'

Maya let out a slow breath. 'You know how he is, Sammy. Besides, he knows you can take care of yourself. If anyone can walk into a new situation and run with it, it's you. Remember when I was your lighting assistant at that Wiccan ceremony, the one where they started getting naked while dancing around the fire? I was so sceptical, but you turned that shoot into the most soulful, enchanting photos. Or that time we got lost on our Bear Mountain hike and you stayed calm and talked me through a panic attack?' She made a shuddering noise before continuing. 'You're the most caring, resourceful person I know. Your father sees that too.'

Samara shrugged, even though Maya couldn't see her. 'Maybe. Still, it's nice to be the caree instead of the carer for a change.'

'*Caree* is not a word.'

'It should be. Anyway'—she exhaled—'I thought I could put together a photo collection of the Khanna family as a thank-you gift for hosting me. Get the best ones framed and put the rest into a nice album.'

'That's a great idea! You've told me so little about them. What are they like?'

'They're . . . complicated.' Samara would have said more, but she heard the roar of a souped-up car engine coming from outside. 'Hang on a second.'

She padded over to the window and peeked out. A sleek black BMW had stopped at their gate, muffled music pulsating forcefully out of its tinted windows. A man sat behind the wheel, but his face was obscured. Then Samara saw a shadowy figure emerge from the house and scurry towards the gate. The person carried a small bag and constantly looked over their shoulder to make sure no one was watching.

It was Diya.

'Uh-oh.'

'What?' asked Maya. 'What's going on?'

'Diya's sneaking out of the house, and there's an obnoxious car parked outside,' she replied just as Diya bent to unlock the gate and exit.

'Ooh. Is she alone?'

The car's engine turned off, and the driver's-side door opened. A man stepped out and sauntered over, talking to Diya in a low voice—which was kind of ironic, given that he'd just blasted the street with his revved-up motor like he was in a monster-truck rally. He laughed when Diya entered his waiting arms. A kiss followed.

'Nope,' replied Samara. 'Definitely not alone. There's a guy.'

'Of course there's a guy. There's always a guy. So what're they doing?'

She sighed. 'Kissing. So that's the reason she didn't want to be matched with Yash. Perfectly understandable, but why the secrecy?'

'Maybe Mystery Man is married. Or maybe he's as obnoxious as his car.'

Samara gave a humourless chuckle. 'I've met enough grooms to know that obnoxiousness has never disqualified anyone from becoming a husband. No, something's up here. I'm pretty sure the Khannas wouldn't be against a love match for Diya, even if they didn't like him. Sharav's fiancée, Nonita, is a real piece of work, and they accepted her, for God's sake. So why is Diya hiding her boyfriend?'

Now it was Maya's turn to chuckle. 'You're going to find out, aren't you?'

Samara watched Diya get into the car and drive away. 'That's right.'

'I don't suppose you could just mind your own business, Sammy?'

'When have I ever minded my own business?'

'Never,' declared Maya. 'You're the most lovable busybody I know. Be careful, though. Remember when you told that girl her boyfriend was cheating on her during our graduation party?'

'She had a right to know.'

'She trashed our apartment! We lost the deposit!'

'Fine, fine,' Samara conceded. 'I'll tread carefully.' She ambled over to her bed and opened a photo of Yash and Diya in the garden on her laptop. 'I actually like Yash, by the way. I think he'd be good for Diya. I mean, he dresses like a young Prince Charles, so there is that . . . hmm, maybe I can help there.'

'What about the others? The mom?'

'Jyoti Aunty is lovely.' Samara opened up a photo of Jyoti. She was laughing, with the sun shining on her face, encircled by the flowers and foliage of her beloved garden. A small smudge of mud sat on her cheek, and her eyes sparkled with joy that someone was taking an interest in her life's work. This one was definitely going in the framing pile. 'She's got so much grief inside her and yet manages to be so warm. Not that anyone appreciates it.'

She scrolled through the photos to one of Sharav and Nonita sitting on the pink garden bench. Sharav wore a strained smile, and Nonita held a practised pose, her face exactly the right angle to perfectly showcase her cheekbones. He had an arm placed around his fiancée's shoulders, and her hand rested lightly on his thigh, as Samara had instructed. Flowers surrounded them, and golden sunlight framed their faces, adding a dreamy glow to the setting. The portrait would look delectably intimate if Sharav didn't appear so uncomfortable.

Samara huffed.

'What?' asked Maya. The sound of fingers typing on a keyboard clacked in the background.

'Nothing.' The less time she spent thinking about Sharav Khanna, the better.

She scrolled to a photo of Dhruv, the one she'd taken in the driveaway. He stared at the camera with a surprised smile on his face, which made him look, for a brief moment, unguarded.

Her smile returned. They'd done good today, and Dhruv seemed to be opening up to her and his family. Plus, with the garage cleaned, he'd be spending more time at home. It was a start. 'I think I'm on the right track here. These people could use my help.'

Maya sighed. 'It would shock me if you thought otherwise.' The typing paused. 'I have to go, Sammy. But promise me that you'll focus more on your future than theirs. You have contracts to wrap up and job follow-ups to do. Don't lose track of the end goal: coming back here.'

'I won't, I promise. You get back to work, and let's chat in a couple of days. Love you.'

'Love you. Bye.'

Samara plopped the phone on the bed and stared at the faces on her laptop's screen. New York seemed so far away, and the Khannas were right in front of her. She thought back to Dhruv's surprise and elation at being allowed to use the garage for band practice and Jyoti's grateful hug—the camaraderie of today's garage cleanup. There could be more moments like that. Moments of healing, of joy. Of coming together as a family. She could help make that happen.

For the Khannas, if not for herself.

CHAPTER 11

Diya caught hold of his wrist just as he began sliding his hand underneath her dress, towards the junction of her thighs. Squirming, she pushed against his chest with her other hand, but he ignored it.

'Ari, stop,' she said, scanning the dark street outside the car to make sure no one was looking. They were parked on a lane that ran along the front of her neighbourhood, only a few houses away from the main road. Anyone walking past would be able to see them.

She pushed at him harder. 'Ari, stop it!'

'Relax. It'll be fine,' he replied against her collarbone. One hand made another bid at her thighs while the other tried to push the dress off her shoulder.

Panic arose in her chest at the unyielding weight of him. Without thinking, she lashed out, a sharp fingernail poking into his eye.

'Ow!' He finally pulled back, squinting. 'Bloody hell!'

'I said stop!'

Clutching his injured eye, Ari rapped the steering wheel in anger.

Hard. 'What is *wrong* with you?'

Diya flinched and drew back. 'I'm sorry. I panicked.'

'Over what? It's not like I'm trying to rape you or something.' He shook his head and glowered at her with his good eye.

Shame and apprehension washed over Diya. She and Ariyan had been dating for almost six months now, and they still hadn't had sex. In the beginning, Ari had been pretty understanding about it, laughing away her resistance and calling her his 'virgin princess,' but now it had become a point of contention.

Part of her just wanted to get it over with—power ahead and do the deed. The *virgin* label was hardly on trend in this day and age. And yet every make-out session with him inevitably wound up with her calling a premature end to the proceedings. It felt like all Ari wanted was to race to a finish line, and Diya just couldn't keep up with him, either physically or emotionally. It wasn't like she wanted music and fireworks when they kissed or anything, but it would be nice if she felt like she was a partner in the experience, as opposed to a collection of body parts he could enter. She wanted to feel ready, that's all.

If only Diya could tell him that without making him think there was something wrong with her.

Was there something wrong with her?

'I'm sorry,' she repeated. 'It's just that we're in the middle of the road—'

'It's two a.m.!' he snapped.

She tried to speak in a calm voice so as not to further aggravate his temper. 'There are night watchmen everywhere, and my family knows people on this street, Ari.'

He fell back into his seat and rubbed his injured eye. 'How am I supposed to drive half-blind? Did you think of that?'

'Let's stay here for a while until it feels better, okay? Can we talk?'

He laughed, scorn on the part of his face she could see. 'Talk away, princess. That's all you're good for, anyway.' He turned and looked out of his window.

Tears stabbed at her eyes, but she blinked them away, resolving not to crumple into a sobbing mess. Not today. Instead, she placed a hand on the back of his neck, alternating between softly kneading and stroking. He always liked that. 'I'm sorry,' she said yet again, this time in a soft, intimate murmur. 'Don't be angry with me. I love you.'

For a few moments Ari sat silently, sulking as he glared into the darkness outside. Then he replied, in an equally low murmur, 'You have a funny way of showing it.' He took his hand away from his eye and blinked rapidly, demonstrating his discomfort for her benefit.

She exhaled, relieved that he'd calmed down at least. She leaned over and kissed his cheek. 'How was work today?'

He shrugged, his tone still sullen. 'Whatever. Papa says jump, I ask how high. It's the same every day.'

'Did you speak to him about your ideas for expanding into semiprecious jewellery?'

Ari shrugged again. 'No point.' He put on an imperious tone in imitation of his father. '"Mehra and Sons only sells the very best quality gemstones to the richest families in India!"' Shaking his head, he reverted back to his normal voice and said, 'He'll never agree. Why do you think he insisted on making your amethyst design in platinum? Sterling silver is too *downmarket* for him. Anyway, I don't want to talk about it.'

Diya remembered Ari's father looking over her designs and remarking that many of them didn't 'lend themselves' to precious jewellery. That she should design more classic pieces, with more and bigger diamonds. That he didn't stock minimalist designs because they weighed less and were therefore cheaper. 'Never marry a man whose mother gifts you flimsy jewellery on the pretext of fashion,' Mr Mehra had advised her. 'She's either a cheapskate or she doesn't like you.'

Little did he know that Diya was planning to marry his son.

When Ari proposed, obviously.

If he proposed.

A wave of uncertainty hit her as she watched Ari fidget with his eye and stare out his window. He'd said he loved her but wasn't ready for the pressure of their families getting involved. Surely it was just a matter of time before he came around. Once they were engaged, the whole sex thing would sort itself out.

She would be ready then.

Diya took a deep breath. 'I need to tell you something.'

'What?'

'I met Yash Malhotra, the match that Ma and Sharav arranged.'

Ari shrugged, still not looking at her. 'Great. So when's the wedding?'

She huffed. 'Be serious. They want me to marry him.'

'So marry him, then, princess.'

'What about *us*?' she choked out, on the verge of breaking down.

Chuckling, he finally turned. 'What about us? You get married and have babies, and I'll have to find myself another princess to adore.'

Diya knew he was teasing, but she wasn't in the mood for his nonchalance. She turned her face away.

He laughed. 'Fine, don't marry him.'

'And then what?'

'What?'

She turned around, her temper rising. 'If I don't marry him, then what about us?'

Shrugging, he replied, 'I don't know. We live in the moment, have fun, make some memories!' He waggled his eyebrows in a suggestive way, something that never failed to make her smile.

Not tonight. Even though he was being good-humoured again, outburst forgotten, she needed some answers. 'I want to settle down, Ari. Get married, have kids.'

He leaned over and nipped her ear gently, then whispered with a smile, 'You say the word, sweetheart, and we'll make a kid right here, right now.'

'Ari!'

'Fine, fine.' He threw up his hands in mock surrender. Assuming a dramatic air, he said, '"Diya wants to get married. She wants to come live in our house and design jewellery for our showrooms while she pops out two kids, a girl and a boy. Gets a dog and goes for ladies' lunches to complain about sloppy maids and school chat groups." I get it, trust me—and I know that's in the future. But we're still young, princess. We've got the rest of our lives to be an old married couple. Let's just have fun right now.'

Diya's voice bordered on desperate. 'You're twenty-nine, Ari. Your parents are looking for potential brides, and you haven't even told them about me!'

Unfortunately for her, Ari had apparently decided he'd had enough of this conversation. He chucked her chin and asked in a playful tone, 'How about we name our dog Cinnamon, after your gorgeous eyes?'

After a fraught moment, Diya realised there was no point in pushing him anymore tonight. He'd just get angry again. She gave him a small, reluctant smile, even as the weight of her disappointment pressed on her shoulders.

Ari grinned. 'There's my pretty little prude. Now, let's get to this party, shall we?' He turned on the engine, and loud music burst into the air as the car surged forward.

Diya held on to her seat.

A short while later, they arrived at a large bungalow in another long-standing and even more posh neighbourhood, Vasant Vihar, where a party was in full swing. Ari entered the gathering like a war hero, to a chorus of raucous cheers and catcalls. He fist-pumped, hugged, high-fived, and thumped backs and shoulders. Most of his friends were there with their wives—women who sat scattered around in groups, eating canapés and conversing while waving diamond-laden hands at their husbands' drunken antics. They were older than Diya, had already achieved that coveted *wife* status, and regarded her with superior, slightly pitying attitudes. To them, she was irrelevant until she was official.

Not to mention that Diya was a bit of an oddball in their circle. Dressed in a simple black dress—with only an antique pendant on a leather chain for adornment—with her natural curls untamed by smoothening salon treatments and very little makeup on her face, she didn't quite fit the mould of Ariyan Mehra's future wife. As the sole heir to a sizable jewellery business, Ari could have his pick of Delhi debutantes.

Why would he pick her? Diya could almost hear them wondering behind their polite smiles and small talk.

She sometimes wondered that too.

'Mousse with cold-smoked wild salmon, century egg, and avocado on a caviar-infused almond wafer, ma'am?'

Diya looked up to see a waiter waving a tray in front of her. On it was what looked like greenish-pink soft serve topped with black specks. Her stomach recoiled at the thought of eating raw fish, old egg, and avocado mush on a fish-egg cracker. She shook her head. Only a handful of the other women were actually eating the pretentious appetiser. But with it, the hosts had made a valuable point—they weren't just rich; they were sophisticated and rich.

Big difference.

What she wouldn't give for a kebab right now.

A hand thumped her shoulder a little too hard. 'Disha!' a deep voice declared. 'How are you, babe?'

Her insides shrank as a sweaty, drunk man plopped down in a chair next to her. Ari's friend Nikhil. Given a choice between talking to him and eating that appetiser, she'd have emptied the tray.

She sighed. 'Diya.'

He squinted at her in confusion. 'What?'

'My name is Diya.'

'Right, right.' He laughed as his eyes roamed the contours of her chest, hips, and legs. The corner of his lips glistened with saliva. 'I hear you're campaigning to become the missus, eh?'

Dread replaced revulsion. 'I have no idea what you're talking about, Nikhil.'

His laugh was knowing as he leaned over and put a hand on her exposed knee, his thumb moving an inch higher on her thigh. Diya stiffened. He reeked of whisky and sweat.

'Ari's a difficult one to pin down,' he whispered way too loudly. 'You want my advice? Better give up the goods, babe. A man can only wait so long.' His thumb stroked her thigh, presumably to illustrate his point and conveniently cop a feel at the same time.

Diya gasped, mortified that Ari would share the most private parts of their relationship with his friends. As if she were just some hookup. How *could* he?

Without thinking, she threw Nikhil's hand off, got up, and strode over to Ari, who was ensconced within a large group of men at the bar. Elbowing away whoever was in her path, she made her way to him. 'We need to talk.'

'Princess!' Ari pulled her under his arm as he drunkenly swayed against the man next to him. 'What're you drinking?'

'Ari, I need to talk to you.'

He gestured to the bartender as though summoning a dog. 'The gin cocktail.' Turning to her with a smile, he said, 'You'll love this new gin. It's got wasabi and truffles in it. Karan got it when he went to Tokyo to have dinner at Kaiseki last week.'

She caught hold of his arm and shook it, barely holding back. 'I said, we need to talk.'

He brushed her off without a glance. 'We'll talk later,' he replied, with a hint of steel in his laughing voice.

Diya once again fought off tears. She knew he'd never forgive her if she made a scene in front of his friends. For all his outward breeziness, Ari's reputation mattered to him.

More than she did, obviously.

She waited at his side for her cocktail before excusing herself. No one spared her a second glance as she walked out into a dazzlingly decorated hallway and kept going until she hit the kitchen. It was a frenetic beehive of activity, and cooks, servers, and helpers bustled about while a catering chef with a heavy French accent barked instructions that were mostly indecipherable to her ears.

Quickening her steps, Diya slipped past and into the back garden, where cooking implements were more widely spread out and there were fewer people. She sat down on a bench in a dark corner, watching fragrant curls of smoke billow up from pots and pans into Delhi's smoggy night sky. Leaning forward and covering her face with her palms, she allowed her tears to finally fall.

It was a wonder she'd been able to hold on to them this long. After a few minutes of quiet sobbing, she heard a rustle next to her.

A woman in a sous chef's jacket was perched on a baluster nearby, a lunch box in her hand.

Diya wiped away her tears and pointed to the bench, which was large enough for three people. 'You can sit here, if you want.'

The woman gave her a compassionate glance. 'I don't want to disturb you, ma'am.'

'No problem. Please, sit. You must be tired from standing all evening.'

The sous chef came over and plunked down next to Diya with a tired puff. 'Thank you.' She quickly opened her lunch box.

'Is that your dinner?' Diya asked.

The sous chef nodded. 'Yes, ma'am.'

'Can't you just eat the food you prepare for the party?'

The woman gave her a look that said she felt exactly the same way about the party food as Diya did. 'We can, but I prefer to bring my own.' She unwrapped the cloth-covered contents of her dinner and held it out to Diya. 'Would you like some? It's just mutton-kebab sandwiches.'

Diya stared at the box containing four sandwiches stuffed with kebabs and melted cheese and almost cried again. 'I'd love one, thanks.'

CHAPTER 12

The injured woman ran down a lonely forest road, wet from the pouring rain. Rivulets of bloody water ran down her petrified face. She screamed into the darkness as the slimy, fanged creature stalked her. It didn't once occur to her to run back to her friends instead of weaving through trees in the opposite direction. No, this was a character that was meant to die early on—the writer had given her poor judgement and a ridiculously high-pitched voice, along with Marilyn Monroe hair and skimpy clothing. Let's face it: What horror-movie buff didn't secretly want the sexiest girl to die a gruesome death?

Ominous music pelted out from the TV and escalated, a sure sign that the creature was going to pop out from somewhere soon. Samara knew this, but that didn't stop her breath from hitching and her body from tightening as she lounged on the sofa in the upstairs TV room. It had been a killer of a day. She had photographed a wedding lunch, where the bride had insisted on directing every single photo that Samara took. No matter how often Samara told the couple to be natural and have fun, that candid photos were better when they were actually candid, Bridezilla had pushed back and browbeaten her groom and guests into posing like they were exhibits at a wax museum.

Which was why Samara was watching a horror flick and imagining the bride's face on every character that got mutilated and eaten by the creature.

The music ramped up, and she felt adrenaline rush through her body. Any second now. Any second . . .

The sofa cushion suddenly dipped next to her, and she shrieked, instinctively kicking out with her leg in a judo move she'd learnt in self-defence classes as a college student.

'Oww!'

Samara gasped for air as her heart slowed, and she tried to blink away the glare of the TV and focus on the person who'd just sat down next to her on the sofa. As her eyes adjusted to the dimly lit room, she saw Sharav, bent over in pain and clutching his nose.

'Oh my God, I'm so sorry!' she exclaimed, just as the woman in the movie let loose a bloodcurdling scream. The creature attacked and the slaughter commenced, with more screaming, roaring, and clanging.

'What on earth are you watching?' snapped Sharav as he grimaced at the TV, his hands still over his nose.

Samara quickly hit the pause button. 'A horror movie.' She slid across the sofa and examined Sharav's face, trying to see his nose through his fingers. 'Are you okay?'

He glared at her. 'Do I *look* okay?'

'I'm sorry. You scared me!'

'By *sitting on the sofa*?'

Samara shook off his bluster and gently tried to pry his fingers away from his nose. 'Let's assess the damage.'

They didn't budge. 'It hurts,' grumbled Sharav.

'I know,' she replied in a soothing voice, trying not to roll her eyes. She pulled his fingers a little harder. 'Come on, you big baby. Let me see.'

'No.'

'Give an inch, Sharav. It won't kill you.'

'I was going to watch!'

She frowned. 'What?'

He leaned back against the sofa and grunted. 'I was going to sit with you and watch the movie. I thought maybe we could hang out, try to get along for a change. Then you kicked me in the face.'

Samara stared at him for a moment, absorbing his admission, before giving him an apologetic look. 'The movie had me all amped up, and I reacted without thinking. I *would* like it if we could watch the movie together. Can we start again?'

Sharav nodded. He gingerly removed his hands from his nose and tested the bone. 'It doesn't feel broken.'

'Great!'

He looked at the on-screen carnage. 'Why a horror movie?'

'I like horror,' replied Samara as she paused the film and rewound it back to the point where she'd left off. 'It's like sitting on a roller coaster. You get the rush of excitement and fear without any actual danger. Like exercise for the nerves.'

'Well, I think my nerves have been exercised enough for today,' he said, chuckling.

A trickle of blood came out of one of his nostrils, and Samara felt a pang of regret. She reached over and grabbed a tissue box from the side table. 'You're bleeding a little. Here.' She handed him a tissue.

To his credit, Sharav didn't complain any further. Instead, he cleaned up the blood and held his nostrils together, breathing through his mouth to stop the bleeding. 'So how's the photography going?'

Relieved, she smiled. 'I had a bride from hell this morning, but most days it's going really well. I should have a good amount saved up by the end of wedding season.'

He seemed to consider her words before asking, 'What do wedding photographers do between March and October?'

'Corporate events, parties, baby showers, social media shoots . . .' she replied. 'But destination weddings are the best because I get to explore the destinations in between events. I love to travel. Hopefully, I'll get a job that involves travel when I return to New York.' Samara grinned.

Even though he was probably still in pain, Sharav smiled back. 'Any job offers yet?'

She shook her head. 'Not yet. I'm sure something will come along soon.'

He looked like he couldn't decide whether her optimism was refreshing or misplaced. 'How do you know?'

'How do I know what?'

'If something will come along.'

She shrugged. 'I don't, but I trust that it will.' She chuckled at his baffled expression. 'You won't understand because you're a control freak.'

'Is that a bad thing?'

'No,' Samara admitted. 'I do sometimes wish I was less impulsive. Although'—she pointed a finger at him—'*you're* a bit extreme. I mean, what will you write in your memoir if you never take any risks, do anything spontaneous or silly? Don't you ever get tired of being so wound up all the time?'

'I'm wound up because I'm responsible for the welfare of other people,' Sharav stated in an even voice, not seeming offended by her bluntness—for once. 'My family members, hundreds of employees, and their families.' After a reflective moment, he added, 'I'm wound up because my mother is sad, my sister is starring in her very own melodrama, Biba is always upset with me for one reason or the other, and my brother is practically a stranger. Not to mention our current houseguest'—he smiled to take the sting out of his words—'has made me her kickboxing bag. Also, I don't plan to ever write a memoir.'

'Why not?'

He shrugged. 'Who would read it?'

Her eyes widened, surprised that he would even ask. 'You, of course. You'd be eighty years old and would have lived a life worth reading about!'

Laughing, Sharav asked, 'So you're going to write a memoir?'

'Absolutely!'

'What will you write in it?'

She thought about it for a minute. 'Today's events will be included in a chapter called "Berserk Bridezillas," where I will reveal how the pressure of wedding planning makes some women lose control. It will include the time a bride threw a cup of hot coffee at me because the groom said I was attractive and the time a bride attempted to climb a pole holding the pavilion up because the flowers at the top were the wrong shade of purple.'

His smile grew wider. 'What else?'

Samara sighed, returning his smile. 'About my travels. The sights and sounds, tastes and smells. Like that first breath of fresh air when you hit the Himalayan foothills and roll your car windows down, the sweetness of a European summer strawberry versus the tartness of an Asian winter strawberry. All the tunnels I've walked through—from the underwater aquarium in Singapore to the Shinto torii gates tunnel in Kyoto. From the shafts that run through the Giza pyramids to the graffiti-lined subway tunnels in New York City to the Cradle of Humankind in Johannesburg.'

'Hold on. You've walked in the subway tunnels of New York? You're not supposed to do that.'

She laughed. Of course he would pick up on that, of all things. 'College kids do reckless things.'

After a moment, he asked, in a voice laced with gravel, 'What other reckless things have you done?'

Her breath caught. She'd been doing a lot of pretty wild things in her thoughts lately. With him. Not that she'd ever tell him that—even though he was studying her with eyes that suddenly seemed darker than before. Black holes that were rapidly consuming her coherence. She cleared her throat. 'Um, you don't want to know.'

He swallowed and replied, 'Probably not.'

Silence sprang, charged with something that felt way more electric than awkwardness. Samara bit her lip, trying to tamp down the awareness making her insides flutter, to make herself stop thinking about nudging closer to him and running her hands over those strapping shoulders stretching out his shirt. Maybe even slipping her fingers inside to feel the warm, solid contours of his chest, his abdomen, his—

Whoa! No, abort. *Abort!*

The man is engaged, she scolded her heart as it thrashed against the walls of her chest. Before the last ten minutes, they'd barely been able to be in the same room together without fighting like cats, and now that they were *finally* talking like normal people, she was going to hit on him? No, uh-uh. Sharav Khanna was off limits, destined to live a long, healthy, utterly predictable life with his perfect trophy wife in Delhi, while Samara would be on the other end of the world, having adventures and feeding her soul.

That was the plan, and she was going to stick to it. No HDD for her!

'HDD?'

Oh no, she'd said it out loud.

'Actually, I meant to ask you about that,' said Sharav, clearing the rasp out of his throat. 'You called me HDD the day you moved in.'

'I did?'

'You did. What does it mean?'

Hot Designated Driver. It still fit him perfectly. 'Nothing, just a bunch of initials.'

'What do they stand for?'

'Nothing.'

He continued to hold her under his gaze, his eyes now intrigued. 'You're lying. Why're you lying? It stands for something bad, doesn't it?'

'Don't be ridiculous.' She attempted an airy dismissal, adding a small huff for effect.

He smiled. Not his usual one. This smile was almost roguish, and it set her pulse racing again. 'I don't believe you.' He leaned forward. 'Hmm, HDD . . . Hairy, Dumb Dimwit?'

'Of course not!' she exclaimed. 'I would never call you that.'

He grinned. 'So it's something good, then. Okay, how about Humble, Diligent . . . Decision-Maker? Honourable, Distinguished, and Dynamic?'

'You wish.'

Undeterred, he continued, 'Highly Dashing and Dapper!'

Samara snorted. 'Yeah, because it's the eighteenth century and my name is Elizabeth.'

'Hot . . .'

She stiffened and then mentally kicked herself.

'Hot!' He leaned in, his expression triumphant. '*Hot* is correct.' He chuckled. 'So you think I'm hot, huh?'

Where was an earthquake when you needed one? 'Shut up!' Great, now she'd been reduced to fourth-grade comebacks.

'What could the other two words be? Hmm . . .' Sharav was thoroughly enjoying her discomfiture—a cream-sated cat couldn't compare. 'Delectable and Debonair. Desirable and Dreamy. Dishy?' He lifted an inquiring eyebrow, scrutinising her reaction as his shoulders shook with smug merriment.

'That's it.' Samara stood up, her cheeks blazing with mortification. 'I'm out of here.' She began a dash towards her room.

Sharav, however, wasn't having it. 'Oh, no, you don't!' Laughing, he leapt up behind her, caught hold of her wrist, and spun her around. Her front collided with his chest just as his arms went around her, holding tight. 'Tell me!'

Samara wrestled against his grip. 'Not a chance in hell!' She pushed as hard as she could, but it was like fighting a wall, so she pinched his arm and aimed a kick at his shin.

He dodged it deftly and caught her other wrist, pinning her hands down. 'Doable? Darling? Tell me!'

'When big fat pigs fly!' she shrieked as she threw herself backward, putting all her weight into it so he would be

forced to let go or fall himself. As it turned out, Sharav didn't let go. They fell on the couch together. Him on top of her.

For a reflexive moment, Samara squirmed, trying to free her legs from under the weight of his. Unfortunately, that meant she not only ended up with her legs on either side of his hips, but her twisting body and flailing limbs tugged him even closer.

Fitting him snugly between her thighs.

That's when she noticed that Sharav wasn't laughing anymore.

CHAPTER 13

He was drowning.

Sprawled beneath him, inadvertently cradling his hips between her legs, was the most aggravating and the most enticing woman he'd ever met. Her lips, devoid of her sunshiny smile, panted hot breaths into his face. Her chest rose and fell rapidly under his. Her eyes—her big, beautiful eyes—stared up at him, rapt, mirroring the pulsating lust raging through him. Lust barely restrained by a hair on the back of a single scruple.

Samara whimpered. A wisp of a sound yet heavy with ache and frustration.

It shot straight through him.

Sucking in a breath, he heaved himself off the sofa. 'I'm so sorry.' His voice was guttural. He ran a hand through his hair. 'Are you okay?

She nodded, seemingly unable to say anything. Or move, apparently. She just lay there in exactly the same position he'd left her in. Blinking up at him, her legs splayed open, breasts heaving.

He looked away.

For at least a minute, neither of them said anything. Sharav stared at the frozen horror movie on the screen, focusing on the grisly scene to calm his body. He heard Samara shuffling behind him, seating herself back on the sofa and coughing delicately. Then she announced in a high-pitched, overly enthusiastic voice, 'The sound system!'

Sharav frowned and turned back. 'What?'

'It's not working. The surround sound speakers, in the walls. *On* the walls. Installed, I mean.' Samara huffed. Apparently, horniness turned her into Yoda.

'Oh.' He pretended to inspect the room. 'I'll get it repaired.'

With a flappy, almost-cartoonish wave of her hand, Samara nodded. 'You should. You have such a huge TV screen. Why don't you use this room more often?'

It took a few seconds for him to process her words, but Sharav managed to organise his thoughts enough to reply, 'Er, I don't know. We should.'

'You *totally* should,' she parroted, with more eagerness than the discussion warranted.

Sharav nodded. 'We should.' He stood over her, undecided as to what to say or do next. Wanting to leave but also not wanting to leave.

As though realising this, Samara pointed to the screen. 'Want to watch the rest of the movie with me?'

He nodded with relief and gratitude for being let off the hook. He sat on the opposite end of the sofa. 'Catch me up on the story.'

'College kids in a secluded cabin. Monster in the woods. Three have been devoured. Six are left.'

He exhaled. 'Okay. Un-pause.'

With the press of a button, the room was once again filled with spine-chilling screams. The pair on the sofa gasped and squeezed their eyes shut at all the right moments, their heartbeats synced to the rise and fall of the movie soundtrack. By the end of the film, Sharav felt wrung out, exhilarated, and on edge at the same time. It was a new, not entirely unpleasant feeling. He looked over at Samara. She looked relaxed and sleepy, hugging a large cushion like a kitten curled around its favourite ball of yarn. Her small frame barely took up any room on the large sectional. He laughed. 'This was fun. We should do it more often.'

She turned her face, stroked by the lamplight, and gave him a languid, almost-sultry smile. The kind that she might give someone who woke her up to . . .

His spine snapped straight. Searching the room, his frantic eyes landed on the empty bar counter and shelves. He gestured towards them as though he were waving a handkerchief at a departing ship. 'Drinks! I'll stock in the bar. Up. Stock *up* the bar. So we can have drinks. Next time. Anyway, good night.'

He fled.

CHAPTER 14

Boring was the only way to describe it.

Samara scowled at Yash Malhotra's clean but characterless desk in the big, fancy YBS Bank corporate office. The space had an open-concept design, with sleek lines, ultra-modern fixtures, and a space-age feel to it. There was a lot of grey, and any natural light was obstructed by windows with steel slats on the outside. Overhead fluorescents threw a bright, uniform light over everything, neither highlighting nor hiding, creating a canvas that painted everyone below in pasty white.

It was as if the place had been designed by vampires.

She turned to Yash, who stood next to his chair with an uncomfortable smile. It was after office hours, and most of the employees had left. Yash was working late, as he'd patiently explained when Samara called him earlier that day. In fact, his exact words were 'I'm sorry, I'm working late and eating at the office' when she'd asked what he was doing for dinner, *clearly* implying that he didn't want to meet.

'I hope I'm not interrupting your work,' Samara asked with a smile, knowing that was exactly what she was doing. There was no time for guilt, though. The morning after Diya had sneaked out of the house, Samara had walked past Diya's room and heard her sobbing. At dinner, her eyes were red and puffy, and she hadn't eaten a thing.

Mystery Man was obviously bad news. Samara had decided in that moment to try to bring Yash and Diya together. She'd been plotting ever since, despite being chronically distracted by the memory of Sharav between her . . . *Nope, not now,* she scolded herself. Tonight was about getting to know Yash.

'No, not at all,' replied Yash with a polite shake of his head. No matter how baffled he might be at Samara's sudden interest in meeting him, he was far too well mannered to let it show. 'It's nice to see you again.'

'I like your desk.' She waved a weak hand at it. 'It's got good . . . er, air circulation.'

He smiled and shrugged. 'It's okay for now. I'm not very high up in the ranks yet, but I'm hoping I'll get a corner desk in a year or two. Those are next to the windows and have a small side table.'

Samara suppressed a small shudder. The thought of slogging for years in this colourless cavern just to get a window seat made her soul die a little. 'Right, well . . . it's good to have goals.'

Yash nodded. Then, after a moment of fidgeting indecisively, he asked, 'Have you eaten dinner?'

'No, not yet. You?'

'No. I was planning to eat something in our micro-kitchen here.

They allow us to invite guests, so you can join me if you like.'

'I'd love to,' she replied, relieved he wasn't going to kick her out. 'Lead the way!'

He led her down a few hallways and into what looked like a small café, with bar tables, a countertop covered with snacks, and vending machines arranged against the wall. Here, finally, were splashes of colour—walls and furniture painted in blues, greens, and reds with a kitschy-chic vibe.

Yash gathered up cups and saucers and turned to her. 'Coffee, tea, or hot chocolate? They've also got green, mint, and chamomile teas. And masala chai, which is sweet but really good.'

'Then I'll have that, thanks.'

He poured them both steaming cups of chai from a fancy machine and put one in front of her. Samara lifted it to her nose and sighed at the fragrant smell of ginger, cardamom, and . . . vanilla? She took a sip and almost moaned. 'Oh my God, it's like masala-chai ice cream!'

Yash chuckled as he sipped his own. 'Good, right?'

'*So* good!'

Just like that, the lingering awkwardness of their situation dissipated into easy camaraderie. Yash gave her an enthusiastic grin and said, 'Okay, so for dinner, we have a few options. The sandwiches are usually finished by now, but there are cookies, chips, chocolate, cheese, crackers, and cereal here.' He waved at the counter. 'Or you could get hot instant noodles and buttered sweet corn from the vending machines.'

He turned to her, and his smile became a little mischievous. '*Or* I could make you a Yash Special, which is my own recipe for instant noodles.'

Finally, he was opening up! Samara grinned right back. 'In that case, I'll have the Yash Special, please.'

'You sure? It's a little unusual.'

'I can't wait!'

He laughed and got to work. While Samara wasn't the least bit attracted to him, she couldn't help but notice how handsome Yash looked when he laughed—as opposed to those nervous, longing looks he'd given Diya the other day.

Speaking of Diya . . .

'Are you in touch with any of the Khannas?'

He stiffened very slightly as he pressed buttons on one of the vending machines, which began creaking in response. 'Not recently. How are they?' His nonchalant tone had a gruff quality to it.

Samara smiled to herself. He had it bad. 'They're good. Diya's started working on a collection of designs inspired by glassblowing.'

He smiled as he pulled out two steaming plastic bowls of instant masala-flavoured noodles from the machine and put them on the counter. 'She's very talented. Her design at Mehra and Sons is amazing.' He turned and dispensed two bowls of buttered sweet corn from the other vending machine. Without ceremony, he dumped the corn into the noodles and folded them in with a fork.

Watching his practised movements, Samara asked, 'You've seen that amethyst set?'

His hand stilled for a second over a packet of cheese slices in a refrigerated display box. 'I, er, was accompanying my mother while she shopped. Mr Mehra pointed it out.' Taking a breath, he gingerly picked up four slices of cheese, unwrapped them, and dropped two into each bowl. The steaming-hot noodles immediately began to melt the cheese.

'That looks good,' Samara murmured as she watched him stir the mixture into a buttery, cheesy, spicy bowl of carby comfort.

Yash shook his head. 'I'm not done yet.' He walked over to one side and picked up two bags of masala potato chips. Then he took everything to a table. 'Have a seat.'

As Samara sat, he put a noodle bowl and a bag of chips in front of each of them. He then tore open the chips, took one out, and piled a generous spoonful of noodles, corn, and cheese on top of it. 'This is the Yash Special,' he declared as he shoved the entire thing into his mouth and crunched down on it with a satisfied grin.

Samara returned his enthusiasm with a grin of her own as she copied his actions. The combination of flavours and textures burst forth in her mouth. It was probably the unhealthiest thing she'd eaten all week, and she *loved* it. 'Yum! Creamy, crunchy, and double the masala!'

'Exactly! Some of my colleagues put cookies or even chocolate syrup on their noodles, but I prefer mine salty and spicy.'

They ate in hungry silence for a while. Then Samara sat back, her tummy warm and full, and took a sip of her now-tepid chai. 'So how long have you been in love with Diya?'

Yash choked.

Leaning over and thumping his back firmly while he gagged and coughed, Samara exclaimed, 'Sorry, sorry! I didn't mean to startle you.'

He shook his head, lips clamped together to keep from spurting a mouthful of food all over her. It was admirable and endearing that he managed to maintain his good manners even when he had spicy food lodged in his windpipe.

Once he'd settled down, Samara apologised again. 'Sometimes I just say things without thinking—but I mean well, I promise,' she said. 'It's just that I've seen the way you look at Diya.'

After a moment of indecision, Yash gave up with a resigned sigh. 'Is it that obvious?'

'Only to someone very observant. How long have you felt this way?' He sat back and fiddled with his tea mug. 'Since we were kids.' He gave a humourless chortle. 'I was a pretty small and shy child, so I got bullied a lot. One day, we were in a large group of families, having a picnic in Lodi Gardens, when two of the other boys began hitting me.' He smiled. 'Diya not only pushed them away, but she punched them back. Until one of them gave her a bloody nose, and then the parents got involved.'

He looked up at Samara. 'She didn't have to defend me. We weren't close. But even as a child, she had integrity and courage. She was also bossy, always telling the other kids what to do, making sure everyone had fun.' His smile became tender. 'She had fire.'

'And you worshipped her from a distance?'

Another laugh. 'Pretty much.'

'Have you ever told her how you feel?'

He shrugged. 'I've said I'm interested but nothing about love. My mom figured it out, though. That's why she's trying to fix us up.'

A buzzing sound came from his pocket. He took out his phone and looked at the screen. 'Excuse me, I have to take this.'

'Of course.'

Yash leaned away and held the phone up to his ear. 'Hi, Nishant. Yeah, I saw the presentation. No, it still needs revisions before we submit. I've marked it up, so please make the changes and get it to me by tomorrow.' After a pause, his jaw flexed. 'No, it's not presentable yet. Yes, I understand it's your friend's birthday, and while I appreciate your effort, I also want to point out that you've had all week to make these changes. As I mentioned, please have it on my desk by tomorrow. Thanks. Bye.' He hung up.

'Everything okay?' asked Samara.

He nodded. 'Just a guy who always has an excuse for everything. Never mind. What were we talking about?'

Samara tilted her head and gave him a teasing smile. 'About how you can lay down the law with Nishant but don't have the guts to go for it with Diya.'

That made him laugh. 'I know where I stand with Nishant. Diya's a closed book. Besides, she's already—' He hesitated and then kept quiet.

'Already what?'

'Nothing.'

Samara shook her head. 'It's not nothing. Tell me. I promise I'll keep it to myself.'

Yash sighed. 'I don't know if Jyoti Aunty and Sharav know, but she's been hanging out with Mr Mehra's son, Ariyan.'

Ah, that explained a lot. 'Are they serious?'

A scornful sound left him. 'I don't think Ariyan has been serious about anything a day in his life.'

'That could change, depending on the situation. Are they in love?'

He hesitated for another moment before his expression turned angry. 'He's also been seen with other women. I doubt Diya knows.'

Samara couldn't help a growl of outrage. 'Forget about Ariyan,' she stated in a firm voice. 'Hypothetically, if Diya were single, would you be interested in pursuing her?'

Shrugging, Yash replied, 'Of course, but I—'

'No *buts*,' she interrupted. 'If you're serious about her, I can help you.'

He gave her a sceptical look. 'How?'

'Just trust me.'

That brought on an amused smile and a lift of his eyebrow. 'Really?'

'See, right there—that look!' Samara waved a finger in his face. 'That's incredibly attractive to a woman. It changes your vibe completely. Even during your call with slacker Nishant, your persona was completely different from the person I met the last time. You're assertive. You have a sense of humour. It's very attractive.'

Yash shook his head with an embarrassed laugh.

'No,' she insisted, 'don't brush it off. Own it. Next time you're with Diya, I want her to see the Yash you are with me.'

He laughed again. 'Won't make a difference. Have you seen Ariyan? He looks like he stepped out of a Tom Ford ad.'

She waved a dismissive hand. 'That doesn't matter. I'll tell you a secret.' Samara leaned forward. 'Most women don't care what a man looks like—not really. It's about a vibe. Women are attracted to confidence. It's far, far more attractive than big biceps.'

Yash replied with a grimace, 'Ariyan's pretty confident.'

'Yes, and maybe Diya likes that in him. But attraction is only the first step. Once that's taken care of, the next thing that matters is substance. Which, given that he's fooling around behind Diya's back, I'm guessing Ariyan lacks. Right?'

He nodded. 'From what I've heard. We don't exactly run in the same crowd.'

'So I think you should step in. Spend some time with her outside of the whole arranged-marriage business. Allow her to get to know you and see you as the man you are and not the child you were. Smile, laugh, and have fun. Look her in the eyes, express your opinions. Show her your true self instead of peeking at her like a lovesick puppy every time you meet.'

A rueful smile. 'Do I really do that?'

'Kind of.' She smiled back, glad he'd taken her words in the right spirit. 'No one likes being put on a pedestal. I mean, it's fun for a while, sure, but it boxes you in, makes you into a stereotype instead of a multidimensional, flawed human being. I'm sure Diya would see you differently if you saw *her* differently.'

'Well, all that's fine, but it's not like we hang out every day for her to notice a difference in me.'

Samara's smile widened. 'Don't worry. We'll figure that out.'

'How?'

'We'll make her think *I'm* interested in you.'

'Huh?'

She took a deep breath. 'It's the perfect plan. Right now, you're just a childhood friend who's being pushed upon her by the family. She doesn't see you as a man.'

'Okay,' he responded in a sardonic tone.

'Relax, it's not you—it's her. A matter of perception, which can change.' Samara pointed at herself. 'If *I* show an interest, she might begin to see you as an object of attraction. Once she's hooked, I'll back off and let her feel like she's won. That you chose her over me. Then I leave for New York, and everyone lives happily ever after!'

Yash frowned. 'You're going to pretend to like me?'

'I already like you. I'm going to pretend to be *attracted* to you.'

'Am I supposed to pretend too?'

'Not at all. You just behave normally, and leave the rest to me.'

It was a credit to Yash's integrity that he seemed uncomfortable with her machinations. Especially when he replied, 'I don't know, Samara. It sounds manipulative.'

'Oh, it is, absolutely.'

He looked surprised by her ready admission and shook his head. 'Not to mention that it probably won't work.'

A scenario Samara had already considered and dismissed. 'Then no harm done! At least you tried. You gave it a shot, it didn't work, and you can move on without regret and find the future Mrs Malhotra elsewhere.'

Moments passed, fraught with apprehension. Then Yash took a deep breath. 'You know what . . .'

Samara held hers. 'What?'

'Ariyan is a jerk.'

'He *totally* is.'

'Diya deserves better.'

'She *totally* does.'

'Fine,' he uttered with a resolute nod. 'Nothing ventured, nothing gained.'

She felt like jumping up and hugging him. 'Wonderful! Just one other small, teeny-tiny, little thing.'

'What?'

'You need a new wardrobe.'

CHAPTER 15

'Nope, not taking it off.'

Everyone watched Dhruv adjust the tie-dyed purple-and-green guitar strap on his shoulder with a slightly defiant air. The rest of his bass guitar was fairly conventional—four strings, a sleek black-and-white body, and an unassuming fretboard. His strap, on the other hand, was totally out of place, as his bandmate and drummer, Ira, had just pointed out.

'Why not?' Ira tilted her elfin face, which was dotted with piercings. 'That thing is hideous!'

Laz, the gangly keyboard player, grinned from behind his stand. 'Dude, it belongs on a sixty-year-old stoner.'

Ira laughed, but Dhruv didn't, noted Samara as she sat in the garage, watching the band set up their instruments. She'd brought in drinks from the kitchen and set them up in one corner of the newly revamped space. Dhruv had been good-humoured and chatty right up until she'd asked if she could stay for one song before she left for a wedding. At that point, he'd stiffened and become tight lipped, even though Ira and Laz told her to stay as long as she liked.

Samara wondered why he didn't want her watching them.

Sounds of guitar-tuning, cymbal-cleaning, and keyboard-unpacking filled the room as the three band members got ready for rehearsal. Samara noticed that even though Dhruv and Ira behaved like regular friends and bandmates, there was a certain something between them. An energy, like the vibration you felt in your chest when you stood next to a loud bass speaker. Invisible but electric.

She laughed to herself. Maybe after she was finished with Diya and Yash, she could take on Dhruv and Ira. Become a matchmaker, an occupation that was actually a legitimate, and potentially very lucrative, one in this part of the world. In millions of joint families like the Khannas, where multiple generations all lived under the same roof, the choice of spouse affected everybody in the house, and so there was an entire industry dedicated to getting it right.

Slam!

'Ladies and gentlemen, brace yourselves!'

Sid, the band's lead guitarist, had just walked in after almost taking the garage door off its hinges and was now standing in a dramatic pose, grinning at them. He was tall, like Dhruv, and had a peppy enthusiasm that complemented Dhruv's reserve. According to Jyoti, they were the best of friends.

'Braced and ready, dude,' Laz intoned in his deep, unruffled voice. 'What's up?'

Bowing low with a flourish, Sid replied, 'I got us our first gig.'

'What? No way!' exclaimed Ira.

'My mom's cousin owns a bar in Hauz Khas Village,' Sid said. 'I showed him our demo, and he said we can do one weeknight a month for the next three months. No money, obviously, but we'll get draft beer, and it's a great opportunity to actually perform!'

Laz's eyes brightened. 'Free beer?'

Sid rolled his eyes, his grin breaking into a laugh. 'Focus, dude! We got a gig! A real one, with an actual audience. I even got him to give us a Wednesday slot. Ladies' night, baby!'

Laz gave a roguish howl, and Ira did a little drumroll as she whooped. Dhruv, however, stood still, breathing unsteadily as he watched his bandmates celebrate. Samara frowned. He was obviously shocked, but it was unclear whether it was good shocked or bad shocked.

'Dhruv, what do you think?' said Sid, turning to him. 'Amazing, right?'

'Amazing!' replied Dhruv, with excitement that was clearly feigned. 'When do we go on?' His hands were balled into fists at his side, and his feet fidgeted, as though he itched to run out of the room.

Sid must have been too elated to notice anything off with Dhruv. 'Our first one is next week, Wednesday night at the Royal Hauz, opening for their regular band.' He turned and started to unzip his guitar bag. 'We need to start rehearsing ASAP!'

Dhruv got a panicky look on his face for a brief moment, and Samara almost got up and went to him before stopping herself.

'Next week is *soon*, bro,' drawled Laz.

Ira whooshed out a breath. 'Better get started. I was going to leave before lunch, but I think we better keep going now.'

Sid nodded. 'Yeah. For the next few days, let's buckle down.'

'Full-day rehearsals!' declared Laz.

'Dude, we've still got *college*,' objected Sid.

'Fine—full nights, then. First, let's sort out the set list.'

'First, let's sort out lunch,' said Ira, rubbing her stomach. 'I haven't eaten since last night and need to slay my grooves.' She did another drumroll with a dramatic crash to drive the point home.

'I'll ask Biba to make something,' offered Samara, keeping an eye on Dhruv, who was still just standing there. 'She usually doesn't like ordering food from outside.'

'Okay, great,' replied Ira. 'Samara's got lunch covered. Sid, set up your guitar, and let's run through some tunes.'

Sid bounded over to the large amp and plugged in his electric guitar. 'We should open with a crowd-pleaser.'

'They should all be crowd-pleasers!' That was Ira.

Laz hummed. 'A couple of ballads, too, in the middle. And a showstopper at the end.'

'How long should the set be?' asked Sid, looking around for suggestions.

Dhruv now gripped his forehead, swaying a little and holding his bass guitar *way* too tight. Samara's mind raced. She had to do something, find out what was wrong with him. 'Dhruv?'

His head jerked towards her.

'Can I talk to you outside for a minute?'

He nodded, seeming to get a sense of his surrounds. 'Yeah,' he all but croaked. He began to walk to the garage door with Samara.

'Dhruv!' shouted Sid. 'Where're you going, bro? We need to rehearse!'

Before Dhruv could say anything, Samara quickly called out with a cheery smile, 'Sorry! I'm just stealing him for a moment. Will return him ASAP!'

Sid, who'd been making puppy eyes at her ever since they'd met at the garage clear-out, returned her smile. 'Sure, no problem. We'll finish setting up in the meantime. Maybe you could join us for lunch?'

'I would love to, but I'm photographing an event,' replied Samara, quickly shepherding Dhruv out of the garage. 'Have fun with your rehearsal!' She exited and shut the door with a decisive clack.

Turning to Dhruv, she asked in a concerned voice, 'What's up with you? Why aren't you happy about the gig?'

With skittish eyes, Dhruv attempted a shrug. 'Who says I'm not?'

'Are you worried about something?'

Dhruv didn't answer that. Instead, he said, 'I'm fine.' Then, after hesitating for moment, he blurted out, 'I need you to not tell my family about the gig!'

Samara regarded him for a few seconds. Was that the problem? He didn't want his family cramping his style? Her gut said no—there was definitely more—but she decided to put him at ease first. 'Okay.'

'I mean, it's not like there's anything *wrong*, per se, but I just don't want anyone at home to know yet.'

'Okay.'

'Only the first one. After that, you can tell them.'

'Okay, no problem,' she replied in a firm voice. 'I won't tell your family, Dhruv.'

He looked suspicious. 'That's it? You're not going to ask me why?'

'You've obviously got your reasons, and I respect them.' That was a half truth. She was *totally* going to find out what was wrong, but he didn't need to know that. Not yet.

'Okay.' Dhruv exhaled, his voice unsteady. He didn't look any happier than before. 'Thanks.'

'You're welcome. You should go back in. There's a lot of work to do before next week, right?'

'Yeah.' He turned back towards the garage, shoulders slumped, footsteps heavy on the ground.

Samara frowned as the door closed behind him. Despite Dhruv's insistence that he didn't want anyone at home to attend his first gig, there was really only one way to figure out what was bothering him.

She had to go to the Royal Hauz on Wednesday night.

CHAPTER 16

'Now I know how Alice felt when she went down the rabbit hole.'

The gold-painted broom that had just nudged Sharav's foot was being wielded by a leggy blonde woman wearing high heels and a shimmering designer gown that must have cost a fortune. There were more like her, women who looked better suited to competing in an Eastern European beauty pageant than sweeping the floor, à la *Biggest Boss*.

Biggest Boss was a popular reality TV show featuring minor celebrities living in a house and voting each other out in between challenges, catfights, sexual politics, confessions, and a *lot* of cleaning. The show was the theme for the pre-wedding party tonight. Different areas of the field-size tent had been decorated like sets, including the *Biggest Boss* House section, where Sharav and Nonita had just entered.

Ergo, beauty queens with brooms.

'This is ridiculous,' Sharav mumbled, looking at the blindingly opulent excess around him.

Nonita, who was standing next to him, waved off his comment. 'Don't be a spoilsport. The bride is a huge *Biggest Boss* fan—and they've got the money, so why not? Besides, they're supporting a charity that makes incense sticks out of recycled flowers. I forgot the name, but there's a stand around here somewhere. They're doing the aroma for the evening.'

Had the hosts donated a fraction of their party budget, the charity would be flush for a decade, thought Sharav, but he kept silent. Nonita was excited to be here, attending one of the most anticipated weddings in Delhi this month. The bride was a friend of a friend, the daughter of the owner of a luxury gym chain.

Milling around were three thousand other people, along with a few reality TV celebs, their gym bodies on full display.

Nonita nodded towards the eye-catching bar, which had been constructed to look like a royal Rajputana palace, complete with gigantic curtains in rich jewel tones and Rajasthani gold embroidery draped from the towering ceiling. Colossal chandeliers hung in between, lighting a vast display of alcohol on bar counters designed to look like palace walls.

'Apparently, there's also a Confession Room, where they gift you a diamond pendant if you confess your secrets on the Confession Cam. The winner of the Biggest Confession Award gets a Range Rover.' Nonita clutched her chin, suddenly looking contemplative.

Sharav's eyes widened. 'You're not actually thinking of going in there, are you?'

She shrugged. 'Why not? It's for a diamond pendant.' Frowning up at him, she asked, 'What's a juicier secret—nose job or eating steak on holidays abroad?'

'You've had a nose job?'

'Of course not! Just a *very* minor procedure for my deviated septum.'

Now Sharav couldn't stop staring at her nose. To distract himself, he asked, 'Why would eating steak on holiday be a secret?'

'The hosts are strict vegetarians. That's why they're serving expensive alcohol.'

Sharav sighed. The only upside of a wedding where he didn't know the hosts was usually the food. Roasted meats fresh out of a tandoor, their charred ends still smoking from tiny flames, wrapped in fluffy, buttery naan. It was one of his favourite things in the world. He didn't care how fat the truffle shavings on a mushroom biryani were. It was a poor substitute. 'Now I actually *do* need a drink. You?'

Nonita brightened up. 'I'll have the wine.'

He nodded. 'Red or white?'

'Whichever one looks more expensive.'

A small wave of irritation tightened Sharav's jaw. Most times, he could ignore Nonita's insatiable hunger for all things high priced regardless of taste, but once in a while, it grated on him. Would she even be with him if he weren't well off? What if the family business suffered losses in the future and they could no longer afford an affluent lifestyle? Would she leave him?

Sharav shook off the niggling apprehension. He was overreacting. So she was a little shallow, overly concerned with appearances, and enamoured with wealth. And perhaps she could be a little insensitive sometimes, especially towards his younger siblings and Biba. Still, Nonita was an intelligent, kind-hearted, go-getting woman from a good family background, who also happened to be tall, beautiful, and athletic.

She got along with his mother too.

He gave a little nod to reassure himself. She was a perfectly fine choice for a wife, and he needed to stop overthinking it and get the drinks. He took a step towards the bar.

Boom!

Sharav whirled around, instinctively shielding Nonita from the explosion while he cast a frantic eye around. Aside from a few gasps, nobody else seemed to be overly worried.

Then the lights went off.

Someone screamed as the sound of thunder rattled the tent and its occupants. Suddenly, spotlights illuminated one of the elaborately decorated entrances. Sharav cursed under his breath as he realised this was part of the 'show.' Apparently, scaring your guests half to death was the new wedding trend.

Deafening sounds of thunder were replaced by an equally deafening remix of the *Biggest Boss* theme song.

An announcer's voice boomed over their heads: 'Ladies and gentlemen, here's the *biggest boss* of them all!' A full-size parade float entered the tent. The bottom half was decorated to look like water, and the top was a bedazzled version of a sleek yacht. Standing at the bow, in sunglasses and a tank top composed entirely of diamonds, was the groom.

The guests clapped politely as the float and the waving groom made their way slowly towards the stage. The lights and music changed again as a contingent of groomsmen skipped onto the stage and, along with the groom, performed a perfectly choreographed Hindi song-and-dance number about men being men and doing manly things, along with various euphemistic references to alcohol and sex.

Pre-recorded sounds of an impassioned, cheering audience filled the air. Like they'd stolen the crowd soundtrack from a boy band concert, complete with screaming preteen girls.

Sharav winced. Now he *really* needed that drink. He made his way to the bar and ordered a wine for Nonita and a single malt for himself. 'A double,' he requested of the bartender, who sympathetically poured him a triple.

At this point, as if Sharav's senses hadn't already been wrung out, the stage setting changed again. Pink-and-purple lights traversed the stage, along with the jingling of ankle bells, signalling the imminent arrival of the bride.

A spotlight shot high above the stage towards the ceiling of the tent. Suspended overhead was a golden cage. As apocalyptic music thrashed around them, the cage slowly lowered to rest on an onstage platform shaped like a rocky precipice. Inside, dressed like an Indian princess in a royal-blue lehenga, the bride knelt in a forlorn pose. Which made perfect sense because she was apparently being craned around like a zoo animal while the groom got to ride in a yacht.

Sharav squinted to get a closer look at the bride. Cradled in one of her arms, dressed in the same royal blue, was a small, furry dog.

'That's the bride's dog, Whisky,' said a voice behind Sharav. 'She wanted him to be part of the performance.'

Sharav took a sip of his drink, feeling sorry for the dog, who squirmed in his mommy's embrace and glanced around nervously at the bright stage lights and crowd.

The groom now charged up the five-foot-tall rock and pretended to strike the golden bars of the cage with a sword. The bars collapsed in a dramatic flourish of laser beams, kettle drums, and frantic barking from Whisky as the bride and groom reunited. The groom hugged his bride and her fur-baby to his chest, their faces all smiles.

Unfortunately, in their enthusiasm, the couple must have squeezed poor Whisky a little too tight between their jewel-encrusted bodies. The dog panicked and snapped at the bride's hand, resulting in her dropping him onto the stage.

At this point, a popular Hindi song about Indian women being much hotter than their international counterparts blasted through the speakers. The groom, obviously a fan of the old maxim 'the show must go on,' ignored the wayward dog and swept the bride into dance steps that they'd probably practised for months with a professional choreographer. The bride, after a brief second of indecision, decided to follow his example. The only problem was that her left arm, the one that was supposed to be holding Whisky during the dance, was now empty, and she didn't seem to know what to do with it. Instead of trying to improvise, she tucked it against her body, as though she were still cradling him, and proceeded with the performance.

Meanwhile, Whisky had decided he wanted to leave. Immediately. He began running around on the stage, weaving precariously in and out of backdrops and props. Lights flashed and he barked wildly, almost hurling himself off the stage. A bespectacled man in a suit, obviously some sort of assistant, heaved himself onto the stage and tried to grab the dog, to no avail. Whisky then disappeared backstage for a second, only to reappear with three stagehands running behind him.

Television-style cameras on cranes and tracks caught every moment of the action—the rescued princess bride, cradling empty air with one arm, and her diamond-vested groom, both shimmying their hips to the song and resolutely ignoring the four men running helter-skelter around them as they tried to corner the furry little fugitive.

It was, as the couple had probably hoped, an unforgettable performance.

By the time Sharav made it back to Nonita with their drinks, he'd wiped away a tear of mirth and regained some semblance of composure. His fiancée was standing with three other women. None of them had even cracked a smile.

'Did you see that gorgeous lehenga she was wearing?' gushed one of Nonita's friends.

'Satyabachi,' clarified another one. 'I heard he designed it specially for her.' When the others raised their eyebrows, questioning the validity of her claim—given that Satyabachi was a notoriously private designer who was said to hate brides—she backtracked. 'Well, that's what the bride's cousin told me.'

Nonita took a sip of the wine Sharav had handed her and made a face. 'Doesn't taste *that* expensive.'

'Really?' asked one of the women. 'I have it on good authority that they imported it straight from the Médoc in Bordeaux.'

'Just because a wine is from Bordeaux doesn't mean it's good,' pointed out Sharav, to no one in particular.

All four women turned towards him with puzzled faces, as though he'd spoken in a foreign language. Then Nonita put a hand on his arm and said in a laughing voice, 'Don't mind him.'

A photographer passed by, and Nonita waved to him. 'Here! Take a group photo.' The four women posed for the camera with pursed lips and tilted chins, legs strategically angled to hone their figures. With the moment duly recorded, Nonita returned to Sharav's side.

She held out her phone to take a selfie with Sharav, and he obliged, patiently holding in his tight smile until she'd found the most flattering angle for her face. She then edited and uploaded it to her social media profiles with a few witty hashtags.

'You know, I'd get a lot more traction and followers if I could tag you in our photos together,' said Nonita without looking up.

This was an old argument. Sharav shrugged. 'I told you, I don't have time for social media.'

Nonita's reaction was predictable. 'What kind of person doesn't have a social media account in this day and age? You behave like you're a hundred years old!'

It was never a good idea to argue with Nonita about these things, so Sharav usually didn't bother. But today, his patience was already stretched thin. 'I like my privacy—and besides, I don't think thousands of people online need to see what I look like drinking a glass of whisky.'

Nonita bristled. 'You didn't seem to mind so much when Samara was taking close-ups of you in the garden.'

Samara. The garden. The movie. Wanting to . . . no, not going there. He went on the defensive. 'I *did* mind. I told her I didn't want my photo taken, but she didn't listen.'

'When I walked into the garden, you two were arguing.' Nonita watched him carefully. 'What were you arguing about?'

'About me not wanting my photo taken!'

'It looked like something else.'

Sharav shook his head with an evasive huff. 'Samara insisted and I lost my cool, that's all.' He took a sip of his drink and looked away. He'd been trying to avoid Samara ever since the night in the TV room, without much success. Their bedrooms were directly opposite each other, and sometimes, if she'd left her door open, he caught a whiff of her lemony-floral scent in the corridor. Refreshing, like a cold glass of nimbu pani in the garden.

He'd never felt thirstier.

After scrutinising him for a couple of fraught seconds, Nonita appeared to accept his answer. Still, her eyes were piercing as she said, 'Let's go to the Confession Booth. I want to try and win the car.'

Relieved to do just about anything else except talk about Samara, Sharav followed his determined fiancée towards a pavilion with banners declaring it the Confession Corner and allowed her to pull him inside.

Once the alarm bells in his head had died down, however, he realised that Nonita intended to take him into the Confession Booth with her. 'I don't see why I need to go in. You're the one "confessing."' He added air quotes to the last word.

Nonita shook her head. 'The steak idea isn't juicy enough to win. Nose jobs will be too common. We need to up the ante.'

'How?'

She looked around, where a few people waited to go into the booth. Servers stood alongside the line, passing out themed cocktails with names like the Loose Tongue and the Secret-Spiller.

'I've got an idea,' whispered Nonita, glancing around like she was afraid someone would steal her brain wave.

Sharav felt a small sting of dread. 'What?'

'Let's make out in there.'

'What?'

Nonita nodded as though it made perfect sense. 'We confess that we can't keep our hands off each other, and then we . . . demonstrate for a minute or two. Nothing major, just kissing—and maybe you can grab me a little.'

Rendered almost speechless, Sharav sputtered, 'B-but there's a camera in there.'

'It's a *Range Rover*, Sharav!' whisper-shouted Nonita, as if that should be explanation enough. When it obviously wasn't, she went on, 'This is a wedding, so they'll probably be inclined to give the prize to a love-and-romance-related confession. We can position ourselves as the cute couple, the ones who can't get enough of each other. They do it on *Biggest Boss* all the time. Plus, we'll look really good together on camera. That has to count in our favour.'

She'd officially lost it. 'This isn't some *Biggest Boss* episode you're participating in, Nonita.'

'It's a Ra—'

'Yes, I know the prize is a Range Rover. You mentioned it, twice.' Sharav's tone was acerbic. 'You already have a very nice car. You don't need to create a sex tape for a new one.'

Nonita looked offended. 'I didn't suggest having *sex*!' she whispered. 'Just a little heavy petting.'

'Yes, I know. Look'—Sharav waved a peeved hand and stepped out of the Confession Booth line—'I'm not going in there. You do what you like.'

A flash of panic swept across Nonita's face, like she'd only just comprehended that Sharav was genuinely upset by her plan. She followed him out of the pavilion, her tone placating as she said, 'It was just a suggestion.'

They stopped at a corner away from the crowd at large. Sharav glanced around, determinedly looking for exits. Nonita ran her hand up his chest and cupped his cheek. 'Don't be angry. It was a bad idea.'

Shrugging off her hand, he took a deep breath and tried to disregard the fact that his fiancée had just behaved like a reality show contestant. 'I'm fine. Are we done here?'

Returning her hand to his chest, Nonita stroked him as though he were a dog she could pet into submission. 'We haven't had dinner yet.'

Frustration washed over him. He looked at his watch. It was already midnight, and dinner probably wouldn't be served for another hour. At least. 'If you're hungry, we can stop somewhere on the way. Or we can raid the fridge at home. Biba always leaves something for Dhruv's nighttime snacks.'

Nonita's face was a study in restraint as she obviously battled her disappointment at leaving behind a lavish spread for Biba's leftovers. Still, she wasn't ready to give up. 'All right, we can leave. After I do the confession. By myself,' she added as a concession. 'Then at least I'll get the pendant.'

'Fine.' Sharav crossed his arms and held on to his drink like it was a life buoy in the open ocean. 'I'll wait here.'

Anger flashed in her eyes, but Nonita simply nodded and turned. 'Fine.' She began walking back to the Confession Booth.

'Fine.' Sharav watched her leave. He swirled his glass, and a few drops of whisky splashed on his shoes. 'Just fine.'

CHAPTER 17

Hauz Khas, once a village, was now a Delhi destination filled with upmarket designer boutiques, overpriced antique shops, trendy cafés, and pubs and bars in old, dilapidated buildings that were supposedly unchanged to retain the 'village charm' of the neighbourhood.

At least, that's what the tourists thronging its alleys were told.

It was not, as most Delhi residents knew, a motley collection of illegal structures containing many establishments that operated without valid licences. No, that would be bad for business.

And business, as Samara deduced from the lively interior of the Royal Hauz on a Wednesday night, was booming. The bar's patrons were a mixed bunch, she noted. Some were young professionals, groups from nearby offices that had decided to go out for a drink straight from work. Others were tourists staying in the neighbourhood's hostels, hotels, and guesthouses. A few were students, and the rest, constituting a large table at the back of the house, were friends and family of Dhruv's bandmates. As far as she could tell, Sid's parents were hosting, ordering round after round for everyone, the group getting more raucous with every passing minute.

The fact that Dhruv hadn't invited the Khannas spoke volumes.

Her stomach began to churn with dread. Dhruv and his band, currently standing behind the stage, talking to a large man she presumed was Sid's uncle, were due to start their set any moment now, and she had no idea what to expect.

Sid, Laz, and Ira were all fidgeting in nervous excitement, but Dhruv stood motionless, a vacant look in his eyes.

The churning in her stomach quickened.

Sid's uncle ambled up to the onstage mic and squashed his mouth against it. His muffled, amplified voice rang out over the commotion in the bar: 'Testing, testing. One, two, three.' Feedback from the speakers screeched loudly, making some people cover their ears, but he quickly resolved the problem by thumping loudly on the mic and waving it around as if to catch a mobile phone signal with it. The feedback magically stopped.

'Ladies' night!' Sid's uncle woohoo-ed and shimmied his hips as though he were a thirtysomething woman dancing to a Beyoncé single. Very few women in the audience joined in, but he seemed too enthused to notice as he boomed, 'Welcome to the Royal Hauz, ladies! It's two-for-one sangrias and masala martinis at the bar, and don't forget to try our special flavoured-gin menu at twenty percent off, only this week! Now, to open for the Royal Hauz Band, please welcome onstage Stone Breed!'

Loud clapping and cheering from the band's table answered his call, but most of the audience just frowned at the stage, waiting either for some music to start or for this dude to stop talking so they could resume their conversations.

Sid was the first one onstage. He grabbed his guitar and twanged a chord in a theatrical attempt to rouse the onlookers. Dhruv followed Ira out and picked up his bass guitar, looped the strap over his shoulder, and stepped up to the mic at the front, looking out over the large assortment of faces staring at him.

Ira, Sid, and Laz played a few chords to test their mics, but Dhruv didn't make a sound, even though he held his fingers on the fretboard and strings. He just stood there, expressionless, while his bandmates nervously generated loud, discordant practice notes. Most of the bar patrons had lost interest at this point, and the hubbub resumed. Sid's uncle waved his hand impatiently, urging the band to start their set.

Samara felt trickles of icy dread creeping up her spine. She realised, for the first time, that Dhruv's reluctance to sing for her earlier hadn't come from normal teenage petulance or even shyness. It came from fear.

Dhruv was petrified.

'Come on, kid. You can do this,' she murmured.

'Do what?' asked a cheery waitress who'd arrived to take her order.

Distracted, Samara shook her head. 'Nothing. I'll have the special. Thanks.'

Rather than nodding and dashing off to return with whatever candy-coloured blend of sugar and alcohol was deemed feminine enough for ladies' night, the waitress decided to offer Samara some ill-timed advice. 'We have two specials tonight. I would order the masala martini. Trust me, you don't want to know what's in the sangria!' She leaned down near Samara's ear and told her anyway. 'They empty all the leftover wine into it.'

Giving her a tense smile, Samara replied, 'Martini, then. Hurry, I think I'm going to need it.'

The waitress nodded with wide eyes and scurried off.

Samara turned her attention back to Dhruv, who still hadn't moved. Sid, Ira, and Laz were now ready, and Ira counted down with her drumsticks before Laz broke in with the opening notes of 'Don't Stop Believin'.'

It was a highly recognisable classic-rock power ballad, so a few patrons turned their attention to the stage with expectant faces, but the rest just carried on talking at a higher volume to offset the music. Some heads started to bob in time with Laz's skillful keyboard melody, ready to chant the well-loved lyrics along with the lead singer.

The only problem was, the lead singer still stood at the front, neither playing his bass guitar nor giving any indication that he knew he had to start singing. Sid, the only band member who stood in front alongside Dhruv, gave him a confused glance.

'Come on, Dhruv,' whispered Samara. 'Push through it!'

He didn't. Dhruv missed his cue and continued to stare out, a blank look on his face. The three other band members glanced at each other in worry. Laz kept playing the opening notes on repeat, nodding at Sid to go find out what was wrong with Dhruv.

By now, most members of the audience had figured out that something was wrong, and more people turned confused faces towards the stage. Sid walked up to Dhruv and prompted him, but Dhruv didn't seem to register his friend's words. At the back, Ira did a little improvised drumroll in a weak attempt at deceiving the audience into believing that the delay was intentional. Sid turned and joined her, twanging his guitar with a mini solo as a distraction.

They didn't fool anyone.

The hum of conversation in the bar had now completely died down. All eyes—and some phone cameras—were on Dhruv, everyone seeming to wonder what he would do next. Break into song? Start crying? Protest something? Breaths were bated. It was a post-worthy moment.

Samara's heart tossed around in her chest as she waited to see what would happen. Dhruv was still young. This experience could potentially scar him for life. Rarely did she ever pray, but she found herself clutching her palms together and mouthing 'Please' over and over again.

Her prayers, however, were not answered. Dhruv drew a jerky breath, blinking rapidly, like he'd just woken up from sleepwalking. He looked around at his bandmates, playing their instruments with anxious faces, and shook his head. 'I'm sorry,' he said into the mic. Then he turned and strode offstage, hurrying into a corridor that led to the back of the building.

Sid, Laz and Ira looked stunned, completely clueless about what to do next. For a second, it seemed like they would stop playing as well, but then Sid hurried up to Dhruv's mic stand with a resolute expression and announced, 'Our first song is "Don't Stop Believin'" by Journey,' and started to strum the song's melody on his guitar, effectively turning their performance into an instrumental one.

The audience, visibly disappointed, either went back to chatting amongst themselves or sang along with the melody as if it were karaoke. A couple of drunk *boo*s were thrown out from the back, but they didn't catch on. The moment had passed.

Samara got up, instinct driving her to follow Dhruv, but she held back, fighting the urge. She wasn't supposed to be here, wasn't supposed to know what had just occurred. Dhruv had *explicitly* told her he didn't want anyone from the Khanna house to attend.

Now she knew why.

She ditched her drink, paid her bill, and forced herself to drive back to the house at a sedate pace, frantically thinking about ways she could help Dhruv without letting on that she'd witnessed him bomb tonight.

As the night wore on, she paced her room, watching from the window as Sid, Ira, and Laz drove up to drop off their instruments. Ira and Laz went home, but Sid hung back in the garage for a while. Dhruv was probably in there, she thought, undoubtedly beating himself up about what had happened.

Finally, after Sid had been in the garage for an hour, Samara couldn't take it anymore. Yes, it was highly likely that Dhruv would be furious with her. However, there was a small chance that he might welcome her help, like he had with clearing out the garage.

She'd never know unless she tried.

After hurrying downstairs and through the kitchen, she opened the garage door and peeked inside. The lights were off, but she could make out Dhruv's and Sid's shadowy figures sitting on stools in the middle of the room. Dhruv was hunched over, holding on to his bass guitar like it was a life raft in a stormy ocean.

'Samara?' asked Sid, squinting up at her silhouette.

'Yeah,' she replied softly. 'I'm coming in.'

Silence greeted her as she entered the garage, shut the door behind her, and used the flashlight on her phone to pull up an old dining chair to sit on. Nobody said anything for a while.

Then Sid spoke into the darkness. 'I have to head back home, dude. Will you be okay?'

After a tense moment, Dhruv's croaky voice replied, 'I'll be fine.' Sid sighed. 'See you in class tomorrow?'

'Yeah.'

Once Sid left, Dhruv went quiet again. Samara sat back and waited, relieved that her entrance hadn't been met by an angry outburst. Long minutes passed.

'You were there, weren't you?'

Samara nodded, even though she knew he couldn't see. 'I was. I'm sorry I didn't tell you.'

Dhruv took a shaky breath. 'Will you tell my family?'

'Of course not.'

A small sniff escaped, and he cleared his throat, obviously trying to push back his tears. Samara didn't react, didn't put a hand on his shoulder or offer meaningless platitudes. She just stayed still, hoping he would come to her when ready.

After what seemed like an age, Dhruv said with a wobbly chuckle, 'For someone who never shuts up, you're awfully quiet.'

'I'm not the one who needs to talk right now.'

He exhaled. 'I don't want to talk.'

'Then we won't.'

More silence. This time, however, it was punctuated by Dhruv's sniffs, which he'd stopped trying to hide. When he eventually spoke, he said, 'I forgot the words.'

Samara shifted in her seat. 'Words?'

'The words to the song,' replied Dhruv, his voice forlorn. '"Don't Stop Believin'" is one of the most popular rock songs of all time. I've known the lyrics since I was a kid, sung them a billion times. Those words have been an anthem in my life, and today, standing up there . . . I forgot them.' His voice quivered. 'I just blanked.'

'Has it happened before?'

Dhruv cleared his throat again. 'Once. When I was thirteen, after my dad died. Our teacher gave me the lead role in the class play, probably because she felt sorry for me, and it was exactly the same.'

'Was it because of your dad?'

'I don't know. I did perform in school after that. Things were fine as long as I was in the back or only had a couple of lines.' He took a deep breath. 'I'm just not meant to be the front person. There's too much riding on me, and I can't handle the pressure. Obviously.' He gave a bitter laugh.

Samara didn't say anything. Dhruv carried on speaking as though she'd agreed with him. 'The Royal Hauz is giving us another chance, in a month. I've told Sid I'll play bass, but I can't sing. It's the right thing to do, you know? For the band. I'll be fine if I'm in the back, and we can find someone else to sing.' His breath shuddered. 'I let them down tonight. They deserve better.'

Now Samara took a deep breath. 'And what about you?'

'What?'

'What do *you* deserve?'

Dhruv shifted on his stool, making it creak. 'It's not that straightforward.'

'Dhruv?' Her voice was tentative. 'Yeah?'

'Do you like singing in the band?'

After a moment, he replied, 'Yeah, of course, but—'

'In an ideal world, if there were no issues with blanking, would you want to be the lead singer?'

'Yes, but—'

'Dhruv?'

He exhaled in irritation. *'What?'*

'Then you have to try.'

The anger arrived, as she'd expected. 'You saw me up there, Samara. I made a fool of myself!'

She didn't try to deny it. 'You had a moment.'

'I failed!'

'You did.'

Dhruv let out another laugh. 'Great, so we both agree: I failed. Now what?'

'You reverse it. By singing. Right here, right now.'

He was stumped. 'Huh?'

'You sing the song you were meant to sing tonight. One of the most popular rock songs of all time. A song that's been your anthem since you were a kid.'

'Now? Here? For you and an audience of spiders and lizards?'

Samara ignored the sarcasm in his voice. 'Yes.'

'Why?'

She shrugged. 'So it gets sung.' When he didn't say anything, she murmured, 'It's dark. No one can see you, not even me. Sing the song you were meant to sing, Dhruv, for no other reason than it deserves to be sung tonight.'

Minutes flew by, heavy with uncertainty and ache. Then Dhruv sighed. 'Fine.' His clothing rustled as he positioned the bass on his lap and then played the opening chords, to Samara's utter relief. His voice joined in, hoarse and unsteady at first.

Slowly, steadily, Dhruv's voice grew, stronger and more confident with each verse, as he sang about people, strangers to each other, trying to find hope and feel alive while their days and nights felt like a never-ending train ride to nowhere. About those people finding joy in the little things, about trusting that their lives can and will get better if only they don't stop believing in themselves.

By the end, it was as if Dhruv had forgotten Samara was in the room, forgotten he was in a small garage and wasn't supposed to belt out the lyrics like he was onstage. He sang the final falsetto with his heart and soul: 'Don't stop believin'.'

Like the song deserved.

Like *he* deserved.

When it was over, he exhaled sharply.

Samara waited until his breathing steadied. 'That was . . . amazing.'

'Thanks. Now what?'

'Well'—her voice was wry in an attempt at humour—'I should probably say something motivational. Like "You're really talented. Never give up," but without sounding cheesy.'

He laughed, much to her delight. 'How about "Tough times don't last but tough people do"? That's my mom's favourite.'

'Good one,' she replied. 'I like "Just keep swimming," from *Finding Nemo*.'

'Be the change you want to see.'

'Where there's a will, there's a way!' she proclaimed.

'If at first you don't succeed, try again.'

'No pain, no gain!' That one made them both laugh.

He snapped his fingers. 'Just do it!'

They laughed some more. Then their mirth shrank into soft chuckles and, finally, silence again.

'Dhruv?'

'Hmm?'

'Don't stop believing.'

He took a deep breath. 'Yeah.'

CHAPTER 18

'I look like I have a squirrel on my face.'

Samara shushed Yash. 'You look rugged and masculine. Stop touching it!'

Yash didn't seem to buy her praise. He scratched his newly unshaven chin and grumbled, 'I thought I would save time shaving, but now I spend *triple* the time every morning, trimming and shaping, applying all those ridiculous beard products you made me buy. Who cares if it's three millimetres or five millimetres long? Why can't I just let it grow out naturally?'

Rolling her eyes and pushing his hand away from his face, Samara replied, 'Because then you'd look like someone who lives in a forest. Look, a well-maintained beard is a fashion accessory. Think of it as the male equivalent of high heels. Uncomfortable and impractical but sexy.'

'Women don't have to wear high heels all the time, especially in the summer.' Yash looked a little panicky at the thought of walking around with face fuzz in the searing heat of a Delhi summer.

Samara sighed. After their impromptu dinner in Yash's office, she'd convinced him to grow a short beard and even taken him to a barber so he could learn how to care for it. Then they'd gone clothes-shopping, which involved Yash modelling outfits Samara had selected for him with a long-suffering look on his face. While he'd drawn the line at wearing cropped pants and pretty much anything distressed, Yash had allowed Samara to put together a low-key but smart, well-fitted wardrobe for him. Combined with the beard and new hairstyle he was sporting, it was quite the makeover. Still inherently Yash-like, but hotter.

Now they just had to wait and see Diya's reaction.

Which was why Yash was at the Khanna household today, helping Samara set up a musical performance in the driveway. In the last couple of weeks, she'd been working daily with Dhruv to help him overcome his fear of singing onstage. They'd rehearsed, written worry journals, done scenario-planning, visualisation, and meditation. Dhruv had even attended a public-speaking workshop. Last night, with Samara's encouragement, Dhruv had finally told his family, apologising for not telling them sooner and for not inviting them to his performance. So thrilled was Jyoti to have her son confide in her that she invited the band for dinner at Dhruv's favourite eatery, a hole-in-the-wall restaurant in Old Delhi that only served parathas stuffed with various fillings that ranged from potatoes, paneer, cheese, onions, nuts, and vegetables to herbs, lentils, sugar, yogurt, and even bananas.

Sharav had accompanied them, once again the designated driver. Over finger-searing parathas, he'd regaled them with stories from his college days and even laughed with everyone else when Biba claimed she could make better parathas at home. It was a sunnier side to him that Samara hadn't yet experienced, and she liked it, a lot. After dinner, they'd strolled around Old Delhi, soaking in the vibrant ambiance, smelling handfuls of spices in the spice market, and trying on silver jewellery. Samara, Ira, and Diya even tried on bichiyas—silver toe rings—much to Jyoti's consternation. 'You're not supposed to wear bichiyas till you get married, girls!' she objected, but she ended up buying the toe rings as a gift after they'd promised to wait until they were married to wear them.

All in all, Samara was quite pleased with how things were progressing, at least on the Delhi front. She still hadn't heard back about her job applications in Manhattan, and it was already January. The wedding season was going to start winding down in less than two months as the summer heat set in. Summer and the monsoon season were what wedding planners called the Blackout Period, when stifling temperatures and muggy downpours made prancing around in heavy formal outfits unbearable.

Which meant Samara was going to have to use her savings to fly to New York and hustle for a job. Find an apartment to share with Maya, go to their favourite comedy club, catch a show. Eat a bagel that actually tasted like a bagel. Sounded like fun!

In theory.

She was going to miss the Khannas. Even Sharav. Ever since movie night—or *missionary* night, given that their accidental embrace had been far more memorable than the movie—they'd declared a truce. But that was even worse because now Samara had no reason to dislike him. A reasonable, friendly Sharav, combined with all that magnetism in close quarters, was downright dangerous.

As demonstrated by her turncoat of a body. Every time he was in the vicinity, it was all systems go, and she had to keep reminding herself that he had a fiancée. A thoroughly dislikeable one but a fiancée nevertheless.

That was the bottom line.

'Samara!' shouted Diya as she came out of the house, carrying a chrome desk lamp. 'Where do you want this?'

Ah, the driveway performance. She had to focus! There was a small army of people who needed her to not be distracted right now. Samara pointed at the line of chairs that had been set up to face the dining table, which had been moved into the driveway to serve as a makeshift stage for Dhruv. 'Put it on one of the chairs and plug it into the extension cord,' she instructed.

Diya frowned as she walked up to them, casting an inquisitive glance at Yash before asking Samara, 'What do you need a lamp for, anyway? It's the middle of the day.'

'Oh, that's our spotlight. We'll shine it on Dhruv when he's singing. Just to give him an authentic spotlight feel.'

Then she recalled that this was the first time Diya and Yash had met since that disastrous morning tea—since his makeover. She held her breath and waited.

'Hi,' said Yash, looking a little confused that Diya hadn't greeted him.

She gave him a hesitant smile. 'Hi. I'm Diya.'

Samara blinked. *Oh my God, she doesn't recognise him!* Holding back a grin with Herculean effort, she watched as Yash replied, 'Diya, it's me.'

Diya's eyes widened. She scanned his face and body in blatant perusal. 'Yash?'

'In the flesh.'

'What *happened* to you?' Diya blurted out before slapping a hand over her mouth. 'I'm so sorry, that was *so* rude—'

'It's fine. Samara and I went shopping, and she'—he gave Samara a wry grin—'had some thoughts about my wardrobe and, er, grooming choices.'

Now it was Samara's turn to laugh. This was going better than expected. 'Yash is being polite, as usual. I totally bullied him into buying new clothes. Doesn't he look great, though?'

Diya looked a little dazed. 'Um, yeah.' Then she frowned. 'You guys went shopping together?'

Bingo. 'We did,' said Samara, patting Yash's forearm. '*So* much fun! Anyway . . .' She flicked her hair back and batted her lashes at Yash. 'I can't wait to hang out again, but right now I have to get this performance organised. Yash, will you help Diya with the . . .' She pointed to the lone lamp in Diya's hand. 'Lights?'

Yash smirked as he replied, 'Sure.' He turned to Diya as Samara moved away. 'Want me to get an extension cord for that?'

Still frowning, Diya blinked up at him. 'Extension cord?'

'To plug the lamp in.'

Diya looked down at the lamp and then back at him, seemingly still surprised by the sight that met her eyes. 'Okay.' Then she shook her head. 'Wait, no. There's an extension cord already.' She pointed to the side of the driveway. 'There.'

'Great. You want me to plug it in?'

'It's plugged in.'

'I meant the lamp.'

'Uh, okay.'

Samara slipped into the kitchen and watched from behind a window as Yash helped Diya set up their makeshift spotlight, keeping up a steady flow of conversation. Diya's dazed reaction had obviously given him a boost in confidence. She rubbed her hands together and smiled. The bait had been set. Now they just had to wait for the fish to bite.

'You look like Mr Burns from *The Simpsons*, just before he's about to blow something up.'

Samara turned to see Sharav walk into the kitchen. Since it was Saturday, he was in his usual weekend jeans. A small, wistful sigh escaped her lips. If she were a pervert, she would take a sneaky photo of his butt in them just so she could have something pretty to stare at on lonely nights during her destination shoots.

'I do have nefarious plans in motion,' she replied and then nodded at Yash and Diya.

Sharav came and stood next to her, looking out of the window. His cologne, combined with his warmth, smelled divine, and Samara felt herself swaying towards him involuntarily. Ugh, why did the man have to be so attractive? And interesting, once you took the stick out of his perfect butt and got a couple of parathas in him.

'Is that Yash?' he asked.

She grinned. 'Yeah.'

He stared outside for a few more seconds. 'I hope you know what you're doing.'

'You're not going to tell me off for poking my nose where it doesn't belong? For being bossy?'

A small smile broke through his resting frowny face. 'You *are* bossy.'

'Said the pot. Besides, I'm a lightweight compared to you.'

He turned to her, an unidentifiable glint in his eye. 'Is that so? Then tell me—why am I so completely, hopelessly, *infuriatingly* incompetent at bossing *you* around?' He took a step closer, nudging towards inappropriate territory. Reminding her of what it had felt like for their bodies to be flush against each other.

Samara's breath caught in her throat, her voice a gasp. 'Do you want to?'

His piercing gaze never left hers as Sharav lifted a hand to move a wavy tendril of hair off her face. His fingers grazed her cheek slowly as he replied in a voice as throaty as her own, 'I do.'

Oh God. It wasn't just her. *He feels this too!* Samara's chest heaved as she fought against closing her eyes and turning into his touch, into the solid, citrusy heat of his body.

Sharav's hand balled into a fist behind her ear, as if to stop himself from touching her any further, even as his face swayed closer to hers. 'Samara, we . . .'

A shrill squeal came from the living room, and they jumped apart.

'Samara!' Jyoti shouted shortly after. Then another squeal.

Sharav broke eye contact first. 'What's going on?'

It took a few moments for Samara to register his question and realise what the commotion was about. 'Oh, right. The photos.' She gave Sharav a shaky laugh. 'I had a few photos of the garden framed for Jyoti Aunty.'

'Samara!'

The intensity in Sharav's eyes softened. 'That was nice of you.'

She shrugged. 'She's been so wonderful. I wanted to thank her. Anyway . . .' She smiled. 'I'd better get over there before she loses her voice.' Without waiting for Sharav to respond, Samara rushed out of the kitchen. It was too much, this knowledge that he felt the same attraction she did. She didn't know what to do with it.

The fact that Nonita was in the living room when she got there was a reminder of exactly how inappropriate her moment with Sharav in the kitchen had been.

'Samara!' Jyoti rushed towards her the second she entered the room. 'Oh, I don't know what to say! These are *beautiful*! Thank you! *Thank you!*' On the coffee table behind her was a set of six enlarged photos that Samara had taken of the garden, framed in vintage white cast iron. They were large, ornate, and feminine, and she'd known Jyoti would love them.

Jyoti pulled her into a bear hug and shimmied them both in her excitement, making Samara laugh. It was exactly the balm she needed right now. Putting Sharav out of her mind, she focused on his mother, who was much less complicated. 'I thought you could hang them in your bedroom,' she said. 'They would be a lovely contrast against the dark wood of your bed.' She knew Jyoti hadn't changed anything in her bedroom since Rajeev Uncle had passed. This could perhaps be the first step forward.

Speaking of steps forward . . . 'Oh, and one more thing, Aunty.' She reached into the back pocket of her jeans and fished out a folded piece of paper. Holding it out to Jyoti while crossing her fingers behind her back, she said, 'This is the second part of the gift.'

Jyoti put a hand on her heart as she took it. 'Child, you've already done a great deal! This is too much!'

Samara shook her head. 'It's not. Just read what it says.'

With an overwhelmed giggle, Jyoti unfolded the paper and began to read aloud. '"Dear Mrs Jyoti Khanna, we are pleased to invite you to participate in . . ."' She gasped, her eyes widening in astonishment. She covered her mouth with a trembling hand, looked up at Samara, and whispered, 'The Delhi Flower Show?'

'Their amateur competition. I applied on your behalf, and you got selected out of hundreds of applicants.' She pointed out the window into the garden. 'Your garden is a work of art, Aunty, and deserves to be appreciated by more than just your visitors. So'—she pointed to the paper in Jyoti's hands—'you're now competing in the Mixed-Flower category. Contestants display their best blooms, and the organisers give a trophy and cash prize to the best bunch. It'll be a great opportunity for you to showcase your skills, and even if you don't win, you could get involved in the community. Maybe even participate in the landscape competition next year.' She smiled. 'What do you think? Will you do it?'

Jyoti was struck dumb, one hand still shielding the lower half of her face. Tears brimmed in her eyes and soon began to trickle down. With a sob, she launched herself at Samara again, clasping her tightly in a hug. 'Oh, *child*' was all she was able to say for a few confusing, angst-ridden minutes while she cried in Samara's arms.

Behind her, Nonita frowned at Samara. With a shake of her head, she grabbed a small pack of tissues from her purse and solicitously stuffed a few in Jyoti's hand, saying, 'Don't worry, Mummy. You don't have to take part in any silly competitions. I'll write to them and refuse.'

'No!' blubbered Jyoti, pulling back from Samara. She quickly wiped her tears with the tissues Nonita had handed her and blew her nose while the two younger women waited with barely held back impatience. Finally, she found her voice. 'I want to. I want to take part! Oh, my darling girl.' She cupped Samara's face with the hand that wasn't holding tissues, her eyes shining with love. 'My darling, *darling* girl. You are such a joy. No one else has *ever* done anything like this for me before.' She seemed to be fighting back another round of tears. 'You've given me something to look forward to.' Her voice broke. 'After Rajeev, and with the kids grown, I've been . . . stuck. And then you came to live with us.' She squeezed Samara's cheek. 'Thank you for lifting my spirits, my child.'

Now it was Samara's turn to whimper. 'Aunty, you're going to make me cry too.'

Jyoti shook her head. 'Not Aunty. Call me Jyoti-Mom. You've been no less than a daughter to me, and now I'm officially a mother to you. And'—she lifted Samara's chin so she could meet her gaze—'that will always be the case, no matter where you are in the world. Okay?'

'Okay,' replied Samara, losing the waterworks battle. She hugged Jyoti and allowed herself to cry, triggering Jyoti's tears too. She'd had many self-proclaimed moms in her life—friend's mothers, her dad's secretaries, neighbours—but this was the first time that any of them had ever actually felt like one.

God, she was going to miss this.

The two women wept in each other's arms, unrestrained, until Nonita spoke in a harsh tone, 'Mummy, please stop. You're upsetting Sharav.'

'Sorry, sorry,' sniffed Jyoti, looking over Samara's shoulder. 'I'll stop, son. But don't worry—these are happy tears!'

Samara turned and saw a blurry Sharav standing in the doorway. She blinked to make him clearer. He'd obviously followed her from the kitchen and heard everything because he had a worried, slightly mystified grimace on his face. But he wasn't looking at his mother.

He was looking at her.

Standing next to him, Nonita was eyeing them both, a furious expression on her face.

Oh crap.

'Right, we'd better get a move on if we want to make this performance happen today,' Samara declared with a shaky laugh. With a deftness she didn't even think she was capable of in this moment, Samara herded them all out into the driveway. She then proceeded to round up every domestic helper, security guard, gardener, and staffer in a five-house radius and install them on the seats facing the dining table. A wireless speaker and phone provided background music while Dhruv very reluctantly climbed on to the 'stage' with a speaker-microphone he'd bought in a toy shop the previous day. He didn't sing, but he did manage to stand onstage for the duration for an entire song, which was a win as far as Samara was concerned. He even laughed a little at the desk lamp pointed directly at his face.

A lamp operated by Yash and Diya, who looked cordial, if not cosy, standing next to each other on the side.

Afterwards, once the Khannas had gone inside and Samara had tipped and dispatched the motley audience, she leaned against the driveway wall and took a deep breath, unsure how to process the veritable stew of emotions roiling within her.

She'd sobbed for the first time in years today. Also, for the first time, she didn't *want* to be distracted from her feelings by thinking about the future or reviewing her travel plans or taking a hot shower.

These weren't feelings that could be washed away.

CHAPTER 19

'You're not seriously going to buy those, are you?'

Nonita scowled at Samara's feet, which were encased in traditional Kolhapuri slippers, brightly decorated with pom-poms, mirrors, and embroidery in a myriad of colours.

Samara modelled the slippers in front of a standing mirror and asked, 'What's wrong with them?' She thought her feet looked cheerful.

After a hesitant moment, Nonita shrugged. 'They're so DM.'

'Direct message?'

'Downmarket.'

Samara stopped herself from rolling her eyes. It was becoming increasingly clear with every passing moment that shopping in Dilli Haat with Nonita was a mistake. While Samara enjoyed buying unique things, Nonita was extremely conscious about labels. In fact, everything she was currently wearing belonged to a luxury brand, from her Vuitton bag to her Dior sunglasses and Gucci belt. Even her ripped jeans were D&G. Inviting her to an Indian handicrafts market might have been, in some twisted way, almost insulting.

She eyed Nonita's tapping foot and crossed arms and put the slippers back on the display pile. 'I'm sorry for suggesting Dilli Haat when you said you wanted to go shopping together. I thought I'd pick up some things to take with me when I leave. Stuff like this is ridiculously expensive in the US.' She held up a hand-painted bamboo-cotton scarf and said, 'This cost me only five hundred rupees, but it would be ten times that in a Manhattan boutique. The box it came in would cost more than this!' She laughed.

If she thought Nonita would laugh along or be a good sport about accompanying her, she was wrong. Nonita simply looked even more annoyed and snapped, 'I know how much things cost in the US. You're not the only one who's travelled.'

Yup, this shopping expedition was a terrible idea. 'Are you hungry? It's almost lunchtime.'

'Fine.'

With as much benevolence as she could muster, Samara steered her to the food section of the market. Dilli Haat was essentially a collection of temporary handicrafts stalls that changed every few weeks, but the food section was permanent, and its kiosks featured regional cuisine from a wide selection of Indian states. From Kashmir in the north to Tamil Nadu in the south, Nagaland in the east to Gujarat in the west, and everything else in the middle—it was all there. Samara loved the variety and made it a point to eat here often. She sat Nonita down at one of the outdoor tables and asked, 'Have you ever eaten here before?'

Nonita shrugged again. 'When I was a kid. But not for many years. I don't like Indian food.'

Okaaay. 'What kind of food do you like?'

'Keto, mostly.'

Samara counted to five in her head before suggesting, 'Why don't I go get a selection of things that we might like?'

'Fine.'

Walking around the kiosks, looking at the familiar menus, and ordering her favourites was a welcome respite. Samara wasn't the sort of person to actively dislike anyone, but Nonita made it so hard to remain friendly. Also, for the life of her, she couldn't figure out why Sharav's fussy fiancée had wanted to go shopping together if she wasn't going to make the slightest effort to engage in any actual conversation.

Still, thought Samara, *it's a sunny winter's day. Perfect for enjoying one of Delhi's best offerings on a rare weekend off from work.*

Maya was going to love the Kashmiri shawl she'd bought her, and the foldable Rajasthani wood puppets she'd gotten at a steal were going to brighten up their future NYC apartment, along with photos she'd taken during the last year.

None of which would remind her of the Khanna family. Of Sharav, who'd be married by then, his moments with Samara a distant memory. Nonita would probably use her room as a closet.

For shoes that weren't Kolhapuri slippers.

Argh! She was becoming way too angsty these days. Whipping her mind back to the task at hand, Samara collected food from various kiosks and hauled her precious cargo back to their table on a large tray. Nonita was busy scrolling on her phone, so Samara said in a loud voice laden with forced cheer, 'Here we go! Goodies galore!'

Nonita looked up from her phone. 'What is it?'

Samara pointed to the spread with the enthusiasm of a travel guide trying to rouse a busload of sullen teenagers on a school trip, 'Here we have fish orly from West Bengal, which is basically fish fried in a masala batter and is absolutely divine. I even got the chef to give us some of their tomato chutney to dip in instead of ketchup.' She winked. 'Next, I got some delicious and healthy momos from Nagaland. And finally'—she waved a hand over a steaming bowl—'what could be better than a hot thukpa on a cold January day? This one is from Arunachal Pradesh. There's also a masala Coke and a fruit beer for you to try.' She smiled. 'Not a curry or roti in sight! Since you didn't want'—she cleared her throat and quashed an eye roll—'Indian food.'

Nonita scanned the dishes with a grimace. 'I don't like fish, and this one is deep-fried, anyway. What's in these momos?'

'Er, pork.'

'I don't eat pork,' her shopping partner said with a lofty air. 'Or red meat.'

Slapping a hand to her forehead, Samara said in an apologetic voice, 'Oh, I'm so sorry I didn't ask earlier. When you said *keto*, I just assumed you weren't vegetarian.'

'I'm not. I eat chicken and egg whites. And low-carb vegetables.'

Right. Samara was officially done playing nice. 'Great. So you can pick the chicken and carrots out of the thukpa.' She sat down with a firm thump and began to help herself to momos. Normally, she'd have ordered the fried ones but got these steamed out of consideration for Nonita. Yet another mistake.

For a while, Nonita simply watched Samara pour generous dollops of chilli-garlic sauce over each momo and dig in with gusto. It was as though she was only really *seeing* Samara for the first time and was both baffled and bothered by what she saw. Finally, she asked in an abrupt tone, 'When are you leaving?'

Now it was Samara's turn to be baffled. 'For where?'

'The US.'

She stopped chewing and regarded her lunch companion carefully. 'Depends on a lot of factors. Why do you ask?'

Samara's answer obviously hadn't been what Nonita was hoping for because she looked annoyed when she replied, 'Nothing. Just wondering.'

Silence reigned between them again, for an uncomfortably long time. Samara occupied herself with lunch while Nonita stared at her phone. At least until she finally said, 'Sharav is a very busy man. He has a lot of responsibilities—taking care of the business, the family, social commitments.'

Samara nodded, thankful her mouth was full of fish. 'Mm-hmm.'

That seemed to further irritate Nonita, who retorted, 'Could you just stop eating for a moment?'

She sighed. The last thing she wanted to do was talk about Sharav with his fiancée. But the woman had her cornered, so she finished her bite and took a sip of fruit beer. 'Okay.'

'Sharav,' huffed Nonita, 'is a very busy man.'

'You mentioned.'

'He doesn't need . . . distractions.'

Ah, so this was the reason behind today's miserable excursion. 'What do you mean?'

Nonita attempted a smile. 'I mean that you're a guest here, and I'm sure you mean well, but Sharav feels that you can be a little . . . you know.'

'No, actually, I don't.'

'A little *too much*.' Nonita cushioned the next blow with another fake smile. 'He didn't want to have you live with them in the first place, and you . . . well, it would be best if you just stayed out of his way until you leave.'

'I see.' Samara felt a ripple of anger fan out under her skin. 'So should I stay out of the rest of the family's way too?'

'It would be best,' replied Nonita, her lofty air returning. 'I mean, things like Diya's marriage, Dhruv's unruly behaviour . . . these are matters usually handled by the head of the house, with support from family members.' She looked at Samara with a pointed, imperious glance that would have put a fairy-tale stepmother to shame. 'Not outsiders.'

'I see,' repeated Samara. She inhaled and exhaled deeply, attempting to tamp down her temper. It didn't work. 'And Sharav asked you to speak to me about this?'

'Well . . .' Nonita shifted in her chair. 'I mean, he hasn't *asked* me outright, but we have discussed it, and since we're getting married soon, I thought it was my duty to speak to you, as an *actual* daughter of the Khanna household.'

Well, there went any hope of dialling it back. Images of fruit beer dribbling down Nonita's perfectly made-up face flashed in Samara's head. 'In that case, I'm sure Sharav will be very grateful that you took it upon yourself to . . . *advise* me on his behalf.' She bared her teeth in a grin she hoped made her look like Hannibal Lector from *Silence of the Lambs*.

Eyes blinking rapidly, Nonita gave her an uneasy smile. 'So you'll take my advice?'

'We'll see,' countered Samara before shoving three momos into her mouth and chewing them loudly with puffed cheeks, partly to irritate Nonita but mostly to ensure that she couldn't tell her where to put that advice. This wasn't the first time someone had told her she was too much, but to hear that Sharav thought so, that he'd discussed her with Nonita? It stung. Did the Khannas really consider her an outsider? Were they just being hospitable when they included her in family matters? Was the whole 'Call me Jyoti Mom' thing just a platitude, declared out of appreciation for Samara's gift? It sure hadn't felt like it at the time. To be fair, Samara hadn't ever been part of an actual family before, so she didn't have much to compare to, but her relationships with Jyoti, Dhruv, and Diya felt . . . real.

They *were* real, dammit!

Chomping on her mouthful like her life depended on it, Samara held back a growl. Nonita was a snake with a natural talent for sensing weakness. Like Kaa from *The Jungle Book*, she'd hit upon the one thing that could actually hurt Samara and used it against her.

The fact that she'd been an outsider all her life.

Down went her masticated bite, followed by a gulp of beer. Then another bite and another.

For the first time in her life, she wanted to hurt someone back. To punish Nonita for managing to breach that place inside her that she'd so successfully protected until now. For reminding her which one of them was really going to be living with the Khannas permanently.

Which one of them would end up with Sharav.

Oh yeah, retribution sounded so good right now. The problem was, as much as she wanted to toss Nonita's untouched thukpa in her face, Samara didn't have it in her to purposefully wound another person.

She settled for buying a pair of Kolhapuri slippers on the way out and wearing them all the way back to the house.

CHAPTER 20

'Bro, at this rate, you'll look pregnant before your wife does.'

Sharav patted the brand-new marriage potbelly his friend Kabir sported on his previously toned abdomen. It was supposed to be a sign of happiness. Given the debacle with Kabir's pre-wedding photo shoot—when the bride and her friends had been doused in champagne by one of the groomsmen, creating a shitstorm between the couple and their families—it was a relief that things were presumably going well on the home front.

That was also the wedding where he'd met all-grown-up Samara for the first time. HDD, she'd called him. He still didn't know what it meant, although the first word had definitely been *Hot*. The thought made him duck his head and grin as he packed his tennis bag after his twice-weekly game.

Kabir shoved his own racket into a bag and wiped his sweaty, heaving face with a towel. 'Don't say the *p* word. The parents and in-laws are on a mission.' He pointed to his belly and rolled his eyes. 'My mom's making me drink almonds and honey in cream twice a day and hanging around outside our door to make sure we're doing it. She even bought Aliya one of those red, lacy nightgowns.' He shook his head and grumbled, 'Every time she puts that thing on, I think of my mom, dude.'

Laughing, Sharav replied, 'Not the best procreation strategy.' Then he stopped, abruptly. Was that going to be him soon? He pictured Nonita, stretched out on his bed, dressed in red, lacy lingerie. She'd look exquisite, perfect, sensual.

Like a painting that would smudge if he touched it.

The thought made him shiver, and not in a good way.

Moving quickly, he zipped up his gym bag and said his goodbyes to Kabir and a few other people around the tennis courts of the five-star hotel, where he was a club member. As he walked through the lobby on his way out, he caught sight of a patisserie counter, gleaming with elaborately adorned treats. All the women in the house *loved* chocolate, so he bought a dozen fudge brownies—and a few lemon tarts just because their sunny swirls reminded him of Samara, and he thought she might like them.

As much as he'd been against her coming to stay with them, Sharav had to admit that she'd done wonders for the household. There was a lighter, brighter feeling when she was around that was difficult to explain. She infused the air around her with energy. And lavender, after she'd bought these essential oil diffusers and planted them all over the house. Since their movie night, he'd stocked the bar in the TV room, and they were now doing family movie-and-cocktail nights regularly, with Dhruv and Diya locked in an ongoing competition to see who could dream up better cocktails. His mother seemed more cheerful, too, he thought, remembering the scene he'd witnessed in the living room, when she'd called Samara her daughter and the two of them had sobbed in each other's arms.

A sliver of guilt wedged its way into that happy recollection. *He* should have been the one to notice that his mother needed some kind of purpose. *He* should have helped her move on from his father's death. They were all his responsibility, and he'd been so wrapped up with the business and his own issues that he'd failed to see what was right in front of him.

Sharav sighed. At least things were on the right track now.

Thanks to Samara.

It was worth the out-of-control feeling he got every time she was within a two-foot range of him. Like an emergency response that was triggered by her presence. He either wanted to hightail it out of the room to save his sanity or, even worse, he wanted to move closer, crowd her, lift her up, and press against her. Wedge and weld her body to his in sweet relief. Extract some of that sweet sunniness from her lips. Claim her in a visceral body-and-soul way that he'd never felt before or even known he was capable of feeling.

If Samara were a painting, Sharav would want to jump in and smudge it until it was a dishevelled, breathless collection of pieces that had been soaked in bliss.

Yeah, totally worth all that torment, just to see the smiles on his family's faces.

He parked his car in the driveway and retrieved the pastry box from the back seat. Walking into the kitchen, he saw Biba and his mother mixing pickles in an oversize glass jar on the floor. Familiar smells inundated him—the comforting pungency of blended spices, the sharp tang of mustard oil, the eye-watering heat of chillies, and the slight sweetness of . . . carrots?

He smiled. 'Is it cauliflower, turnip, and carrot pickle time again?' His mother's pickles were like a calendar in their precision—lime pickle in spring, mango pickle in summer, mixed-vegetable pickle in winter, and ginger pickle once the monsoons were over and a chill began to hang in the air at night. Each was made at the same time every year, without fail.

Well, except for the year his father died.

Jyoti glanced up, her face a little sweaty from the warmth of the kitchen. 'Sharav! How was your game?'

'Good.' He put his tennis bag and the pastry box on the kitchen table. 'That looks like hard work. Let me help you.'

Shaking her head, his mom replied, 'We have to do it ourselves, son. Make sure there are no air pockets in the jar. Otherwise the whole thing will go off.' She then watched

Biba meticulously press a piece of cauliflower into a gap inside the jar.

'Do you really need to make so much?' he asked, even though he knew the answer to his question. The jar was at least two feet tall.

'Of course!' huffed Jyoti. 'Imagine what our relatives and neighbours would say if I didn't send them some!' She ran a loving hand over the jar. 'Besides, your grandmother used this pickle jar, too, you know. It adds its own flavour to every batch. The glass has soaked up all the differently seasoned oils over the decades.'

Her words spread warmth within Sharav. Despite all the expectations that came with being 'the man of the house,' there was also a certain comfort to be found in tradition. In celebrating the tried and true, the things that entwined the lives of people together and gave meaning to them. These pickles were part of a life he believed in. One with stability, honour, and connection. The kind of life that would endure periodic waves of volatility.

Even tsunamis named Samara.

'Fine, I won't help,' he said to his mom with a smile. 'But I'll carry it up to the roof terrace for sunning once you're done.' Pickles needed to slow-bake in the sun for days before their flavours came together and stopped 'cutting the tongue,' as his grandmother used to say.

His mother returned his smile with one of her own. 'Thank you, son. It'll save us the trouble of waiting for the gardener to do it.'

Biba, kneeling on the floor with one gloved hand in the pickle jar, smiled at him too. Something she hadn't done in a while.

Clearing his throat, Sharav said, 'Listen, I wanted to say something.' Both women looked up at him expectantly.

'I haven't been the most pleasant person to be around these last few years.' He shifted on his feet and glanced at Biba. 'I've said things I didn't mean and handled a lot of stuff badly. I just want to say I'm sorry.' He met their gazes with a contrite expression. 'I'm going to try to do better from now on.'

Biba's eyes widened a little as she gave him a nod of affection and acknowledgement—an assurance that things hadn't changed between them.

Jyoti's reaction to his apology was more animated. 'Oh, son. You've been doing your best. We all understand that!'

He shook his head. 'No, I haven't. I'm going to do my best from now on, though. I promise.' Then he took a deep breath and grinned. 'I bought some pastries for everyone!'

For a moment, Jyoti regarded him with eyes that brimmed with unshed tears. Then she wiped her hand across them and looked at Biba. 'Carry on, Biba. I'll be back in a few minutes.' She waved at Sharav, indicating that he follow her out of the kitchen and into the living room.

Once there, she sat next to him and held one of his hands in her own. 'These last six years have been hard on you, son. They've been hard on all of us but especially you.' She shook her head. 'I'm to blame for that.'

Sharav frowned. 'Ma—'

'No, listen for a minute, she interrupted. 'I leaned too heavily on you after your father's death. I was so scared, so . . . bereft, that I became incapable. It was selfish. I should have been there to support my children, help them through it. I should have been strong for you instead of forcing you to be strong for me.' She squeezed his hand. 'I'm sorry for that, son.'

'Don't apologise, Ma. It was my duty to step in, for you all and the business. I would have run it even if Dad was alive, taken it over when he retired.'

'Yes, but not until you were older and better prepared.' She put a hand on Sharav's cheek. 'Ever since then, you've looked like you carry the weight of the world on your shoulders. You know that night in Old Delhi, when we were having parathas and telling stories? You laughed.'

She let out a chuckle. 'Son, you haven't laughed like that in so long I'd forgotten what it sounded like!'

He put a hand over his mother's on his cheek. Had it been difficult to step into his father's shoes at twenty-three? Of course. Would he have done anything differently? Of course not. He was the eldest son, and he'd done nothing more than what had been expected of him, what his father would have wanted. It wasn't Sharav's job to be happy. It was his job to ensure his family was happy. 'If I'm laughing more these days, it's because the rest of you are laughing more.'

Doubt shone from Jyoti's ever-doting face as she regarded him for just a little too long to be comfortable. Then she said, 'Sharav, your happiness is as important as Diya's or Dhruv's, you know. Now that the business is under control, it's okay to take some time for yourself, think about what you want.' She hesitated before continuing, 'Does Nonita make you laugh?'

He crinkled his brow in confusion. 'What?'

Sighing, she said with a wistful smile, 'Rajeev used to make me laugh. Ours was a match arranged by the families, but we shared so much love. We grew together, brought out the best in each other.' Her smile wavered. 'I want that kind of marriage for *you*, too, and I'm asking if you think that you could have that with Nonita.'

For a split second, Sharav thought to brush off her words. It was an uncomfortable question, and courtesy demanded that he laugh it off or just lie to keep his mother happy. But the love, concern, and astuteness on Jyoti's face held his dismissal back. His mother was only just piecing herself together, returning to the world of the living after six years, and she deserved the truth. He breathed to centre himself before answering. 'I don't know, Ma. What I do know is that Nonita shares our values, wants the same future as me, and is willing to support the business and participate in family life. She's intelligent, beautiful, and well meaning. Isn't that a good foundation for love?'

'Of course! But how does she make you feel?'

He fidgeted. Truthfully, one of the things he liked about Nonita was that she didn't rouse any kind of intense feelings in him. Unlike Samara. His unruly brain suddenly pictured Samara eating the lemon tarts he'd bought for her, wondered if her lips would taste of them afterwards. The thought made him shift in his seat, his trousers shrinking inappropriately.

Sharav huffed inwardly. This was *exactly* the problem with . . . feeling things.

At least with Nonita, he would never get aroused in the middle of a bloody conversation with his mother!

He cleared his throat. 'Nonita and I will grow into one another, like you and Dad did—don't worry.' Time to change the subject. 'Let's talk about Diya's marriage instead. Are you still set on Yash?' he asked, hoping his mom would take his lead.

'Well, the Malhotras haven't called since Yash told them that things didn't work out with Diya, after that *disaster* of a morning.' She shuddered. 'I was surprised, you know. He's always been interested in Diya. It was so sweet, how he used to look at her when they were younger. And since then, well, he's done so well professionally, and he's still *such* a nice, respectful boy.' Jyoti smiled a sad smile. 'I thought he'd be perfect for Diya. That's why I pushed so hard.' She shook her head. 'Anyway, no point dwelling on it. If there's anything I've learned lately, it's that we must leave the past behind!'

Sharav debated whether to tell his mother that Samara was trying to push Yash and Diya together with another one of her ridiculous schemes. He decided against it. He didn't want to get her hopes up.

It probably wasn't going to work anyway.

CHAPTER 21

'This is not going to work.'

'It's going to work.'

'I don't think so,' grumbled Diya, her arms crossed in protest. 'You're a lot smaller than me.'

'Trust me,' coaxed Samara, holding out her arms towards Diya. 'I'm stronger than I look.'

A sceptical squint furrowed Diya's face, but she relented with a disclaimer. 'If I fling you into the crowd, just remember you asked for it.'

Samara laughed, taking Diya's hands in her own. She gripped them tightly. Then she called over her shoulder, 'Stand back, Yash!'

Yash took a few steps back with a grin, Samara's camera strap around his neck. 'All clear!'

With a giggle, Samara leaned back and balanced her body weight against Diya's, their hands crossed and clasped in the middle. Diya was smiling despite her earlier objections. Together, they began to whirl around, in the traditional kikli dance. Faster and faster, round and round they spun in a wide circle, laughing and squealing as their speed picked up and the world went by in a rapid eddy. All she could see was Diya's face, mirroring her delight. For a few moments, until they got too dizzy to continue, they enjoyed that rush of adrenaline, the lightheaded *aliveness* that came from pushing your body into an unnatural momentum. That was the beauty of the kikli dance—you didn't need a roller coaster, a race car, or to be zipped into a harness and thrown off a bridge to feel that rush. All you needed was another person.

They broke apart, laughing and giddy. Samara's head spun and her feet stumbled, unable to find purchase because, as Diya had rightfully warned, her larger frame meant that she'd inadvertently flung Samara on the dismount.

Straight into Yash's arms.

'Whoa, easy there,' exclaimed Yash with a laugh as he caught her in a tight hug so she wouldn't fall. He grinned down at her. 'You all right?'

Samara squinted up at him with a lopsided smile. 'There are two of you!' She held out a finger and touched the tip of his nose—or at least, what she thought was the tip of his nose. It was difficult to be sure since her eyes were still trying to focus.

Yash held her until she was able to stand on her own. They parted with beaming faces, and Samara turned to suggest that Diya have another go, this time with Yash as her partner.

Only to find Diya watching them with a scowl.

For a moment, Samara almost rushed to put her at ease, assure her that there was nothing between her and Yash, before she tamped down the urge. This was exactly the kind of jealousy that she'd hoped to see Diya display.

It meant that, as unpleasant as it felt, her plan was working.

She swallowed her qualms and twisted to look around for something that would hopefully distract Diya. And herself, given that when Samara wasn't distracted, her mind would immediately start replaying that horrible conversation with Nonita. They were in the main park of their gated community, which was lit up with fairy lights, coloured lanterns, and a large bonfire for the Resident Welfare Association's annual Lohri celebration signifying the end of winter and the beginning of spring.

Which was wonderful, except that spring weddings weren't as plentiful as winter weddings, and Samara wasn't nearly as busy as she'd have liked. Lohri was a tangible reminder that her time in Delhi was running out.

A tap on her shoulder broke that train of thought, thankfully. She turned to find an elderly lady in a salwar kameez, a small notebook in her hands and an RWA badge on her chest. 'Welcome to the Lohri fair!' she said with a smile. 'Would you like to buy some Lucky Draw tickets? You get a free box of popcorn and puffed rice to throw into the bonfire for good luck!'

'Sure!' replied Samara with equal enthusiasm. 'What are the Lucky Draw prizes?' she asked, reaching for her wallet.

Yash stepped closer. 'Let me get these,' he said, wallet in hand.

The older woman's eyes gleamed at the look of a man who wanted to impress the ladies he was with. 'The bumper prize is an iPhone, the latest model. If you buy five tickets each, you increase your chances!'

Yash bought twenty tickets, then handed ten each to his companions. Samara giggled quietly to herself when Diya blinked up at him in confusion as their hands touched, like she was seeing him for the first time. They then carried their boxes of popcorn and puffed rice and walked over to the bonfire. There was a small crowd of people dancing around it, singing a traditional Lohri song about a Robin Hood–like folktale character named Dulla Bhatti. At the end of each line, the crowd would shout 'Ho!' and laugh, dancing and throwing various edible treats into the flames. Joining in, the three emptied their good-luck grains into the fire and went looking for something more substantial to eat.

Stalls, selling everything from clothing to home decor to food, lined the edges of the park. A crowd had gathered around a counter selling sweet rotis made from millet and jaggery, so they made their way there. The vendor handed them a plate of steaming rotis slathered in ghee, and Samara watched with delight as Diya and Yash shared one, laughingly puffing hot air out of their mouths after they took a bite. By the time they'd polished off their sweet rotis, followed by earthen cups of jaggery-sweetened tea, Diya and Yash were deep in discussion. With heads bent together and arms gesturing animatedly, they almost seemed to have forgotten that Samara was with them.

Leaving them to enjoy each other's company, Samara ambled over to a line of kiosks selling traditional Lohri sweets, usually various combinations of seeds and nuts cooked with jaggery. As the excitement of the evening receded, her mind began running over an internal checklist of tasks. She had to start planning for her move to New York. Setting dates, buying airline tickets, finding a place to stay in the city. Potentially working as an assistant for an established photographer or a website. Maybe doing a temporary internship if nothing else worked out.

A shard of melancholy pricked at her.

No, Samara scolded herself. She wouldn't think like that. Returning to the US was the right thing to do. Her future wasn't in the Khanna household. Delhi had always been a short-term thing. Diya would hopefully get together with Yash, and Nonita would marry Sharav and move in, bringing her unsolicited opinions along with her.

She *definitely* didn't want to stick around for that.

Samara was still angry about what had happened at Dilli Haat. She was going to give Sharav a piece of her mind when she saw him. After all this time, she really thought that he'd come to like her, appreciate her in the same way she did him. That despite the obvious attraction they shared and studiously ignored, they were in a good place. To hear that he wanted her gone?

It hurt.

'Buy the ones with sesame seeds.'

Disconcerted, Samara glanced up. In front of her was the booth's vendor, gazing at her with a mix of compassion and pity. 'Huh?'

The vendor repeated, 'Buy the til rewari, the one with sesame seeds.' He pointed to one of the sweetmeat boxes on display.

Shaking herself off, she asked with forced cheer, 'Is it the best one?'

'No,' the man replied. 'But if you throw sesame seeds into the bonfire, you'll be blessed with a son!' He beamed as if he'd just imparted the secrets of the universe.

Annnd the anger was back.

She glowered at the vendor and strode off. After a few minutes of searching, she found Diya and Yash near the exit, carrying a large box and laughing. 'What's that?' she asked, pointing to the box.

'It's an air purifier,' replied Yash, his eyes twinkling. He looked like the cat that not only got the cream but also the canary, the goldfish, and a belly rub to boot. The man could barely hold back his glee.

Diya held up the box. 'I won it in the Lucky Draw!' she said, with enthusiasm that seemed disproportionately high, given that the Khanna house not only had an air purifier in every room but also in each of their four cars *and* a heavy-duty filter installed in the air-conditioning system.

Putting aside her own issues for the moment, Samara allowed a moment of satisfaction that the prospective couple in front of her were finally getting along. 'That's great! Should we move along? Diya, you have a Lohri party to get to, right?'

Nodding, Diya checked her watch. 'Yeah, we have two parties this evening. The Sandhu family is apparently giving stunt kites from the US as Lohri favours this year, so Dhruv and Sharav are keen to go.' She turned to Yash. 'Are you going to the Bhatts' party?'

He nodded. 'I am. Also to a couple of others, so we should leave.' He smiled. 'Maybe I'll see you at the Bhatts' house, around midnight?'

Suddenly coy, Diya breathed 'Okay' before turning to Samara.

'You'll come with us, right?'

'Can't. I've got to prepare for a shoot this week,' she lied. It was an unfortunate but necessary falsehood. If Sharav was going to these parties, Samara couldn't tag along. The last thing she wanted was to get into an argument with him in front of the family and ruin Lohri for them.

No, she would wait until they were alone to show him exactly how much she could be.

CHAPTER 22

'All the best for tonight.'

Sharav clutched Dhruv's shoulder and squeezed. After weeks of preparing, the day of Dhruv's bar performance had arrived. Unlike the last time, when Dhruv hadn't invited any of them to watch, tonight the whole family was going to the Royal Hauz to support a visibly nervous Dhruv.

His foot bouncing as he styled his hair in the mirror, Dhruv replied in a quiet voice, 'Thanks.'

Sharav watched his younger brother get ready, his fingers itching to dust specks off the boy's dishevelled clothing, correct his slouchy posture, and give him pointers. He held back with great difficulty. Instead, he uttered words that would have seemed alien to him mere months ago. 'Whatever happens, I'm proud of you for getting up there and trying again. It says a lot about the kind of man you are, that you didn't let one setback knock you out of the game.'

For a stunned moment, Dhruv just gawped at Sharav in the mirror. Then he croaked, 'You . . . you're *proud* of me?'

'Very proud.' Sharav took a deep breath and forced out more necessary words. 'Dad would have been proud too.'

Dhruv's stupefaction turned into horror in the blink of his eye. 'Oh my God. You're not *dying*, are you?'

'What? Of course not!' Sharav laughed.

'No, I'm serious. I can't take over the business. I'm only nineteen, and I'm not you. I don't have it in me!'

Sharav turned Dhruv around and held him by his shoulders. 'I'm not dying, and you will not be required to join the business at any age unless you want to, okay?'

'Okay.' Dhruv breathed out a heavy puff of air. 'You really scared me for a second.' He turned back to face the mirror and fiddled with his hair. 'I mean, I might join the business after college, but right now I'm kind of really enjoying my music.' He smiled. 'Samara's really put me through my paces this week. It's been fun.'

Sharav couldn't help a wry chuckle. 'You're not the only one she's been putting through their paces. Trust me.'

They shared an amused glance through the mirror before Dhruv mentioned, 'I saw Yash at the driveway performance. And that stuff she did for Ma? It was really sweet. I like Samara.'

'Me too.' Way too much, but Sharav wasn't going to admit that to his younger brother. 'Anyway, I'll see you at the bar. Break a leg.' He thumped Dhruv on the shoulder and walked out of the room.

Contentment bathed his insides as he walked down the hallway, a big smile on his face. His mother was singing while she gardened, Diya was laughing at the dining table, and Dhruv was talking to him! If anything, having Samara live with them had made Sharav realise just how disconnected they'd been earlier. No more. He swore to be present in his family's lives from now on. Make an effort.

And thank Samara properly for everything she had done. With a gift of some sort. Jewellery? She didn't strike him as a diamond person, but maybe one of those bracelets with the dangly things? A camera lens she didn't already have? A new laptop? Or maybe *yellow* diamonds.

Suddenly, a door opened, and Samara rushed out, crashing into him with a shriek as she wobbled in ridiculously high heels.

Sharav reached out to steady her, instinctively putting his arms around her body. The heels made her taller, brought her face conveniently closer to his. It felt so right that, for a moment, he just let himself enjoy the feeling without guilt, smile down into her sweet face, and feel the gratification that came with—

She kicked his shin.

'Ow!' He let her go, frowning in confusion. 'What the hell?'

'Oh, I'm sorry. Was that *too much* for you?' She stalked off.

For a dazed moment, Sharav just stared at the back of her head as she strode towards the staircase. Then he followed her. 'Samara, what are you talking about?'

Samara zipped down the stairs despite her sky-high footwear. She didn't stop or turn as she shouted, 'I'm not talking to you right now, but I *will* be talking later!'

'Huh? Talking about what? Samara!'

He chased her out the front door and into the driveway, where Jyoti and Diya were waiting, both dressed up for the evening. Before they were within earshot, Sharav reached out and caught Samara by the arm. 'Are you angry with me?'

She rolled her eyes. 'Oh, wow. What gave it away?' When he frowned, she pointed at his forehead. 'Don't you dare try to distract me with that frown line. I'm *very* upset with you!'

'What? *Why?*'

Turning to look over her shoulder at Jyoti and Diya, both of whom now stared at them with bewildered expressions, Samara hissed, 'We'll talk about it later.'

But Sharav was beyond caring what they looked like. 'Tell me now!'

'Don't order me around,' growled Samara, once again in motion. 'Besides, you wanted me to stay away from you, right? I'm giving you what you want.' She swivelled with so much force that she almost tottered again, but she quickly righted herself and continued to sashay down the driveway.

Which was when Sharav noticed what she was wearing.

It was a shirt. A tight, open-necked, silky black *shirt* that hit her thighs, with sparkly boots up to her knees. And nothing but smooth, bare skin in between! *Oh dear God.* He squeezed his eyes shut and clutched his forehead to stop his brain from short-circuiting.

'Sharav?' called out Jyoti. 'Are you all right?'

'Fine,' he rasped. 'Give me a minute.' He bent down, untied and retied his shoelaces with painstaking deliberation, buying enough time to bring his arousal under control. Then he marched up to Samara, who was in the process of telling his mother and sister how nice they looked in their evening wear.

'You're not wearing pants,' he bit out, pointing an accusatory finger at her legs.

Her eyes sparking with barely held temper, Samara squinted up at him. 'It's a shirtdress. Do you have a problem with it?'

'No,' he replied in as even a tone as he could manage. 'I just think you'll be cold. Very cold. It's *winter*.' He pointed to the sky, as if that would aptly illustrate his point.

'I think she looks sexy,' interjected Diya.

Jyoti joined in. 'You can borrow my shawl if you get cold, child.'

Samara gave Sharav an acerbic smile. 'You see? I can borrow Jyoti Mom's shawl if I get cold. Now . . .' She gestured towards her car. 'Who's riding with me?'

Between her belligerent attitude and the effects of her clothing, Sharav wasn't exactly at his best, but he was still capable of driving to the bar. 'There's only four of us. We'll take my car.'

'You take your car and I'll take mine,' snapped Samara over her shoulder, walking to the driver's side and opening the door. 'Jyoti Mom, you want to come with me? We can discuss your plans for the flower show.'

His mother looked as baffled as Sharav felt, but she gave him an apologetic smile and followed Samara. The moment they were seated, Samara hit the accelerator and sped off down the road, bounding over a pothole on the way.

Feeling as though she'd run over him instead, Sharav looked at Diya, who was still standing beside him. 'What just happened?'

Diya shrugged. 'She's obviously upset with you.'

'Do you know why?'

Another shrug. 'Maybe because you just behaved like a toxic boyfriend.'

Which was exactly what Samara was thinking as she drove Jyoti towards Hauz Khas Village for Dhruv's big night. Sharav had never commented on her clothing before, and Nonita regularly wore stuff more skimpy than a shirtdress, so his reaction infuriated her even more. He thought her dress was too revealing? Well, she would show him! Precisely *how* she would show him was unclear, but she was too angry to consider that right now.

'Are you all right, child?' came Jyoti's perplexed enquiry.

She took a deep breath, navigating the busy road expertly. 'Sorry. I'm just a little upset with Sharav.'

'Yes, I saw that. Do you want to talk about it?'

'Maybe later, once I cool down.'

Before Jyoti could respond, Samara's phone rang over the car's speaker system. It was Diya's number, so she picked up the call and spoke loudly, 'Hi, Diya. You on the way?'

It was Sharav's voice, however, that resonated inside the car. 'We're right behind you. Slow down.'

Slow down? *Slow down?* Samara had driven all over the world—on both sides of the road—for almost a decade. She could drive from the house to the bar in her sleep! 'Do you *ever* stop telling people what to do?'

She thought she heard Diya giggle before Sharav replied, 'Samara, what on earth is going on? Why are you behaving like this?'

'I told you we'd discuss this later!'

'Why can't you tell me right now?'

'Fine!' Her voice was a whip. 'You want to know? I'll tell you, in front of your mom and sister!' She took a rapid breath. 'You told Nonita that I'm an outsider and you want me to stay away from you and your family!'

Jyoti gasped.

'What?' Sharav's usually deep voice rose a couple of keys. 'I did not!'

'Yes, you did. She told me. You said I was too much. That you didn't want me to stay in your house in the first place. That you wanted me *gone*!' All her hurt came pouring out, and she swallowed a brand-new lump in her throat.

'No, that's not . . . Samara, you've driven around this roundabout twice,' sounded Sharav's worried voice. 'Pull over so we can discuss this.'

'Why? So you can tell me to calm down and put on some pants? I'm perfectly capable of driving, Sharav. And Jyoti Mom and I will go around this roundabout *as many times as we want*!' she yelled, navigating her car so that it coasted around the roundabout in the innermost lane of the road. It was the only way of safely staying away from the bulk of the lane-changing traffic and aggravating Sharav even more.

Jyoti shifted in her seat. 'Well, I—'

'You're behaving like a child!' Sharav's car followed hers into the lane and drove directly behind them.

'Are you denying you said those things to Nonita?'

'Samara . . .'

'Are you?'

There was silence for a moment. Samara peeked in the rearview mirror and saw Sharav behind the wheel, his face a worried scowl.

'I might have said something along those lines—'

Jyoti gasped again. 'Sharav!'

'But it was *before*!' he stressed. 'Before I . . . before we . . .'

A small splinter of hope nudged out of the relentless plane of her anger. 'Before what?'

Sharav gave a helpless huff. 'Samara, can we discuss this privately? Please pull over.'

'Before *what*, Sharav?'

'Before we got to know you—before *I* got to know you, okay? Before I was able to appreciate everything you've done for us.' She heard him take a breath. 'You've been really good for this family, Samara. And yes, I didn't want you to stay initially, and I might have thought you were too much in the beginning, but that *completely* changed, and I feel the opposite way now.'

Warmth slowly began to rinse away the bitterness. 'So you think I'm the opposite of too much?'

He laughed. 'I think you're just right.'

'And?'

After sighing, Sharav muttered, 'And I'm sorry for saying those things to Nonita. I shouldn't have, and I'm going to speak to her about it too. Okay?'

Samara smiled. 'Okay.'

'Okay,' he repeated with palpable relief. 'Now, can you *please* stop circling the roundabout?'

'Maybe just once more.'

'Dammit, Samara!'

CHAPTER 23

Three men turned their heads when she walked up to the bar, Diya noted.

One was greasy haired, with stubble that looked as if it'd been painted onto his face, another wore a tartan T-shirt with way-too-skinny jeans, and the third had at least six gold chains around his neck. His fingers were full of gemstone rings, too, a clear indication that some wily astrologer was fishing in his pockets.

Maybe this was why she put up with Ari. The dating market around Diya consisted either of arranged matches whom she was expected to marry after a month of awkward tea parties . . .

. . . or these three.

To be fair, Diya hadn't tried any of the numerous dating apps out there, even before she and Ari became a couple.

She sighed. The word *couple* was a bit of a stretch these days.

It had been weeks since he'd called her first. His replies to her texts were vague, never committing to an actual assignation. No amount of 'sweetheart' and 'princess' texts made up for the fact that he didn't feel any urgency to see her, be near her. Apprehension slithered up her spine. Had he become bored because she wouldn't have sex with him? Maybe if she agreed to . . .

Diya shook her head, shaking off the thought. She wouldn't use sex as a negotiating point in a relationship. It wasn't unreasonable to expect a man to give you more than a quick bang on the way to a party for your very first time. To expect intimacy and tenderness.

Glaring at the three would-be suitors until they turned away, Diya leaned over the bar and ordered an Old-Fashioned, partly because she actually liked the cocktail and partly to prove to herself that there was nothing wrong with being a little old-fashioned in a world obsessed with newness.

The Royal Hauz bar was crowded for a Wednesday night, so she leaned back against a high stool and waited until the bartender got to making her drink. Besides, after what had happened on the drive over, she really didn't want to go back to the table and be around Sharav and Samara right now.

'Need any help?'

She turned to find Yash behind her, dressed in fitted jeans and a black shirt that hugged his body without being tight. Smiling at her, like always. Being the recipient of Yash's unguarded smile had always felt mildly annoying growing up.

Now it felt a little special.

Not because he'd gone and grown a beard—which, admittedly, made him look almost like a different person—but because they'd actually talked like equals the last few times they'd met. Without the weight of family expectations, childhood history, or unrequited feelings. It underlined the fact that they had both grown up. That he, too, had developed into his own person, just like her. Someone who was still unguarded and a little geeky but also really smart and funny and interesting. And confident, which was more attractive than Diya cared to acknowledge right now.

'No, I'm just getting a drink for myself,' she replied, smiling back at him.

He looked around. 'Where's your family?'

She rolled her eyes and gave a dramatic chuckle. 'At a table. Sharav and Samara had a *huge* argument on the way over, and they're still snapping at each other, so I had to get away.'

Yash frowned in concern. 'Is Samara okay?'

Diya's sunniness dimmed a little. Yash and Samara. Was that a thing? They had been kind of cosy with each other lately. Had Yash transferred his affections from Diya over to Samara in a matter of weeks? If so, that would be a little shallow of him.

And why did the idea of them together bother her so much? *She* was already in a relationship.

Technically.

She watched Yash order himself a pretentious Japanese whisky that was sitting on the top shelf of the bar. Smirking, she said, 'You know that's probably been rotting up there for years, right?'

He gave her a teasing grin. 'Whisky *ages*, not rots.'

Diya returned the tone. 'Like fine wine?'

'And fine women.' He winked.

A spark of heat sizzled through Diya unexpectedly, leaving her breathless and more than a little dazed. *Where did that come from?* She squinted, scrutinising him in a way she'd never done before. His jaw framed lips instead of just a mouth, and his shoulders were wider than they'd been a minute ago. His shirt had two buttons open at the front, exposing a sprinkling of chest hair. *Yash has hair on his chest! He has lips!* She dropped her gaze, winded from the realisation. His fingers, long and firm, were curled around a whisky glass, his index finger rubbing idly against the curve. Her ovaries somersaulted, like puppies leaping for a treat.

She caught hold of the stool she was leaning against. Yash shot out a hand to grip her elbow. 'You okay?'

She gaped at his hand, now touching her skin, sending frissons through her body. Glancing up, she met his eyes, warm and resonant. The spark within her began to simmer, turning her belly molten.

Oh my God!

She was attracted to Yash!

'Diya? Are you feeling unwell?'

Her reply came out in a gasp. 'No.' She needed to distract him, distract herself. 'Er . . . you know Samara's leaving soon, right?'

Seeming surprised at her erratic behaviour, Yash peered at her for a worried moment before he answered. 'Yes, I know. Do you want to sit down?'

'I'm fine.' Diya shrugged a little too frantically for it to be believable. As epiphanies went, this one was a whopper. Suddenly, she *really* wanted to know how Yash felt about Samara. 'Do you like Samara?' She shook her head. 'I don't mean just like—I mean, *like* like.' Great, now she sounded like a high schooler.

Yash smirked. 'I like her. Not *like* like her, but I like her. Like, in a liking way.'

'Yash!' Diya huffed. 'Do you have feelings for her?'

'No.' His eyes pierced into hers. 'I have feelings for you, as I mentioned that morning. When you told me to lie to my parents and say I wasn't interested. Remember?'

Her breath turned inexplicably steadier. 'You still feel that way? Towards me?'

He nodded. 'I still do.' His expression was open, unafraid to be vulnerable. That was the rare thing about Yash—he didn't play games. Diya always knew where she stood with him.

A fact she'd never appreciated before now.

She gulped. 'Yash, I'm seeing Ariyan Mehra.'

He nodded again. 'I know.'

'You know?'

'People talk.'

Right, obviously. This *was* Delhi.

After a moment, during which Yash seemed thoughtful, he asked, 'Diya, are you happy with Ariyan?'

No. 'Yeah.' She gave him a shaky smile.

'Does he treat you like you deserve to be treated?'

The question brought sudden tears to Diya's eyes. She cried easily on a good day, but right now, overwhelmed by her sudden awareness of Yash and weeks of frustration over Ari, she couldn't hold them back anymore. 'I . . . he . . . I don't know,' she blubbered before the tears spilled over and started rolling down her cheeks.

Immediately, before she could get ahold of herself, Yash's arms came around her, cradling her head against his shoulder. 'Hey, it's okay.' His hands rubbed her back. 'You're okay.'

'No, I'm not,' she mumbled into his chest, crying freely. She hadn't been able to disclose her relationship problems to anyone before now, given that Ari wanted to keep it secret. Having a warm shoulder to cry on, strong arms supporting and soothing her, felt heaven sent.

Like spotting land after months on a stormy sea.

The bar and its noise fell away for a few seconds. All she could feel was Yash and a rising tide of shame—shame for the way she'd treated him earlier, shame for the way she'd allowed herself to be treated by Ari.

Yash said nothing, but she could feel anger radiating in his embrace. The last thing she wanted was for him to confront Ari on her behalf, for her relationship issues to turn into a quarrel between the Malhotra and Mehra families. The thought grounded Diya, made her belatedly realise that so much more was at stake in this situation than just her feelings. She took a few deep breaths and wiped her tears, attempting to defuse his anger by saying in a flippant tone, 'Not what you expected from a Wednesday night, huh?'

It worked. Yash replied with a small chortle, 'I never know what to expect with you. It's pretty exciting, actually.'

'I've wet your shirt.'

'It'll dry.'

She looked up and caught his eye. 'I'm sorry, Yash.'

He wiped a tear off her cheek with his thumb. 'There's no reason to be sorry, Diya.'

'There is,' she insisted. 'I behaved like a spoiled child that morning with your parents.'

He shrugged. 'You kind of did, honestly, but they know you. They've seen you growing up.'

Diya shook her head. 'Yeah, but that's no excuse. I'm grown up now.' Her jaw tightened. 'Time to start behaving like it.'

CHAPTER 24

'So now you're going to avoid me?'

Sharav rolled his eyes and glanced down, briefly skimming over Samara's shirtdress before quickly turning away. 'I'm not avoiding you,' he told her.

She pointed to the pool table, virtually hidden in an L-shaped corner of the bar, where two men played against each other with a slightly bored cluster of onlookers. 'You're actually interested in watching these two try to play pool?'

'Yes.'

'Fine,' replied Samara, crossing her arms. 'Then you won't mind me watching with you.'

Sharav gritted his teeth, making a muscle in his jaw twitch. He didn't reply, but she could sense the cacophony of thoughts swirling around in his brain.

Turning to the pool table, Samara fumed silently too. Never one to hold a grudge, she'd genuinely forgiven Sharav for what he'd said to Nonita. She was still, however, irrationally angry. After their moment in the kitchen, on the day of the driveway performance, when he'd touched her face, Samara had lain awake most of the night, wondering what would have happened if they hadn't been interrupted. If he might have kissed her. And the more she thought about it, the more certain she was about one terrifying fact.

She would have kissed him back.

She would've tossed the thought of his troublemaking fiancée into the recesses of her brain and climbed him like an apple tree in the Garden of Eden.

So, Samara was angry, both with Sharav and herself. Sharav, for being forbidden fruit, and herself for . . . wanting to eat it.

One of the men playing pool bent down to take a complicated shot with his cue, aiming to shoot a red-striped ball into the closest pocket. She shook her head, perversely annoyed by the man's misjudgement in her current state. 'Won't go in.'

The man turned to her with an irritated look. 'Excuse me?' He glanced at Sharav for a brief second, his expression conveying what he couldn't say out loud. *Control your woman.*

Which, for obvious reasons, sent Samara's already-frayed temper rocketing into the stratosphere. 'That's the wrong angle,' she explained with a dismissive flick of her hair. 'You have to aim more to the left of the ball.'

Sharav rumbled a warning. 'Samara, let him do the shot the way he wants.'

'Well, he's doing it wrong.'

The man glowered at Samara with condescension written all over his face. 'Really? You think you can do better?'

She shrugged. 'I know I can.'

Beside her, Sharav's voice was a growl. 'Samara . . .'

'Really?' the man said again with a sneer. 'Fine, then *you* do it.' He flipped his cue around and held it out to her. 'Unless you need a child-size one?'

'This one will be fine,' answered Samara, snatching the cue from him. Maybe she'd been wrong in pointing out the man's mistake initially, but she wasn't going to sit back and excuse misogynistic behaviour.

Walking around the table, she gauged the positions of the ball and pocket before lining up her cue and aiming. Before she made her strike, though, she glanced up to see if Sharav was watching. He was, looking possibly even more aggravated than she felt. Like a flame with a vat of hot oil being poured into it, her determination to show up the men around her flared higher. She made the strike.

And pocketed the ball.

Sharav's jaw clenched even harder as a couple of the onlookers clapped, and Samara smiled. She proceeded to pocket another ball, with a strike that had as much flair as accuracy.

The second man playing the pool game laughed. 'You're too good for me. I'm out.' He put down his cue and picked up his drink.

Samara looked up at Sharav with a raised eyebrow. 'Anyone willing to take his place?'

A blaze lit up Sharav's eyes, the challenge clearly firing his pride. They flashed at her for a moment, and then he stepped forward and seized the discarded cue like he was trying to choke it with his fist.

She knew she was pushing him, but Samara desperately wanted him to feel what she was feeling. This frustration coupled with gut-wrenching, soul-searing *want*. Which was why she walked around the table, stood in front of Sharav, and bent over to aim her cue, knowing full well that her dress would hike up from behind. Knowing that he'd look and be both enraged and aroused.

'It's such a pity,' she announced over her shoulder, right before pocketing a ball, 'that decent pool players'—Samara walked to the opposite side of the table and bent over again, this time giving Sharav a preview down the front of her shirtdress—'are so hard to find these days.' She aimed and looked up at him from under her lashes, giving him a saucy smile that she would have thought completely inappropriate if she were thinking clearly. Then she struck and pocketed another ball.

For a few transfixed moments, Sharav just stared at her, his eyes tempestuous. His cue looked about ready to snap in two, and that muscle in his jaw clenched. But then, as if in slow motion, she saw his face transform as he grasped the game she was playing. He returned her smile.

The saucy one.

Samara's hand, holding the cue in position to strike the next ball, slipped. The ball nudged forward uselessly.

Sharav stepped forward and rubbed some chalk on the tip of his cue, somehow managing to make it look ridiculously carnal. He aimed it towards the ball she'd just missed. 'I'd say it's even more of a pity,' he stated as he pocketed the ball easily, 'that decent pool players'—he walked around the table and made another strike—'allow their vanity to get the better of them.' He looked up and winked, making her breath stop in its tracks.

There were only three solids and the eight ball left on the table. Brushing past her, Sharav bent down to take another strike. 'You see, being too cocky affects their concentration.' He pocketed the solid balls in quick succession before indicating the pocket he'd chosen for the eight ball with his cue, leaning to take aim. 'And eventually'—he glanced up at Samara, smugness all over his face—'they lose.'

His cue struck the eight ball so hard it flew into the pocket with a loud thud. The game was over.

Everyone around them started clapping. Sharav straightened and stared at Samara, who stared right back at him from the other side of the table. The smirk fell off his face. He was as breathless as she was. As if a current had suddenly sucked out all the air between them, pulling them in even as they fought against it. Suddenly, there was no pool game, no audience, no bar, and no noise. There were no future plans and no fiancées. No misgivings, no principles, no guilty consciences.

There was only Sharav and Samara. Eyes saying what lips couldn't.

The screech of microphone feedback filled the cavernous room, and air gushed into their bubble, breaking the moment. Something always did, as though the universe were playing a perverse game of tug-of-war with them for its own entertainment.

The bustle in the bar quieted a little as the high-pitched feedback sounded again. Samara caught herself. In all the drama, she'd completely forgotten the reason they were here in the first place.

'Dhruv's performance!' she squealed.

Sharav blinked for a disconcerted second. Then he cleared his throat and nodded. 'Let's get back to the group.'

Together, they elbowed and nudged their way to their table, where Jyoti happily conversed with Sid's parents about the health benefits of black pepper tea while throwing inquisitive glances at Diya and Yash, who were huddled up at one end in deep discussion.

'It's time,' Samara announced with a grin, taking a seat next to Sharav. The atmosphere at the table, which also included a few friends of the band, was charged with a mix of expectancy and dread. Would Dhruv sing, or would there be a repeat of last time? As confident as Samara was that they'd prepared Dhruv for every eventuality, there was always the possibility that he wouldn't be able to see it through.

The owner of the bar, Sid's uncle, stood behind the mic stand onstage, where the band's instruments were already laid out. His voice resounded with contrived enthusiasm as he woohoo-ed with a little jiggle of his bottom, exactly as he'd done the previous time she was here. *'Ladies' night!'* He proceeded to rattle off the specials while the band stood behind him, their faces anxious. 'Now, to open for the Royal Hauz Band, please welcome onstage Stone Breed!'

Samara's foot twitched in nervous anticipation as Dhruv walked onstage with his band members. Sid, Laz, and Ira looked visibly on edge, throwing furtive glances at Dhruv the entire time. Dhruv, on the other hand, had that same numb look from last time. Samara's breath hitched. *Don't let him freak out now,* she prayed. He'd never get up onstage again if he did.

She shared a worried look with Sharav, who was clutching his jaw to hide his apprehension from the rest of the group.

The audience fell silent as Dhruv walked up to the mic. He strapped on his bass and turned to look at Sid, who nodded at him and murmured something only he could hear. Dhruv didn't nod in return. When he turned back to the audience, his expression hadn't changed.

He looked dumbstruck.

The audience began to get restless when the music didn't start. Then Dhruv looked at his feet, took a deep breath, and murmured 'Lights' into the mic. Two seconds later, the spotlight illuminating him on the stage turned off, transforming him into a shadowy silhouette.

From the dark, a deep bass note twanged, and Dhruv's voice filled the room. 'Ladies and gentlemen, thank you for giving us a chance to perform for you tonight.' Another note escaped in the dark. 'It's been a journey getting here, a journey that had some bumps along the way. But just like the song we're about to perform, we didn't stop believing, and neither should you.' A final bass note, loud and forceful. 'Hit it, guys!'

Laz's keyboard began the opening notes to 'Don't Stop Believin',' and Samara's heart began to pound. She felt a hand reach over and clutch hers, squeezing it tightly. She turned to find Sharav looking as tense as she felt. She squeezed his hand back and they held on, waiting.

Dhruv had spoken, but would he sing?

He did.

Samara let out a gasp she didn't know she was keeping inside when Dhruv sang the first verse, his voice pulsating through the bar with emotion. Still cast in silhouette on the stage as he was, the effect was dramatic and unexpected. A minute later, Sid's guitar joined in with a stylish lick, and finally, Ira burst in with the drums, bringing the spotlight back on and the song in full swing. Dhruv's now-illuminated face was exultant, and his vocals rang with confidence. The audience began to sing the chorus with the band, and the whole place throbbed with the rousing spirit of a classic anthem that had inspired people for generations.

It was perfect. Just perfect.

Sharav's hand pulled her into his shoulder, where his arm went around her. That was when Samara realised she was crying. She laid her head in the crook of Sharav's shoulder and allowed it to happen.

'Thank you, Samara,' murmured Sharav into her ear, hugging her to him. 'This was all you.'

Funny, how being in Sharav's arms could make her feel so turned on one minute and so soothed the next. How his deep voice could make her knees weak in two totally different ways. She sniffed. 'It was mostly Dhruv, but I'll take your thanks.' She looked up at him with a wobbly smile. 'Since it's all I'm going to get from you.'

His shoulders shook in rueful laughter, and he wiped her tears with his thumb. 'I'm sorry. For everything.'

'I'm sorry too.'

'For the record'—his eyes went sad, but his smile stayed—'I think you're amazing.'

She didn't want to see him sad. For all her frustration with the current state of affairs between them, she wanted to see Sharav happy. 'I *am* amazing.'

That made him laugh again. Soon, they were set upon by a gleeful Diya and Jyoti, both thanking Samara for helping Dhruv. There were hugs and celebratory rounds of drinks, and Jyoti drank enough alcohol to loudly proclaim, 'Trousseaus be damned! We're going to *use* the Wedgwood dinner set tomorrow!'

That brought on more celebration, even though most of the people at the table had absolutely no idea what she was talking about.

Finally, after two more songs—both of which Dhruv killed—the band took their bows to an enthusiastic round of applause and vigorous backslapping from Sid's uncle, who went on to introduce the regular house band to the stage. After a while, Dhruv and his bandmates came to the table, amid more hugs, cheers and backslapping.

After giving his delighted mother a quick hug, Dhruv hurried to Samara, picked her up off the ground, and spun her around in his exhilaration. 'Thank you, thank you, *thank you*!'

Samara laughed and squeezed his shoulder. 'You were fabulous!'

He put her down, and his expression became solemn. 'I couldn't have done this without you. Thank you so much.'

She brushed it off. 'You did the work. I just helped. Anyway . . .' She hugged him and declared, *'Time to celebrate!'*

The others woohoo-ed and clapped in agreement. Dhruv moved on to be congratulated individually by his family and friends, and Samara took a step into the shadows, watching with a wobbly grin on her face.

Her phone vibrated in her pocket. That was the great thing about shirtdresses—they not only filled men's heads with confusing thoughts but also had pockets.

She fished it out and saw Maya's name on the screen. 'He sang!' she yelled into the phone as she picked up the call.

'Who sang?' asked Maya.

'Dhruv sang!'

'Er, yay?' responded Maya in confusion. 'Where are you?'

'At the Royal Hauz bar! Drinking a . . .' She held up her mud-coloured drink. 'I don't know what I'm drinking, but it tastes disgusting!'

'Are you sober?' asked Maya with a laugh. 'I have some news! Great news!'

'I am,' Samara replied. 'Hang on, let me move to a quieter place!' She walked out the main door and onto the sidewalk outside. 'What's up?'

'Okay, you're not going to believe this,' started Maya in an excited voice. 'I was at a book launch and got talking with this guy who's the visuals editor at *Vanity Fair*. He said they're looking for a freelance photographer to cover features for Paris Fashion Week. Street fashion, underground fashion scene, et cetera, but not in a been-there-done-that way. So I showed him your online profile, and he loved it, so I showed him the portfolio on your web page, and he loved that too. He took your number and email and said he'd get in touch with you this week!'

Samara stood stock still, her pulse racing. 'Huh?'

'Did you hear what I said? *Vanity Fair* wants to send you to Paris Fashion Week! This is it—your big break, Sammy!'

It is, thought Samara. There was no question about it. This was the best-possible solution to all her problems. She'd get to live in New York with her best friend and travel to Paris for *Vanity Fair*, one of the best-paying gigs out there. It was a dream come true.

She waited for the explosion of joy in her chest, similar to the one she'd had when Dhruv sang his song minutes ago.

It didn't come.

Samara frowned, feeling mystifyingly detached from this opportunity of a lifetime. She should be jumping up and down. She should be squealing into Maya's ear, skipping over to the table, and announcing it to even more fanfare. She should get drunk and dance on the bar, buy rounds of drinks for strangers. She should be . . . happy. This was everything she'd wanted.

'Sammy?' Maya's voice sounded concerned now. 'Is this a good silence, or is something wrong?'

A great question, one to which Samara didn't know the answer. She turned around and saw Sharav standing outside the door to the bar. He'd followed her, a concerned look on his face. She gave him a *Don't worry, I'm fine* smile and replied with forced cheer, 'Definitely a good silence. Great, in fact. I'm just in shock. Wow.'

'I know!' laughed Maya. 'Now, buy that ticket, baby! I'm going to start checking out apartments.'

'Yeah, definitely.' Samara looked down at her fidgeting feet. 'Listen, I'm going to call you tomorrow morning, okay?'

'Sure. Sammy?'

'Yeah?'

'This is still what you want, right?'

She had absolutely no idea. 'Uh-huh. I'll call you tomorrow.'

'Okay. Love you!'

'Love you.' She hung up.

Sharav scanned her face carefully as she walked back to him. 'Everything all right?'

Samara nodded. 'Let's get back to the party!' She didn't want to tell him, or anyone, about the *Vanity Fair* thing yet. Not until she knew how she felt about it.

Because right now the only thing she knew for sure was that she wasn't going to call Maya back tomorrow morning.

CHAPTER 25

Sharav felt uncomfortably hot under his sweatshirt—a sign that winter was rapidly waning into what promised to be a sweltering spring.

He fidgeted in his seat. It was a rare Saturday morning that he had the house to himself. Even Biba wasn't home, so there were no loud thuds, clinks, and clangs coming from the kitchen. He should be soaking in the silence with one of the many books he'd bought but still hadn't had the time to read. Instead, he was sitting in the living room with Nonita.

Pretending to listen to what she was saying.

He watched her animated face idly as she narrated a story about something that had happened on social media. With a celebrity . . . or a friend. Either way, there were lots of references to followers, likes, and comments. She checked her phone—securely held in one palm at all times—every two minutes to see if the situation she was talking about had evolved.

Despite her unwarranted conversation with Samara, and the argument it had caused, Nonita was a great girl, Sharav firmly reminded himself. Something he had to do a little too often these days. In the past, he'd been able to immediately list at least a handful of reasons she would make an ideal wife. Nowadays, he was having trouble finishing the thought. Even more unfortunate was that the idea of marriage to Nonita usually made him think of Samara, resulting in an unfair comparison between the two that left him racked with guilt.

Even if he wanted to scrap his carefully planned future and break up with Nonita, it wasn't like Samara was going to stick around. She had a life plan, and it didn't include bogging herself down with him and his family when she could be travelling the world, rootless and free of responsibility.

No, Nonita was the safer choice, with a higher chance of success in the long term. Besides, she was already his commitment, his reality.

Samara was a fantasy.

In more ways than one.

'Sharav, are you listening to me?' interrupted Nonita, a flash of annoyance in her eyes. She quickly blinked it away.

He cleared his throat. 'Sorry, I got distracted for a minute.'

'Are you thirsty? Should I make you some coffee?'

Sharav shook his head with a laugh. 'No, thanks. You don't have to wait on me in my own house, Nonita.'

She looked offended. 'It's going to be my house soon too. Shouldn't I treat it as such?'

That was exactly the kind of thing he'd appreciated before. Now it just got on his nerves. 'Even so. I can get my own drinks.'

If Nonita was confused by his behaviour, she didn't show it. Another thing that now bothered him—she never called him out. Not like Samara.

Wait, he wasn't comparing anymore.

'Sorry, what were you saying earlier?' Sharav tried to refocus.

'I was telling you how my friend Anaya got photobombed by Suleiman Khan. She posted it last night, and there are already . . .'

He zoned out. Again.

Then he got irritated. This was so *not* what he wanted to be doing right now.

He leaned forward, interrupting Nonita midflow. 'Hey, I hate to stop you, but I've got to go to the office. Can I call you next week?'

Her eyes narrowed. 'But it's Saturday.'

'Yeah, there's some urgent work that can't wait.'

She looked over his grey sweatshirt and jeans in suspicion. 'You're going to the office like that?'

It was a fair question. Sharav was normally scrupulous about how he dressed for work. 'I'll change before I go.' He stood up, his eyes shifting away from her face in guilt. For lying, yes, but also for not wanting to spend time with the woman with whom he was going to spend the rest of his life. 'I'll see you out.'

Nonita wasn't happy. Her expression clearly showed it. But the words that came out of her mouth were 'Okay, sure. But I can still wait for Mummy to come home.' She looked around, as if expecting Jyoti to pop out from behind an armchair. 'Where is she, anyway? She's usually here whenever I visit.'

'Mom's gone plant-shopping with Samara, so they'll probably take a while,' replied Sharav, already moving towards the front door. 'I'll tell her you dropped by.'

Nonita had no choice but to stand up and follow him. She asked with a scowl, 'She's gone with Samara? Why didn't Mummy call me if she had no one to take her shopping?'

Sharav opened the front door. 'No, they'd planned it together. To prepare for the flower show.' He couldn't help a wry smile. 'They'll probably come back with a truckload of saplings.'

After staring at his face for a moment, Nonita burst out as though she couldn't help herself, 'Samara's become *very close* to the family all of a sudden.'

The scorn in her voice made Sharav wary. 'Not that sudden. She's been here for a while now. Anyway . . .' He frowned. 'That reminds me of something I've been meaning to discuss with you. Did you tell Samara—'

'Wasn't she supposed to stay only a few weeks? It's already February. Why is that woman still here?'

'She's—'

'I don't know how you all put up with her every day. All that nonstop meddling, giving instructions to everyone as if *she* was the head of the family!'

'That's not—'

'Must be nice,' she said, her voice dripping with sarcasm, 'to go through life making people think you're helping them instead of freeloading off them—'

'Nonita!' snapped Sharav, cutting off her rant. He was both surprised and angry at her unkind assumptions and the fact that she'd so thoughtlessly hurt Samara's feelings, creating unnecessary conflict between them. Still, he knew he had to have this conversation with his fiancée in a calm, nonaccusatory way. For the sake of all parties involved. 'Did you'—he took a breath to make his voice less brusque— 'tell Samara that I wanted her to stay out of everyone's way?'

Nonita's shoulders stiffened, her eyes narrowing. 'What did she say to you?'

'What did *you* say to her?'

After a strained moment, Nonita attempted a casual shrug, which came off as anything but casual. 'Hardly anything. I'm sorry if she took offence, but I was only trying to do my duty. I hope you understand that.' She kept quiet, seeming to gauge his reaction.

Duty. That magic word that made every action justifiable. 'Samara did get upset. Next time,' he said in a deliberately soft tone, 'please don't put words in my mouth. It creates misunderstandings.'

Her eyes burned with barely held back fury, but Nonita nodded. 'Fine. Although *I* am your future wife, Sharav, so you *should* be taking my side.'

'It's not about sides, and it's not about duty!' he retorted, incensed.

Taking a moment to calm down, he tried again. 'Look, I know you mean well. So does Samara.'

'"Means well"?' Nonita tittered. 'Well, if you call encouraging Dhruv to skip college for that silly rock band or flirting with Yash and trying to take him away from Diya . . . or making your mother exert herself in the sun and waste money—'

'Stop!'

She froze at his harsh tone.

'My mother,' he said forcefully, 'hardly ever gets out of the house, so a shopping expedition will do her good. She can spend as much money on plants as she likes because we can well afford it. Yash and Samara are just friends, and Dhruv is just a boy. I regret being so hard on him. He deserves a break.'

Finally, Nonita allowed the full force of her temper to show. Her voice became shrill. '"A break"? You're sounding very progressive these days, Sharav. Has Samara gotten to you too?' She swung her arms out in the air. 'What's next? She decides she's staying permanently? Decides she doesn't want to work anymore and asks you for an allowance? Moves into our bedroom after we're married? *Where does it stop?*'

She pointed a finger in his face and stamped her foot. Actually stamped it on the floor, like a stepsister from a Disney movie. 'Instead of putting your foot down, you're just going along with that woman's schemes! *That's* why I stepped in! So things can go back to normal around here, the way they were before *she* started *squatting in this house!*'

Sharav stared at his fiancée in shock. Nonita had never spoken like this in front of him, so uncontrolled and scathing. In the back of his mind, a small voice questioned how much more of her true self she was holding back. Another voice, a louder one, was aghast that Nonita seemed to think that they'd been a normal family before Samara arrived. That she wanted them to revert to that state.

He clutched his forehead. The funny thing was, if anyone had asked Sharav at the time of his engagement, even *he* would have agreed that the Khannas were a normal family. That it was normal to be constantly stressed out and at odds with each other. To sweep grief and loss under the carpet and pretend that everyone was okay when they weren't. To put duty before attachment, before everything. That was life, Sharav would have told himself.

Until Samara.

He blinked, thunderstruck. Along with everything else, had Samara also changed his outlook on *life*?

'Sharav?'

His eyes focused on Nonita's soft murmur. Now she had a contrite look under her fluttering eyelashes. How long had he been standing at the front door in silence? When had she transitioned from a Fury into an apologetic Aphrodite?

'I'm so sorry!' she exclaimed with an almost-fearful expression. As though she'd seen the shocked realisation on his face and assumed the worst. 'I didn't mean to shout at you.'

He couldn't do this right now. 'Nonita, it's fine. Shout at me as much as you want. Listen'—he gestured for her to walk out the door—'I really have to run. We'll talk later.'

The fear on Nonita's face intensified as she followed him outside. 'I don't normally behave like that!'

He pinched his forehead with tight fingers, still walking. That she felt she had to put on a submissive front for him was so problematic. Why hadn't he noticed before? 'It's perfectly normal to lose one's temper. Please don't worry about it.' They reached her car, which was parked in the driveway. 'Let's talk in a couple of days.'

'You're not angry with me?'

'Not at all.' He shifted impatiently, waiting for her to take out her car keys, get into her sedan, and drive away.

Nonita, on the other hand, seemed to have other plans. With a frantic look at his perturbed face and fidgeting feet, she burst out, 'Mummy!'

Startled, Sharav looked over his shoulder at the empty road beyond.

'No, not your mummy, *my* mummy,' clarified Nonita with a nervous laugh. 'She wanted to speak to you!'

Before he could say anything, Nonita dialled her mother's number, her phone ever ready in the palm of her hand for such emergencies. She put it on speaker so Sharav would hear the ringing and know that it was too late to back out of speaking to his future mother-in-law.

He tried to hide his exasperation as the phone rang and rang until finally, Nonita's mother picked up and barked, 'What? I'm busy,' clearly not expecting to be on speakerphone.

Which was why Nonita immediately crooned, 'Mummy, you're on speaker, and Sharav is here.'

'Hi, Amita Aunty,' added Sharav, trying not to sound as unenthusiastic as he felt.

'Oh, *Sharav*!' The fawning in her mother's voice put Nonita's to shame. 'My *son*! How are you?'

'I'm fine, Aunty.'

'Call me *Mummy*, son,' she sang. 'We're family now. So are you kids enjoying yourselves?' Her tone was almost suggestive.

Sharav cringed inside. 'Nonita was saying you wanted to speak with me.'

Nonita quickly interjected, 'Yes. Mummy, remember you wanted to talk to Sharav? About the wedding?'

A few moments of silence ensued, followed by, 'Yes, I did. The wedding. We'll make it a grand affair. Er, what would you like as a wedding gift, son? A Rolex? A BMW? Perhaps an investment property?'

'Not that, Mummy,' countered Nonita through gritted teeth. 'You wanted to discuss *dates*, remember?'

'Oh, right. Dates,' her mother replied. 'We'll get them straight from Dubai, the very best kind. Stuffed with almonds and coated in chocolate.'

'Not *dates*,' grated Nonita. '*Wedding dates!*'

'Oh! Yes, yes, of course. *Wedding* dates! We'll need to discuss wedding dates, son.'

At this point, Sharav would have said just about anything to end this conversation. 'Sure, no problem. I'll ask my mother to get in touch. Nice speaking to you, Aunty.'

'Not *Aunty*, remember? What did I tell you to call me?' she asked, like a kindergarten teacher asking what letter came after A in the alphabet.

'Mummy,' ground out Sharav.

'Very good! Okay, I'll see you soon. You kids have fu—'

Nonita ended the call, cutting her mother off.

She turned to Sharav and scraped together another smile, anxious energy still crackling around her. 'Are you okay?'

No. 'Yes.'

'Are you still angry with me?'

Yes. 'No.'

Probably sensing that she wasn't going to get anything else out of him this morning, Nonita beat a strategic retreat. 'Okay. I'll call you later.' Standing on tiptoe, she gave him a peck on his cheek, then got into her car and drove off.

Sharav watched her disappear down the road, feeling like a dog inside a cage that it had willingly entered with the promise of a bone, only to discover a carrot instead.

Trapped.

CHAPTER 26

The second they exited the car, Jyoti disappeared into the garden, calling to the gardener in a voice brimming with energy and excitement.

Samara smiled. Spending the morning in a nursery with Jyoti, where they'd bought a trunkful of saplings for the garden, had been an effective distraction from the internal turmoil of the last few days. Since her conversation with Maya.

After downing a glass of water in the kitchen, Samara made her way upstairs with her shopping bags. She dumped them on the floor and sat on the bed, taking a deep breath. A familiar shame, one she'd been ignoring for two days, swept over her. She'd pulled a Dilip Mansingh on Maya by not returning her call. Her best friend deserved better. So she picked up her phone and dialled.

A groggy Maya answered on the seventh ring. 'Who died?'

Samara uttered, 'I'm sorry, babe.'

Shuffling on the other end of the line told her that Maya was sitting up in bed. 'For what? Waking me up at two a.m., or not calling when you said you would?'

'Both.'

Maya sighed. 'Okay. Tell me what's going on?'

Somehow, even now, Samara couldn't verbalise it. 'I bought you a wind chime and a shawl. You'll love them! I bought myself a dream catcher.'

'Samara Mansingh, stop beating around the bush. Spit it out!'

She sighed. 'My dreams are all messed up.'

'Okaaay. How?'

'Well, earlier I used to dream of obvious things. Travelling and taking stop-scrolling-and-stare photos, swimming under waterfalls, eating Black Forest cake in the Black Forest . . . that sort of thing, you know?'

'Uh-huh.'

'Now I dream of movie nights and family dinners. And Sharav. A lot about Sharav. The other night, I dreamt we were sitting in the garden at night and looking up at the stars. There's this pink bench there, which he thinks is too girly, but he was sitting on it with me. We were bickering about whether birds prefer to eat prawns or chocolate.'

Maya snorted. 'Chocolate, obviously.'

'That's what I said, but Sharav insisted prawns were healthier. And then we kind of digressed . . .'

'Ah,' murmured Maya.

'Dream-Sharav knows what he's doing. Plus, he's warm, smells like heaven, and likes to cuddle.'

'Cuddling? You've got it bad, huh?'

Another sigh. 'So bad.'

'Isn't he engaged?'

'Yeah, he is. But the way I see it, Dream-Sharav isn't like Real-Sharav. He's a fantasy, a nocturnal manifestation of my infatuation. I don't need to feel guilty about doing stuff with a fantasy, right?'

'Sure,' replied Maya. 'Keep telling yourself that.'

A frustrated groan escaped her. 'What do I do, babe? I can't stop thinking about him.'

'Is he the reason for your subdued reaction when I told you about *Vanity Fair*?'

'Partly,' Samara answered. 'I got the email from the visuals editor and sent him all the information he requested. Thank you, by the way. I didn't thank you when you called.'

'You don't have to thank me, Sammy.' Maya's voice was soft. 'You know I really want you to come back, but I only want that if you do too. You can tell me if you've changed your mind, you know.'

'I know, and I love you for saying that,' she said. 'I'm going through something right now, but I'll figure it out. I have to.' She cleared her throat. 'All right, you go back to sleep. Let's talk in a couple of days.'

Maya yawned. 'Okay.'

For a moment after she hung up, Samara felt lighter, relieved that she'd cleared the air with Maya. The feeling only lasted for a moment, though, before all the angst came rushing back in. With a growl of impatience, she swung open the door to her room, determined to distract herself before she regressed into a teenager.

Just outside, however, she ran into the star of her dreams, who had been about to knock on her door. Samara felt a guilty flush rise from her neck and into her cheeks. She prayed Sharav wouldn't notice, wouldn't guess the kinds of thoughts she was regularly having about him.

'Hi,' said Sharav with a small wave of his hand. Dream-Sharav would have greeted her *very* differently.

Samara cleared her throat. 'Hi!' It came out too high-pitched.

'How was plant-shopping?' Sharav looked over her shoulder at the shopping bags. 'What did you buy?'

She tried to normalise her tone. 'Oh, just a few gifts.' Damn, she'd overcompensated, and now her low-pitched tone sounded like she was trying to scare a toddler.

He lifted one eyebrow. 'You okay?'

Outside of the dirty dreams and crushing indecision?

'Yeah, great!'

Shuffling his feet, Sharav put his hands in his pockets and asked, 'If you're not too busy, I thought maybe I could take you out for lunch.'

Surprised, Samara blinked up at him. 'Lunch? Just you and me?'

'Yeah, why not?' He shrugged. 'Mom's going to be busy, and I haven't thanked you properly for helping out so much around the house.'

'You got me lemon tarts.'

He smiled. 'I can do better.'

'Sure.' She smiled back. She went back into her room and picked up her handbag from the floor where she'd dropped it. 'All set.'

One corner of his lips twitched. 'Your room looks cleaner. I'm glad to see I'm rubbing off on you,' he said with a wink.

Samara barely suppressed a groan. The man knew how to make a corny joke and wink without looking like a creepy uncle at a family gathering. An impossibly difficult task. She attempted a smirk but probably ended up looking like a creepy uncle herself. 'Uh-huh. Let's go. Since you're feeling so generous, I feel like eating a bucket of caviar for lunch.'

Laughing, Sharav herded her out to his SUV, which had clean, buttery leather and smelled like him.

On the way, she convinced him she didn't really want to eat caviar and would much prefer to go to her favourite Asian-fusion restaurant in Khan Market.

Once there, Sharav parked, and they walked past lane after narrow lane of stores. The paths were riddled with cracks and potholes, deep and deadly, but Samara navigated them in her blue boots with practised ease, just like all the other women around her.

After climbing a dingy staircase, Samara and Sharav arrived at the restaurant she'd chosen. The decor was light and airy, decorated with pan-Asian motifs and smelling of delicious garlicky things sautéing in a poorly ventilated kitchen. A waiter seated them next to a window and handed them menus.

'The sushi and dim sum here are my favourite,' said Samara. 'They do them with Indian flavours. Spicy edamame, wasabi rolls, maki with Tabasco sauce, and chilli-cheese dim sum.' She kissed her fingers. '*So* good.'

Leaning back in his chair, Sharav barely glanced at the menu. 'I'm sensing a trend here.'

She nodded, perusing the offerings intently. 'Samara like spicy.'

Sharav pressed his lips together to quell his amusement. 'Samara talks about herself in the third person like a weirdo.'

'Samara will order Sharav only wasabi and water.'

He held his hands up, laughing. 'Sorry. Spicy *is* good.' His voice was a rumble. 'Sharav like spicy too.'

Her lady bits leapt. *Down, girl!* 'Great,' she croaked. 'I'm ordering you a chilli-cucumber fizzy drink.'

'Order away. Just ask for some water too.'

She held up her hand to get the waiter's attention and mouthed 'Water,' to which he nodded and scurried off to the side station. Samara turned to Sharav. 'So how's work?'

'Good.'

She tilted her head and regarded him thoughtfully. 'You never talk about your work.'

He shrugged. 'Not much to talk about. We manufacture machines that manufacture other things. It's pretty straightforward.'

'Do you like your job?'

Sharav chuckled. 'Stop it.'

'Stop what?'

He smiled. 'What you usually do. Ask questions and break people down until they're crying on your shoulder over their problems, after which you promptly try to solve them.'

Samara rested her chin in her palm and leaned forward. 'What's wrong with that?'

'Nothing,' he clarified. 'As I've said before, I'm very grateful for your help with the family. But I'm different.'

'You don't have problems.'

'I don't need your help.'

'So you *do* have problems.'

Sharav rolled his eyes and muttered, 'You just can't help it, can you?'

'Not really.' She shook her head. 'I grew up by myself, mostly. Dad was busy and the house was always empty, so I got involved in the lives of my neighbours and friends. It became a habit.'

'So helping people is how you overcome boredom?'

'No,' she replied. 'Helping people is how I feel less alone.'

After a moment, Sharav murmured, 'Sorry. I appreciate your helping habit greatly, but I'm still not talking about my problems. Assuming I have any, which you shouldn't.'

'Fine,' huffed Samara. 'Then I'll tell you about my problems.' She threw out her hands as if she were Hamlet about to deliver a monologue. 'You're looking at—'

Unfortunately, just then, her right hand collided with the jug of mint-and-cucumber water that the waiter had been bringing to their table. The waiter squawked as the jug overturned and poured its contents all over the front of his pants.

'Oh my God,' exclaimed Samara, springing out of her chair. 'I'm so sorry!'

The waiter, rendered immobile by shock, stared down at the front of his pants. A sprig of mint had gotten caught in his zipper, and a long sliver of cucumber had rolled down his leg and flopped onto the front of his shoe like a dead eel.

It looked like he'd wet himself. And foliage had sprouted from it.

Grabbing her napkin without any thought, Samara quickly bent down to his groin level, her face inches away from the scene of destruction. 'Here, let me help you.' She began forcefully scrubbing his crotch with her napkin, trying to dislodge the mint and soak up the water at the same time.

'Ma'am!' The waiter jumped back.

Sharav clutched his forehead, his shoulders shaking. 'Samara, stop touching him!'

Realising where her face was and what her hands were doing, Samara snapped up. 'Oh my *God!*' The waiter gaped at her, now shielding his privates with the jug. 'I'm so, *so* sorry. I didn't mean to'—she waved at the jug with the napkin—'touch it.' She shook her head. 'I mean you, touch *you*. Like *that*.'

'It's fine, ma'am,' the waiter muttered before hurrying off.

'No, it's not fine. It's completely unacceptable! *I'm so sorry!*' Samara called out after him, but he'd disappeared behind the kitchen door. She turned back to the table, where Sharav was shaking his head and barely holding back a guffaw. 'It was a genuine mistake!' She sat back down with a plunk, filled with self-loathing. 'I'm a monster.'

'It's not so bad.' Sharav grinned.

'I groped our waiter!' She dropped her head in her hands and groaned.

'You tried to help him.' Sharav reached over and pulled her hands away from her face, tilting her chin up with his finger. 'It's an admirable quality, done with the best of intentions.' He glanced at the cucumber-mint-infused puddle on the floor. 'Collateral damage aside.'

Samara attempted a weak smile, her chin bobbing in his hand. 'So I shouldn't go into the kitchen to apologise again?'

'Absolutely not. Give the man his privacy.' Sharav sat back and crossed his arms. 'So what problem were you talking about before?'

Sighing, she took a moment to collect herself before saying, 'I was about to say that I don't know what I'm doing—what I'm supposed to do or want to do with my life. I'm confused and feeling pulled in different directions.' She exhaled. Even though she wasn't going to tell Sharav about the Paris Fashion Week gig, it felt good to finally say that out loud.

Sharav considered her words. 'Has what you want changed?'

'I don't know,' she replied honestly. She met his eyes. 'What seemed so clear before just keeps getting murkier by the minute. I love the idea of working in New York, living with my best friend, doing the whole American dream thing. At the same time, I love so many aspects of my current job, and I'm already making a name for myself on the wedding circuit. The money is great, and the travel is amazing.' Plus, there was what she couldn't say out loud. The fact that she loved living with the Khannas, being part of a family unit.

The fact that, without her even realising it, that lonely void she'd always carried around seemed to have disappeared.

The Khannas thought she'd helped them. They had no idea what they'd done for her.

Still, she couldn't carry on living with them, even if she stayed on in Delhi. At some point, before Nonita moved in, Samara would have to move out and find her own place. Be alone again. At least if she went to New York, she would have Maya.

A waitress arrived, presumably to replace the stricken waiter, and Sharav proceeded to order every spicy thing on the menu with an occasional smile of acknowledgement in her direction. Samara felt a pang of longing every time he did. Sharav. Strong, steady, smart, and sexy Sharav—always so close and yet so far out of her reach.

If Delhi and the Khanna household were a biryani, Sharav would be the meat. Nonita would be the bones, the only hard, inedible thing in an otherwise melt-in-your-mouth delicacy.

A spiral of unfamiliar self-pity suddenly wrapped around her, at the spectacular unfairness of meeting this man, this imperfect-perfect man who wanted her as much as she wanted him, at a time in both their lives when being together was an impossibility.

The universe had a sick sense of humour.

Sharav put the menu down after the waitress left and refocused on Samara's admission. 'What does your dad say about this decision you have to make?'

Nothing. Her dad was busy with his own life and hadn't picked up her last two calls. The self-pity now morphed from a spiral into a whirlpool, surprising her with its strength. Samara swallowed a lump in her throat and gave her stock answer for questions about her father's involvement in her life, 'He wants me to be happy, so he'll support whatever I do.' Which was technically true and didn't invite any sympathy. 'Anyway . . .' She mentally shook herself. 'Speaking of fathers, what was yours like?'

Sharav blinked at her sudden about-face. 'Er, well . . .' He took a breath, his expression turning contemplative. 'He had a big personality. He liked his food and drink. Laughed often but was serious when needed.' He smiled. 'We spent a great deal of time together. He taught me a lot.'

'You must miss him terribly.'

'We all do,' agreed Sharav. Then he shifted in his seat. 'Although . . .' He shook his head. 'Never mind.'

'No, no. You can't do that. You can't make me confide in you and then not do the same. Tell me!'

Laughing, Sharav tilted his head at her. 'Only if you promise not to go on a crusade to fix it.'

Samara held up her palm. 'I promise I will forget everything you've said after this lunch.'

'Okay.' Sharav paused for a moment. 'I guess it's been hard to transition since he passed. For everybody. Six years on, I'm the one who's running everything, but it's still Dad's business in everyone's mind. At home, it's still Dad's study and Dad's seat at the dining table.' He shrugged, clearly trying to make light of something that was obviously not. 'Some days, I feel like I'm living up to his expectations. Other days, I feel like a poor substitute. But he's just always there.'

'You feel like you're being made to live his life instead of your own. Like a seat-filler.'

'Yeah, and I feel disloyal for thinking it and for wanting to move on. But I *do* want to move on. Run the business *my* way, make decisions based on what *I* think is best. Not always be answerable to the ghost of what my dad would have wanted.' Sharav let out a dry laugh. 'Wow. I've never actually said that out loud before.' He circled a finger at her. 'You're good.'

She ignored the finger. 'Would you do anything differently? Choose another life?'

'God, no. I love the business and love living at home. My family is everything to me, and as it turns out, I'm not a bad businessman,' he added with a slightly embarrassed tilt of his lips.

'Are you happy, though?'

Sharav looked into her eyes and held them for a few long seconds, as if battling with his next words. Then he leaned over and took her hand in his. 'I have been since you arrived,' he murmured.

The breath got sucked right out of her body. 'We're talking about you and your father.' She tried to pull her hand away, but he held tight.

'Since you arrived, Samara Mansingh,' he continued without looking away, 'my mother, sister, and Biba smile at me, and my brother *actually* high-fived me yesterday. No one storms out of the dining room or avoids me in the hallways anymore. They laugh, like before. And me? I buy lemon tarts and take *you* out for lunch when I'm supposed to be having lunch with my fiancée.'

'Sharav,' she whispered.

'You know what else I do?' His thumb stroked over her palm as he spoke. 'I sit in the TV room and watch nightmare-inducing movies because I know you like them. I smile for photographs. The other day I left a damp towel on my bed for five whole minutes.'

She choked out a laugh.

'I think about you constantly.'

Her pulse began to race. 'Sharav, stop.'

'I can't stop.' His eyes burned into hers. 'Since you arrived, Samara Mansingh, I can't stop thinking about you. There. Maybe that's something you could help me with.'

'You want me to leave?'

His hand immediately tightened on hers. 'God, no.'

'Then what do you want?' Her voice was a gasp.

Sharav's jaw clenched, his stare turning molten. 'Should I say it?' She gulped, her heart thrashing against the walls of her chest. 'No, don't.'

'Samara . . .' he whispered.

'Wasabi rolls!'

A platter clunked onto the table between them, forcing their hands apart. The waitress, beaming, with arms holding a large tray of food, proceeded to deposit each plate with a short description of what was on it. There were too many dishes for the small table they were seated at, so another one was quickly added to theirs by the waitstaff.

It was both a welcome and unwelcome respite from their conversation. As much as Samara wanted Sharav to acknowledge the squall of fire and feelings between them, at the end of the day, he was an engaged man. Hearing it would only hurt more. So she forced herself to do what she always did—focus on the future. The immediate future, in this case, was a table laden with spicy dim sum and sushi that was way too much for two people. When it came to food, the Khannas believed in feasting.

I will always remember that about them, thought Samara as she piled up her plate while trying to look at Sharav as little as possible. The wasabi went up her nose, and the chillies stung her lips and tongue, but she didn't stop eating. Sharav picked at his lunch, watching her stuff her mouth in silence. Once in a while, they gave each other a strained smile.

It was like street theatre or a poker game. They could win awards for their bluffing faces.

The end came, Sharav paid the bill, and Samara duly thanked him. He opened the restaurant door for her, and she thanked him again. They descended the stairs, and he asked her if she wanted ice cream, to which she said no and thanked him for offering. It was all very civilised.

Right up until they sat in his car.

Sharav slammed his car door shut and twisted so he could face her. 'We have to talk about it.'

She rolled her eyes and muttered, 'Funny, that's usually my line.'

He reached for her chin and turned it towards him. 'Speak to me, Samara.'

'I can't speak at all right now.' She met his gaze, against her better judgement. 'My lips are burning.' They actually were.

Sharav's eyes fell to her lips. As though he were in a trance, he ran his thumb over her bottom lip, smoothing it.

Once, twice. 'They're swollen from the chillies.' He swayed towards her, his voice a strangled rasp.

Oh God. His eyes had gone almost onyx-like in their intensity, radiating that focused, forceful look of a man who was about to kiss a woman.

Heat pooled and coiled at the bottom of her belly, like a snake getting ready to strike. Hot, shaky breaths fanned his fingers, making his thumb stroke over her lips again. Faster, a little rougher this time. Samara barely held back a moan. Now. He would kiss her now. She pushed against his hand, tilting her chin up in invitation. Damn the consequences.

If one kiss was all she ever got from Sharav Khanna, she'd take it.

A low growl emerged from Sharav's mouth as he slowly slanted her chin, taking control of the movement with a firm grip, aligning her face with his. *This is how he would kiss,* thought Samara to herself. How he would touch, make love. Gentle but strong. Attentive but assertive. Needing to be in charge. It was so Sharav. She closed her eyes and yielded, letting him lead.

Just this once.

Moments passed. She heard Sharav's gulps of air, felt his gaze like a brand on her skin. His heat emanated towards her, closer and closer. His hand slid from her chin to the back of her neck, where it pulled her lightly forward. He was almost there. She could feel his breath on her lips now. Any moment now, she'd feel his kiss.

Instead, Samara felt his forehead rest against hers.

'I can't.'

CHAPTER 27

I can't.

Two tiny words, and yet they carried the titanic weight of his guilt.

Sharav gripped the steering wheel tighter as he drove back home, a silent Samara in the passenger seat. He'd been so close to kissing her, to finally giving in and feeling her softness against him, tasting her spice-swollen lips. The depth of his want in that moment had been almost savage. And yet he couldn't bring himself to do it. To cross that line he'd been skirting for so long.

He was an engaged man. No matter that Samara had pierced his very being and taken it over with the strength of the tornado that she was, he was still an engaged man. He'd made a commitment to Nonita. They'd had a ceremony, officially connecting the families.

In the eyes of society, they were as good as married.

But not actually married, argued a voice inside his head. A self-serving voice he'd never paid much attention to before but now seemed to be growing in strength. Every time he pushed it away, it sprang back.

Just like Samara.

'I'm sorry,' he said for the tenth time.

Samara shook her head, her eyes fixed on a spot outside the window, her shoulders stiff. 'Don't apologise. We got carried away.'

He frowned. The words *carried away* suggested they were like a couple of teenagers who'd lost control of their hormones. This was so much more than just physical attraction. 'I don't want this to change things between us.'

She pressed her lips together, obviously hurt and understandably angry. 'It won't. Besides, I probably won't be around much longer anyway.'

Goose bumps rose on his arm—the kind that were a portent for bad things. 'What do you mean?'

She was silent for a minute, as though debating whether to answer him. Then she straightened her shoulders and replied in a sharp tone, 'I got a gig from *Vanity Fair*, to photograph feature stories at Paris Fashion Week.'

His heart sank. 'Oh. You didn't mention that over lunch.'

'I didn't want to tell anyone until I'd decided.'

'I see.' He paused, aching to know if she'd decided. She'd leave permanently if she accepted that job. As much as the thought of never seeing her again destroyed him, Sharav had to concede that it would probably be for the best. Samara had grown up all over the world. She wasn't built to be tethered to one place. The best thing for both of them would be to let her go. 'Congratulations.'

'Thanks.' She sounded as if she were being strangled.

He felt exactly the same way. 'When do you leave?'

She didn't answer.

'Samara?' He glanced over and saw her lip wobbling. 'Samara, don't cry. Please,' he whispered. He wouldn't be able to take it. He'd pull the car over on the side of the road and kiss her tears away. Abandon every bit of judiciousness he'd drummed up.

'I'm *not* crying,' she sniffed. After a few moments, she whispered back, 'Do you want me to leave, Sharav?'

His fingers grasped the steering wheel so hard he was surprised it didn't crack. How could he beg her to stay when he couldn't promise her anything? 'Don't ask me that.'

She didn't let up. Or couldn't. 'Do you want me to stay?'

'Please, Samara.'

A sob disguised as a gasp escaped her. 'Hurry up and drive.'

'I . . .'

She shook her head. 'It's fine. I'm fine. Just drive, Sharav.'

Can anyone forget they're driving *while* they're actually driving? Because he'd come pretty close. There was nothing left to say. She had a job; he had a fiancée.

He drove home.

The living room was full when they walked in through the front door. The sombre faces of Jyoti, Diya, Dhruv, and Biba peered back at them.

'What's happened?' asked Sharav.

Jyoti was the first to speak. 'Oh, nothing. Just chatting about a phone call I had,' she replied a little morosely. 'Come, sit with us. How was your lunch?'

'It was nice,' answered Samara, sitting on the sofa next to his mother. He noticed the swelling in her lips had diminished, but her eyes were drawn. 'What phone call?' she asked.

Jyoti hesitated before replying, 'Nonita's mother, Amita, called. To discuss . . . well, she was saying that the kids have had some time to get to know one another, so . . .' She looked up at Sharav. 'They want to set a date, son. For your wedding.'

Sharav froze, his eyes darting to Samara and catching that fleeting instant when her shock and hurt was evident on her face before she whipped out her phone and pretended to be distracted by notifications. Her head bent low and her shoulders stooped, and Sharav wanted nothing more than to go over and hold her, comfort her.

Say the words he couldn't say.

He mentally shook himself. The wedding. 'When do they want to have it?' His voice sounded raw even to his own ears.

His mother glanced at the trepidatious expressions around her and replied, 'If you agree, they'll bring over their family astrologer to settle on an auspicious date for the ceremony.'

Sharav's mind whirled, unable to stop replaying the moment in the car. Samara, her lips open and inviting, her eyes closed and face tilted up towards his, waiting. Her softness. Her sweet, lemony scent.

The humiliation on her face when he hadn't kissed her.

He clenched his hands into fists, causing his family members to stare worriedly at him. *This is ridiculous,* he chastised himself. Samara was leaving! Sharav couldn't ask her to stay and give up the career she'd always wanted any more than he could break off his engagement and submit Nonita and her family to the vilifying whispers of society.

He opened his mouth, but nothing would come out. His agitated fingers pinched his forehead, and his feet shifted. *She's leaving, she's leaving,* he chanted in his head like a mantra. In a matter of weeks, Samara would be gone. Photographing Paris Fashion Week. Chasing experiences that would fill her memoir.

Curling up against someone else when she watched her atrocious horror movies.

He inhaled and exhaled slowly, even though it hurt to breathe. He *had* to move on and allow her to do the same. 'Fine,' he grated out. 'Call the astrologer.'

Samara's head whipped up, and their eyes met. Hers screamed betrayal for a moment before she looked back down to her phone.

'Oh.' Jyoti frowned up at him and then exchanged glances with everyone else. 'Yes, yes, of course.' She cleared her throat and gave him a weak smile. 'Well, good. Good news. I'll, er, call them back with the good news.' Then she paused and gave Sharav a meaningful look. 'If you're sure?'

'Yes,' he bit out. He needed to leave the room, immediately. Before his family saw him throw something against a wall for the first time in his life. 'I'll be in the study.' He strode out of the living room, exiting into the corridor.

When Samara's voice stopped him.

'Jyoti Mom,' she said quietly. 'Are you okay?'

He frowned. Was something wrong with his mother? He stepped back a little, his ear next to the living room door.

'Oh, nothing, child. I'm fine. Just fine!' His mother's voice sounded anything but fine.

After a moment of silence, he heard Dhruv burst out, 'I can't believe he's actually going to marry her!'

Diya joined in. 'I know. She's going to move in and make our lives hell.'

'Children!' exclaimed their mother softly. 'Don't say such things. It's not right.'

Dhruv's voice continued in a bitter tone, 'How can we not, Ma? The minute they get married, she's going to get up to her tricks, and the house will go back to the way it was before!'

Biba spoke for the first time. 'We're going to have lettuce coming out of our ears.'

'Oh God. Can you imagine meals with her every day? "You shouldn't eat carbs at night. Are you still in that silly band?"' Dhruv sang in a high-pitched parody of Nonita's voice, making Diya laugh.

'Dhruv, children—'

'No, he's right,' interrupted Diya. 'Mom, *how* could you allow Sharav to get engaged to that woman?'

Jyoti replied in a flustered voice, 'Well, it's so difficult to predict these things, child. We didn't know the family personally when they sent the proposal, but we knew about their background, their standing in society, and they came highly recommended by our relatives. Nonita seemed nice, and Sharav liked her. We gave them time to get to know one another. That's how these things are done, you know. I never imagined . . . well, better not to say.'

Sharav leaned back against the corridor wall, his heart twisting into a knot of pain. He'd had no idea his family felt this way about Nonita. Because he'd never asked them. He'd been so disengaged, so bloody blinkered, it had never even occurred to him to ask his own family's opinion about the woman he was bringing into their house as his wife. Someone they'd have to live with every day.

His family didn't like her.

How could he have missed so much?

Samara's soft but firm words interrupted his self-flagellation. 'Everyone,' she said, 'let's not forget that Sharav's choice of spouse needs to be Sharav's decision. If she makes him happy, then no matter how you feel about her, you have to let your love for him override that. You're his family. You should be willing to compromise for him, *especially* given how much he's stepped up for you in the last six years. How much he's sacrificed to make sure your lives run smoothly. Doesn't he deserve your support?' She took a breath. 'Also, can everyone please stop comparing him to Rajeev Uncle all the time? Sharav deserves to be more than just a replacement for his father. It's *his* business, *his* study, *his* seat at the dining table, and *his* marriage. Let's all try to remember that he's a person, too, with his own identity and choices, just like the rest of you.'

Shocked silence greeted her. Even Sharav held his breath, stunned by how she'd managed to express his sentiments without pinning them on him. How she'd stood up for him despite what had just happened between them.

Finally, Dhruv spoke. 'You're right.'

'You are. You absolutely are, child,' added their mother, her words wobbly. 'We've been selfish.'

'Yeah,' said Diya softly. 'He deserves to make his own decisions just as much as the rest of us.'

'So it's decided, then. We're going to support him. If he wants to marry Nonita, then we will give them our blessing and welcome her with open arms. Yes?'

Everyone must have nodded because, after a moment, Jyoti declared, 'Good. Thank you, Samara, darling. You're *such* a godsend!'

Dhruv said, 'Yeah. Too bad you got sent after Nonita.'

No one laughed.

CHAPTER 28

She couldn't breathe.

Then again, she *was* pacing her room, so the oxygen must have been making its way inside her lungs somehow. Even if it didn't feel like it.

Samara trudged over to her bed and sat. Then she stood up and started pacing again. After a minute, she sat down again. Her eyes burned from all the tears.

He'd refused to kiss her. He hadn't asked her to stay. He'd agreed to set a wedding date.

Sharav's choice was pretty clear.

Her phone rang, startling her out of her thoughts. It was Maya, no doubt calling to find out if she'd made a decision, if she was moving to New York soon.

She let it ring.

Once it was silent, she picked up the phone again, scrolling to find her dad's number. How would he react if she told him everything? *Daddy, I got the job I've always wanted, in a city I love, but I don't want to go anymore. Oh, and I'm in love with a man who's about to marry someone else—*

Oh my God. She was in love with Sharav!

The phone dropped out of her hand onto the bed just as a knock sounded on the bedroom door. 'Samara?' It was Jyoti. 'Can I come in, child?'

Her answer lodged in her throat. What came out was a frantic whimper.

Jyoti opened the door and came in, her brow puckered with worry. She took one look at Samara's face and rushed over to the bed. She didn't ask any questions or offer any solutions.

Instead, she took her into her arms in a tight embrace and rocked them both side to side, murmuring, 'It's okay. Mom's here.'

It was too much to bear.

Samara's first sobs came as gut-wrenching coughs, too intense to be dignified. Burying her face in Jyoti's shoulder, she cried her heart out. This time, her tears weren't for someone else's predicament or achievement—they were for herself. This time, she allowed herself to let go, allowed someone else to catch her.

For the very first time in her life.

CHAPTER 29

Five days. What could happen in five days? Well, you could take an intensive course in driving or cooking. You could go on a holiday to the foothills of the Himalayas or go rafting down the Ganges River. A workweek in Delhi typically lasted six days, so that didn't count. The festival of Diwali was supposed to be five days long, but there was an entire season devoted to it.

A course of antibiotics usually lasted five days. Unless you were really sick.

If only there were antibiotics for being heartsick, thought Sharav. He would have started that course five days ago. The day he'd almost kissed Samara, only to find out that she was leaving. The day he'd agreed to marry Nonita, only to find out that his family hated her. By now—he continued to ruminate with surgical precision—the antibiotics would have worked their healing magic, and he would be looking forward to his future. Instead, his heart felt like a washing machine on a never-ending spin cycle.

With a knife clanging inside it.

'Sharav?'

He jolted out of his stupor. Around him, in the lamp-lit living room, sat his mother, sister, and fiancée. He remembered that he'd come home from work early this evening because Nonita's mother was supposed to have arrived an hour ago with Panditji, their family astrologer. To set a date for his wedding.

To Nonita.

Who was currently looking at him as if it were *his* fault that they were late.

'Yeah?' he asked.

Nonita nodded towards his mother. 'Mummy was asking if you have any preferred dates. For the marriage ceremony.'

He looked at his mother, who had been unusually quiet and distracted the past five days. She kept gazing at him with a troubled expression. Sharav tried to smile at her. 'Do *you* have any preferred dates, Ma?' Jyoti shook her head. 'Whatever Panditji decides is fine with me, son.' She turned to Diya. 'What about you, child? Any preferred dates?' Diya shook her head, aiming a polite smile at Nonita, obviously as part of the family's resolution to be welcoming towards her. Sharav was both gratified and irritated by it.

Nonita spoke when the room lapsed back into silence. 'Maybe after Panditji leaves, we can discuss venues. The good ones get booked early—sometimes years in advance. And honeymoon destinations, of course.' She smiled at Sharav. 'I was thinking Bora Bora. Going to the Maldives is so passé.'

Diya chimed in. 'The Maldives will be underwater soon.'

'Then *you* should definitely go, Nonita.' That was Dhruv, who had just walked into the living room with Samara. He had on a cheeky smile that suggested he was baiting her in good humour, but Nonita frowned and looked at Sharav in silent complaint, as though she expected him to reprimand Dhruv.

Sharav sighed. This was what life was going to be like once she moved in. He was tired already.

His mother intervened, thankfully. 'Kids, come and sit with us! Panditji is coming to read Sharav's and Nonita's horoscopes and set a date for the wedding.'

Samara's eyes shot to Sharav for a split second before looking away. With an uncharacteristically subdued expression, she replied 'Sure' and sat down. She gave Nonita a strained smile. 'Hi.'

'Oh, right!' exclaimed Dhruv. 'The astrologer thing is tonight.' He grinned at Samara. 'Hey, maybe we could get him to read our palms.'

'Oh, let's!' Diya piped up. 'He could tell us how long we'll live and how many kids we'll have.'

Dhruv waved his fingers. 'Or how many marriages.'

Nonita scowled at them. 'Panditji isn't a palm reader. He only reads horoscopes.'

'No palms? Then I'm out.' Dhruv turned to Sharav. 'Do you need me to stay?'

Sharav shook his head. 'No.'

'Great. I'll be in the garage.' Dhruv waved to the room at large and exited. Samara watched him leave with a look of envy. Obviously, she'd much rather be in the garage too.

'Dhruv should be here when Panditji arrives,' objected Nonita. 'To pay his respects.' She looked a little offended on Panditji's behalf. Sharav hadn't even met the astrologer yet but already disliked him.

The doorbell rang, much to everyone's relief. Unfortunately, it wasn't his future mother-in-law who walked in, but Yash. Sharav held back a groan. He didn't have the bandwidth for Diya's drama tonight.

Which was why he was stunned when Diya sprang out of her armchair with an excited 'Hi!' and gave Yash a wide, flirtatious grin that suggested Samara's plan had, against all odds, succeeded.

'Hi,' responded Yash, eyes scanning the room and then resting on Diya. His smile had the same edge as Diya's but without the bouncy enthusiasm. He walked over to Jyoti and gave her the requisite 'Aunty' side-hug before turning to Samara. 'What's this I hear about you leaving?'

Samara's returning smile was warm but laboured. 'I can't stay forever.'

'Why not?' asked Yash. 'Stay and become Delhi's top wedding photographer. You'll make millions!'

Diya joined in. 'That's what I told her too. She *should* stay!'

Jyoti nodded, her eyes a little sad. Surprisingly, though, she stayed silent.

Sharav stayed silent, too, even as his heart tried to jam into his throat.

Nonita, however, decided to jump in. 'I'm sure Samara's looking forward to getting back to her exciting life in New York. Besides, even if she did decide to stay on in Delhi, it's not like she could live in this house permanently!'

Diya got a defiant look on her face, looking ready to challenge Nonita's point, but was quickly distracted by Yash, who brushed her arm and said, 'Hey, I was hoping to get a minute to speak with you. Is this a bad time?'

'Not at all!' replied Diya. She swivelled to face their mother. 'Mom, the garden is dark. Can I take Yash upstairs to the terrace?'

Jyoti looked only too happy to sanction the impromptu rendezvous. She and Samara shared a conspiratorial half smile as Yash and Diya left the room together. Nonita looked on, her lip curled in disapproval.

Thankfully, before anyone could voice an opinion on the proceedings, the doorbell rang again.

Finally. Sharav needed this evening to end. Needed to stop looking at Samara's dejected face across from him and being reminded that *he* was the one who'd taken away her sparkle. That sunny, room-lighting-up smile he loved so much.

Amita Kapoor, Nonita's mother, bustled into the room in an overwhelming cloud of Chanel No. 5 and excitement. Behind her was a short man who looked like he had stepped out of a mythological pantomime. Clad in long white robes with a profusion of rudraksha prayer beads covering the entire front of his torso and half his forearms, Panditji had light-grey ash smeared from the tops of his heavily kohled eyes up to the middle of his bald head. Over a dozen gemstone-and-gold rings decorated his fingers, and from the looks of it, he was wearing violet-coloured contact lenses. The only out-of-character thing about him was his watch—a diamond Rolex.

'Oh, Jyoti, so good to see you,' exclaimed Amita Kapoor over her shoulder as she held the door open for Panditji. 'Come, Panditji. Have a seat, please.'

The way Panditji's violet-tinted eyes skimmed the gathering from behind his upturned nose, you'd think the pope himself had walked into the living room. He looked at the large three-seater sofa in the centre that Jyoti was sitting on and sashayed towards it. Standing in front of her, he raised a displeased eyebrow. She immediately stood up and moved out of the way before he seated himself bang in the middle of the sofa.

Then he closed his eyes and kept them shut.

'Jyoti,' whispered Amita, 'Panditji likes to meditate before a reading. We can chat in the meantime.' She held out her hand and lightly drew his mother towards another sofa, where they sat together.

'So nice to see you, Amita,' whispered Jyoti, side-eyeing Panditji as if afraid to wake him. 'How have you been?'

'Good, good.' Nonita's mother seemed only half listening as she rummaged through a large basket that her chauffeur, who'd quietly entered behind her, had laid at her feet. 'Ah, here it is!' She pulled out an elaborately decorated box and handed it to Jyoti. 'The dates from Dubai that I was telling Sharav about. These ones are stuffed with macadamia nuts and wrapped in gold leaf. You must try them.' She then gestured at the basket. 'The rest are just oranges from our orchard in Ludhiana. I know you liked the last batch I sent.'

His mother accepted the box and murmured, 'Thank you. You shouldn't have.'

'Nonsense!' Amita whisper-shouted. 'We're family now.' She looked over and gave Sharav a fawning smile. 'And I didn't forget our groom!' She fished out of her oversize Louis

Vuitton handbag a brand-new iPhone, the latest model, still in its packaging. Walking over, she put her hand on Sharav's head in blessing and held out the phone. 'Just a small present since today is a special occasion.'

Sharav gently pushed the phone back towards her. 'Thank you, Aunty. I'll gladly accept just your blessing.' Expensive gifts were commonly given by a bride's family to the groom and his family, both before and after the wedding. While they were technically supposed to be celebratory tokens, most of the time they were just extravagant replacements for the illegal dowry system. Grooms, fathers, and brothers were given designer watches or fancy cars, while mothers and sisters were given fine jewellery. Honeymoons and higher education were paid for, houses were bought. Sharav detested the practice.

Amita, however, wasn't having his refusal. She held Sharav's chin up with all five fingers, as though he were a show dog, and insisted, 'Of course you can accept it! Such a small gift, only for good luck. Take it, son! Take it!' She shoved it at him, and when he still wouldn't grasp it, she dropped it in his lap and beamed. 'Remember, I'm not Aunty. I'm . . .'

He clenched his jaw so hard it was a miracle his teeth didn't crack. Sharav's upbringing wouldn't let him be rude to his elders or make a scene involving his future in-laws, but if he could, he'd be calling Amita Kapoor something *very* different from 'Mummy.'

'Good, good,' she responded with a satisfied look, patting his cheek and then turning away. Before sitting down, though, she cast her eye about the room and saw Samara. 'Ah, yes. You must be Samara,' she said in a tone that could flash freeze a bonfire.

'Hello, Aunty,' replied Samara softly.

Amita pressed her lips together and fished out a handmade ornate red envelope from her purse, the type usually used to give cash gifts. She marched over to Samara and pushed the envelope into her hand. 'Here. For you,' she stated, as if being forced to be gracious towards the younger woman. 'For your travels.'

'No, thank you.' Samara gave it back with a resolute look. 'I appreciate the gesture, though.'

'Take it. It's fine.'

'I can't.'

After a moment of considering whether Samara was worth the trouble of insisting, Amita obviously decided she wasn't and marched over to sit next to Jyoti, detaining her in a whispered conversation.

Sharav peeked at Samara and then Nonita, both sitting at opposite ends of the room and pretending not to notice each other. Ironically, he was seated bang in the middle, unable to decide which way to turn his head, direct his conversation.

As a metaphor for his life, it was laughably accurate.

'Hmmmm. Hmmmm. *Ahem! Gnnhnh, gnnhnh!* Hmmmmmmm.'

The noises were emanating from Panditji, who seemed to have found his voice, if not his words.

The room silenced, gaping at the humming astrologer with a mix of curiosity and distaste at the gurgling sounds of phlegm in his throat.

Finally, Panditji opened his eyes. He inspected each person in the room with slit-eyed precision, lingering a bit on both Nonita and Samara. Then he gave both the mothers a supercilious scowl.

'Which one is the bride?'

CHAPTER 30

'I broke up with Ari.'

It came out breathlessly, like her body had been working up to this declaration as much as her mind had. Diya peered at Yash's shadowed face in the dim light of the upstairs terrace, trying to gauge his reaction. Beyond, amid distant traffic sounds, an owl hooted and a couple of crickets chirped up a storm. Their shrill calls kept building up in bursts, getting faster and more intense and then erupting in long, drawn-out crescendos. Multiple times.

Lucky crickets.

Yash's response was measured. 'Oh?' His expression stayed neutral.

Diya huffed. '"Oh"? That's all you have to say?'

'What do you want me to say?'

'What do you *want* to say?'

He smiled, finally. 'Why did you break up with Ari?'

Did he look just a tiny bit smug? '*Not* because of you, just to be clear,' retorted Diya.

Yash's smile turned into a grin that couldn't hide his gratification. 'Okay.'

Not smug—just pleased, Diya realised with relief. She thought carefully about her next words, wanting to say them right. 'I don't think it was *anyone's* fault. Neither Ari nor I ever pretended to be anything other than who we were. The problem was, we both wanted the other person to change, fit into the mould we'd made for them.' She swallowed and shrugged. 'I finally understood that it was never going to happen. That at least on my end, I had built him and our future up in my head, almost like a fantasy. But the reality of him was *very* different.'

'What made you realise that?'

She locked her gaze with his. 'You.'

A spark lit up Yash's eyes. 'So I *did* have a little something to do with it, then.'

There it was—that male self-satisfaction she'd been expecting after her confession. Though it didn't aggravate her like she thought it would. His smugness somehow *included* her, like his victory was hers as well.

It felt both weird and wonderful.

'Don't get cocky,' she grumbled before smiling it away. 'It's just that you like me the way I am. You always did. I never really appreciated that before.'

'Why not?'

Diya shrugged again. 'You were always that kid from my childhood. And even though it sounds *totally* shallow, you looking different made me . . . see you differently.' Then she frowned. 'Why *did* you change your look? Was it for Samara?'

Ducking his head, Yash replied, 'It was Samara's idea.'

Jealousy, plain and simple, fluttered in her chest. 'Are you guys going to keep in touch when she leaves?'

'Definitely.'

Diya loved Samara like a sister, but right now she kind of hated her. 'So if things work out long distance, you'll move to New York?'

Yash smiled and stepped closer, meeting her eye again. 'As I've told you before, Samara and I are friends. That's all we'll ever be. She told me to change my look because she wanted *you* to give me a chance romantically. It obviously worked, and I'm very happy about that.' He ran a hand over his closely cropped beard. 'Although I can't say I enjoy spending an hour a day grooming this damned thing. It's like doing geometry on your face.'

Elation promptly replaced the jealousy. He still wanted her! 'Now you know what wearing makeup feels like.'

'I have a new appreciation for women.'

They stood in silence for a full minute. Keening crickets aside.

Finally, Diya couldn't take it anymore. 'What are you thinking?'

After another quiet moment, Yash sighed. 'I was remembering what I told you before, about never wanting to make you uncomfortable or pressure you in any way.'

She nodded, understanding. The ball was in her court. She had to decide what to do with it.

She extended her hand, stroking the scruff on his jaw. 'You can shave it off, if you want,' she murmured. Her fingers fanned out, learning the contours of his face.

It felt . . . right.

Yash stayed still, but his gaze became hooded as he watched her touch him. 'What do *you* want?'

Her heart thumped in her chest, building up her nerve for what she was going to do next. 'This,' she whispered, going up on the tips of her toes and placing her lips on his.

It was as though she'd broken a dam. Yash's arms came around her waist instantly, pulling her against him. His lips, soft yet firm, moved against hers with an intensity she didn't know he possessed. His hands, usually so restrained, ran through her hair, over her neck, her back, her waist. Staying in respectful areas but exploring with confidence and skill. Cancelling out any qualms she might have harboured. Allowing Diya to lose herself in the mating of their mouths, in the feel of his hands and body, while trusting that he would stop the moment she wanted him to. That they would go at her pace because he never wanted her to feel uncomfortable or pressured.

That trust. It made all the difference.

She moaned against his lips, her insides on fire. This man—she still had so much to learn about him. They gasped for breath as their lips broke apart, his moving on to kiss her jaw, nibble and nuzzle her neck. 'Yash,' she whispered.

'Hmm?' He pulled the lobe of her ear between his teeth.

She shook her head. 'Nothing. Just . . . Yash.'

He laughed. Planting a quick kiss on her lips, he looked into her eyes. 'Hi.'

She laughed back. 'Hi.'

CHAPTER 31

She didn't need to be here.

At any point, Samara could have stood up and excused herself. Left, like Dhruv and Diya had. But she didn't do it. She made herself keep sitting in the living room, needing to watch this cuckoo astrologer fix a date for Sharav and Nonita's wedding. Needing to witness Sharav accept it, celebrate it, and embrace Nonita as his future bride. Even though it would break her heart, she needed to see it.

So she could move on.

Buy the ticket, pack her bags, and get on a plane to the rest of her life.

Biba came in with a tray full of things that smelled amazing, as usual. God, she was going to miss Biba's cooking. Her glares and grumbling too. She'd miss Diya's fieriness, Dhruv's soulfulness. Jyoti's hugs.

Laughing and bickering with Sharav—dutiful son, brother, and friend. Her Hot Designated Driver.

She would hold the memories close but move on.

Amita Kapoor waited for Biba to serve the snacks and tea before waving an envelope of cash towards her as if trying to distract a dog with a biscuit. Glowering at Sharav, Biba pretended she didn't see it and stomped off, leading Nonita to shake her head and mumble, 'Attitude problem.'

Sharav just sat quietly, looking as though he wished he were anywhere else.

Jyoti handed a folder to Panditji. 'Here is Sharav's horoscope.' He already had Nonita's in his lap.

Panditji coughed, *hmmm*ed and *ahhrmm*ed over the two folders, flipping pages and poring over diagrams and charts. Once in a while, he shook his head in dramatic disappointment and made a *khhrrrr* sound instead. It was like watching a human version of a diesel generator at work.

Finally, he put the folders down and transferred his gaze towards the gathering at large. 'Bring the groom and bride to me,' he decreed with an air of mystery.

Given that the groom and bride were sitting barely six feet away, it was unclear what he meant. Still, Sharav and Nonita stood up and sat on either side of him on the sofa. Sharav wasn't a small man, so he had to really press himself against the sofa arm so as not to look like he was cuddling his astrologer.

'A wedding, the union of two families, is a sacred event,' began Panditji. 'As is the union between a husband and his wife. If held on an auspicious day, it will herald a life blessed by the gods, with an abundance of wealth and children. If arranged on an inauspicious day, it will be the harbinger of sickness and death. Evil spirits. *Bareness!*' he declared with a wide-eyed grimace that befitted his pantomimic appearance.

Amita Kapoor shuddered.

'Keeping this in mind,' continued Panditji, 'we must look at the stars for guidance. These two horoscopes may be aligned, but the sun and the moon are not. Also, Jupiter is in Mars, and Saturn is in Venus, and Mars is in Saturn, and Mercury is in Jupiter, which makes things a little complicated.' He turned to Sharav on his right. 'The groom should wear a red coral to combat Mars and conduct a Mars prayer ceremony. He must recite a chant to Lord Ganesha one hundred and eight times every morning after his bath and fast on Tuesdays.'

Sharav nodded dismissively. Amita fished out a notebook from her purse and began scribbling notes.

'The bride has already married an earthen pot and destroyed it to combat Mars in her own horoscope.

She is, thus, a symbolic widow and free from curses. This will be a successful union if the marriage ceremony is conducted on the correct date.' He picked up the folders again. 'There are two dates which are fortuitous, but neither is convenient for the families. One is three years in the future, and the other is in three weeks. I strongly advise that you utilise the date set three weeks from now, as it is also inauspicious to have a too-long engagement.'

'Three weeks!' The exclamation came from Jyoti.

Sharav's jaw clenched. 'That's ridiculous!'

Samara could hear Biba muttering outside the living room door. Nonita and her mother, however, were suspiciously silent.

Overcome with contempt, Samara almost laughed out loud at the blatant quackery on display. Unfortunately, given that the Khannas had already agreed to set a date and consult this astrologer, they'd officially been backed into a corner. To question his expertise now would be to offend Nonita's family.

'We can't organise a wedding in three weeks, Panditji,' explained a distressed Jyoti. 'It's impossible!'

'This is ridiculous,' repeated Sharav, glaring at Nonita over the top of the astrologer's head.

Nonita shook her head, refusing to meet his eye. 'I know. It's too soon, but what can we do? We have no choice.'

Her mother piped up with a quasi-sage expression. 'We'll just have to do a small wedding, Jyoti.'

'But, Amita, where can we even find a venue with such short notice?' asked Jyoti. 'Send out invitations, organise caterers . . . it's too much!'

'Maybe we could just have a small ceremony in the garden, Mummy?' suggested Nonita. 'With only close family and friends. I don't need a big wedding,' she added, looking every inch a martyr.

Amita nodded enthusiastically. 'Your front lawn and driveway could easily hold two hundred people. My cousin-in-law is a caterer, so that's no problem.' She smiled at Jyoti. 'We'll organise everything, don't worry. Let them have the marriage ceremony now, and we can put together a grand musical evening and gala reception in a few months. Book out large venues, have performances, and invite around a thousand guests. Or more, if you want. Have Sharav arrive in a brand-new Range Rover.' Her smile became obsequious. 'We are the *bride's* parents, after all. Just tell us what you want, and we'll arrange everything.'

It was as close to an offer of dowry as one could politely—and legally—make.

Sharav huffed, and before Jyoti could say anything, he replied, 'We don't want anything, Aunty. That's not the point. It's too short of notice. We need more time.' He stood up from the sofa and seated himself on an armchair, crossing his arms to underline his point.

For a few silent seconds, there was an impasse.

Then Nonita said in a polite voice, 'Samara, could you give us a few minutes, please?'

After a moment of confusion, Samara realised she was being asked to leave the room because, as much as the Khannas insisted otherwise, she wasn't a family member and thus had no right to be part of a family discussion. She got up and left.

Feeling Sharav's eyes burning into her back the entire way.

In the hallway, however, she ran straight into Biba, who covered her mouth with a finger and pulled her towards the same wall that she was huddled up against. Raising an eyebrow, Biba proprietarily gestured at the people in the living room, as though to justify the fact that she was blatantly eavesdropping.

Samara shrugged and joined her. Partly because of her bruised feelings but mostly because minding her own business had never been one of her strengths.

'I don't know why you're behaving like this,' came Nonita's plaintive voice.

Sharav replied, 'I'm not trying to be difficult for the sake of it, Nonita. To have a wedding here, at home, in three weeks will be too stressful, especially for Mom.'

Amita chimed in with 'I'll organise—'

'Mom, let me speak.' Nonita's tone was sharp. 'Mummy,' she crooned in a completely different voice, 'I know you've organised large parties here in the past but haven't held any since Papa's demise. Wouldn't this be a lovely gesture, in his honour, to hold Sharav's wedding ceremony here? If my family arranged everything, all you would have to do is attend and witness your home being full of light and celebration again. Doesn't that sound lovely?'

Jyoti's voice was tentative. 'Well, yes, but—'

'Great,' interrupted Nonita again. 'So Sharav, Mummy is fine with it, my mother is going to organise it, and Panditji has *specifically* said it is the *only* auspicious date for three years. It's up to you now.'

Next to Samara's ear, Biba whispered, 'I never liked her or her mother. These astrologers are all fake too. My parents were told I'd die as a baby, and here I am, healthy as a horse.'

'It's not that simple,' huffed Sharav in the other room.

'Yes it is!' cried Nonita, her tone agitated. 'It's simple! We met, our families met, everybody liked each other. We decided to get to know one another, and my parents stopped looking for another match for me. We let *everyone* know that I'm promised to you, put my reputation at stake for *months*! We even did a ceremony, made a formal commitment in front of our families. On Saturday, you agreed to set a wedding date, and here's your chance. *What are you waiting for?*'

Samara pushed a fist against her mouth so she wouldn't make a sound. Inside, however, she was screaming at Sharav to pull the cord on this train. Choose *her* instead.

He didn't. A few fraught moments later, she heard him say quietly, 'Nothing. There's nothing to wait for and nothing waiting for me.'

Samara heard Nonita shuffling across the room. Calmer but still sounding intense, she spoke. 'I've done everything right, Sharav. Given up everything waiting for you. Always believed that you were the honourable man you said you were. Do you still believe in honour?'

Biba breathed a quiet 'Manipulative witch' next to her.

The living room stewed in silence, as if everyone held their breath, like Samara. Even the astrologer didn't make a peep.

Finally, Sharav rasped, 'Fine. Do it.'

Samara spun around and ran, not caring if they heard her footsteps.

She had to leave Delhi. In less than three weeks.

CHAPTER 32

'You made the right choice.'

Nonita's voice sounded almost condescending, pinching his heart after it'd already been punched to the ground and kicked repeatedly.

Sharav opened her car door and held it open, his shoulders stiff and uncompromising. Her mother had already left with Panditji, and his mother had gone upstairs. He stared ahead at the road, waiting for Nonita to get into the car.

She stood in front of him and blew out an irritated breath. 'I don't understand, Sharav. Today is supposed to be a happy day. We're getting married!'

It *was* supposed to be a happy day. He should feel excited about spending his life with this woman instead of feeling like he was walking towards a hangman's noose. Sharav was a Punjabi businessman in Delhi, bound to his roots and family, confident of his place in the world, certain of the future he wanted. Samara was a rootless free spirit who wanted to travel the globe, having adventures. Delhi had been nothing more than a pit stop for her. They didn't belong together, he argued against his dejected heart.

It wouldn't listen.

He looked Nonita in the eye. Before he could stop himself, he asked, 'We're doing the right thing, aren't we?'

Her eyes narrowed. 'Yes! We can't wait three years for the next—'

'No,' he interrupted. 'I mean getting married.' His voice was a little unsteady. 'Will we be happy together?'

Nonita looked at him as if the answer were obvious, not a hint of doubt in her tone when she said, 'Of course we will. We've gotten to know each other, and we have similar backgrounds and personalities. We know what to expect, from our relationship and our future. There won't be any surprises down the line.'

'No surprises,' repeated Sharav.

'No,' she said with confidence. 'We have a stable relationship, and we'll have a stable marriage, based on mutual respect, common values, and understanding.' Nonita looked up at him. 'Isn't that what you wanted?'

He swallowed what felt like a fistful of sand in his throat. 'It was.'

'Good.' She nodded. 'Then we're clear.' She smiled and patted his shoulder. 'I'm glad we had this talk.' Reaching up, she pulled his head down to hers and touched their mouths in a kiss, lingering for a few seconds. Their lips didn't move, and neither of them held the other. Tried to take it further. No, this was a deliberate gesture, symbolic of their relationship and devoid of inconvenient ardour. An affectionate, if lukewarm, tribute to the occasion.

She drew back and nodded purposefully. 'I'll see you tomorrow, okay? There's a ton of work to do!'

'Okay.'

She turned, got into her car, and drove away.

Sharav stood in the driveway for a full minute afterwards, watching the car and then the empty street, illuminated by the light from the houses around it. Sounds of the living emanated from them—voices, music, thuds, and clanks. Soon, those lights and sounds would fade away and night watchmen would start their rounds. Tomorrow morning, birds would gather at his mother's bird feeder and sing while she gardened. Bicycles would speed by, ringing their bells to warn pedestrians. Vendors would call, selling their wares, and Biba would argue with them loud enough to rouse the dead. Sharav would wake up early, get ready, and drive to work. He would return in the evening, eat dinner with his family, and catch up on his emails in the study. Sleep at a decent hour so he wouldn't be tired the next day. Play tennis in the winter and swim in the summer. Attend weddings and parties. Go on occasional holidays, when work permitted.

None of that would change when Sharav married Nonita. No surprises.

He sighed and was turning to go back in when a movement in a window upstairs caught his eye. Samara was standing in it, looking down at him. The light behind her cast her frame in silhouette but couldn't hide the misery on her face. His hands turned into fists at his side.

She grabbed the curtain and pulled it shut.

Something inside him snapped.

CHAPTER 33

Well, thought Samara as she sat down on her bed to look for flights from Delhi to New York. If the astrologer's announcement hadn't done the job, the sight of Sharav kissing Nonita certainly had.

Torn her heart into a million little pieces.

The funny thing was, she felt no desire to fix it. No inclination to strategise and come up with a plan to stop this disastrous wedding in its tracks. Despite the fact that, forget the family, even the *groom* so obviously didn't want to marry the bride. Not that he'd ever admit it. That pigheaded man would ride a rodeo bull into a burning building if he thought he was doing the right thing.

No, she wasn't going to get in his way.

As her fingers flew over the laptop's keyboard, however, the door to her room burst open. Sharav stood in the doorway, breathing hard. Without asking for permission, he walked in and pushed the door shut with a slam.

'You!' He pointed at her, his eyes aflame. 'You drive me wild. Fight me at every turn. Make me do things I don't want to do, feel things I don't want to feel.' He waved a distracted arm towards the door behind him. 'You'd have them all dancing in the streets, singing kumbaya with pickpockets and swindlers. There would never be a moment of peace with you!'

That was it. She was done holding back. Leaping off her bed, she advanced on him. 'At least you'd have a life instead of walking around like an uptight zombie all the time. You know, when I first arrived here, I thought you and Nonita were perfect for each other. Stupid, *stupid* me for thinking any differently!'

He didn't back off. 'We *were* perfect for each other! Until *you* came along!'

'At least *I'm* not throwing my life away because of my pride!'

'Why do you care, anyway?' Sharav loomed over her, his chest heaving. 'You got the job you wanted. You're leaving!'

'You never asked me to stay!'

Their breaths were gasps now, their shaking bodies so close she could feel the white heat of desire flaming inside him. It mirrored her own, flicking and stoking until a bonfire raged between them. Visceral, wanton. Irrefutable.

It was too much.

They collided.

Samara whimpered in relief as Sharav's lips clinched hers in a crushing embrace. He bent down and lifted, wrapping her legs around his waist, bringing their faces to the same level and connecting every inch of their bodies below. That solid, warm wall of strength that had fished her out of the pomander pit? It was now walking them to the actual wall, pinning her against it and kissing the hell out of her. She ran her fingers through his hair and arched against him, egging him on as her tongue wrestled with his. Sharav growled when she squeezed her thighs tighter, the sound making her toes curl. There was nothing polite about this kiss. It was as rude, as unfiltered, as their conversations. Sharav slanted his lips over Samara's again and again, biting, sucking, thrusting his tongue into her mouth. His body enclosed hers, making her feel out of control and protected in equal measure. Sealing her off from the rest of the world. Fighting and worshipping her at the same time.

Nothing had ever felt so good.

Nothing had ever felt so right.

They broke apart, panting. 'Samara,' rasped Sharav as he trailed his lips over her jaw, her ear, before burying his face in her neck and trying to catch his breath. Struggling for control.

Samara let her head fall back against the wall. 'Please—'

'Shh, don't say anything. Don't move.' His voice was muffled. His breaths gusted against her neck.

She didn't listen. Obviously. Grabbing his shoulders to pull him impossibly closer, she pled, 'No, Sharav. Don't start thinking. Not yet.'

'I . . . I . . . Samara . . .' Sharav lifted his head. 'I can't.'

'Yes, you can! You—'

'No. Oh God.' He shook his head roughly. 'What am I doing?'

She closed her eyes and fought back a sob of frustration. Their moment was over. The real world had just stepped in.

She allowed him to disentangle her thighs and put her down. He stepped away the second she was steady on her feet. Whirling around and running his hands through his hair repeatedly, his expression thunderstruck. 'What the *hell* am I doing?'

Desire turned to wrath. 'You're doing what you want,' snapped Samara. 'For once in your life.'

Sharav just stood there gaping, as if he hadn't understood a word she said. As if he were so appalled at his own behaviour that nothing could pierce the unconscionability of it. Finally, he turned and spoke. 'This was a mistake. I'm so sorry.'

There it was. Samara understood him well enough to know that his guilt would set in at some point, that the word *mistake* would be bandied around, but knowing hadn't seemed to dim the pain of its arrival. His absolute certainty that what they'd done was wrong infuriated her even more. 'Why can't you see what's right in front of you?' she shouted at him.

But Sharav wasn't listening. 'It was a mistake. I'm an engaged man. I had *no right* to kiss you!'

'The only mistake you're making is marrying Nonita!'

He shook his head again, his eyes simmering with anger at himself. 'I made a commitment to her. In front of our families,' he ground out.

'You don't love her!'

'No,' he replied. 'But that doesn't mean I don't honour her.'

Samara wanted to scream, but instead she snarled, 'Your idea of honour is to trap both of you in a loveless marriage for the rest of your lives? Is *honour* going to keep you both warm at night?'

'Maybe not,' he said, his voice breaking. 'But that doesn't change the fact that I'm engaged. I'm engaged,' he repeated, 'to Nonita.'

She laughed in sad and bitter fury. 'Yes, Sharav, you're engaged. To the wrong woman but definitely engaged. You know what else you are? A coward. A stubborn *coward.* I can't find one good reason to be in love with you.' She blinked back angry tears. 'And yet I am.'

He looked dumbfounded for the second time. 'You're in love with me?'

'Yes. I'm in love with you. Even though I know it changes nothing, you should understand what you're giving up. In fact, you know what?' She whirled around and grabbed her laptop to cancel her flight search. 'Before you came in, I was going to make it easy on you and run away. But now, I'm going to stay for this wedding. And even though I know you'll regret it for the rest of your life, I'm not going to try and stop it. Because, if nothing else, when it's done, I'll be able to close this chapter forever.' She looked up at him, teary eyed but determined. 'You will have to look at me while you get married, Sharav Khanna. Knowing that it could have been us. If only you'd had the guts to make the better choice.'

Sharav just stood there with his jaw dropped, his fingers making untidy tracks in his usually immaculately styled hair. It was almost comical. After all this time, Samara had finally done it: rendered him speechless.

Never had a victory seemed so empty.

'Stop staring at me with your mouth open,' she hissed, punching random keys on her laptop in an effort to ignore him.

'You love me,' he whispered. 'Yes. Now, get out of my room.'

'Samara . . .'

'Get out!' Her voice was shrill. She didn't look up.

For a while, Sharav didn't move. Finally, his shoulders slumped, and he bit out 'I'm sorry' before walking out of the room.

Samara waited for the door to close before touching her kiss-swollen lips. Tears cascaded down her face. Again.

She wiped them away in disgust. Her body was going to get dehydrated at this rate. No more tears, she resolved. She was going to make the most of her remaining time with Jyoti, Diya and Dhruv.

She'd have plenty of time to cry over Sharav in New York.

CHAPTER 34

If someone had told Sharav three months ago that it would be possible for him to feel imprisoned in the home his family had lived in for generations, the one he was born and grew up in, he would have laughed. Yet, in the last two weeks, Sharav had come as close to running away as he ever had in his life. Even closer than when his father had told him he was dying. Then, like now, he'd been petrified of the future. The difference was that back then, he didn't know what the future would bring, and now he knew exactly what was in store for him.

A 'loveless marriage' was what Samara had called it.

Samara, who loved him. Whom he'd kissed with more passion than he had thought himself capable. Whom he would have made love to against that bloody wall had he not been promised to another woman.

Instead, he was reduced to reverse-stalking her in a house that suddenly felt far too small.

To add to his woes, not only was Samara *not* holed up in her room nursing a broken heart, but she was actively helping with the wedding preparations. Buying jewellery and lehengas with his mother and sister. Bedecking bridal hampers and giving instructions to decorators, gardeners, florists, caterers, bartenders, and the multitude of people who seemed to be running around his house like headless chickens day in and day out.

She was taking photos of everything, too, as though she were the official wedding photographer. Making his mother laugh and clicking away. Heckling Dhruv until he cracked a smile. The photographs would be her parting gift to the family, she'd said. With a forced smile on her face.

It had killed him.

Sharav leaned back in his chair and scanned his study, where he was currently hiding. He hadn't told anybody, but ever since his lunch with Samara, he'd been making small changes in here. Moving things around, changing the decor piece by piece. Making it his own. Without feeling guilty that he was somehow being disloyal to the memory of his father. He sighed. Another item in the laundry list of things for which he had to thank Samara.

Funny how he'd been so successful in avoiding her physically but couldn't think of anyone or anything else. Not even his own nuptials, which were less than a week away. The house was in full wedding mode, and he was wallowing in here.

Like the coward she'd called him.

Standing up, he brushed himself off and walked out. Noises, laughter, and bustle came from the living room, so he made his way there, passing three unidentified harried-looking people on the way.

'Sharav!' called Jyoti the minute he entered the living room. 'Come and sit, son. We're putting on a fashion show!'

The scene before him was as bizarre as it was heartwarming. His mother sat on the sofa, nursing a cup of tea, while Diya sorted through a pile of clothes in a large suitcase, and Samara and Dhruv hung up outdoor string lights in the living room. Not on the edges, like normal people, but from the ceiling in the middle of the room, creating a lit-up walkway of sorts.

To make matters worse, Samara was balanced on top of a tall stepladder, attaching equal sections of the long strings to the ceiling with sticky tape. Dhruv stood beneath her, holding and detangling the lights.

She looked precariously close to falling.

Which was why Sharav's 'What on earth are you doing?' came out more sharply than he would have liked.

Dhruv started and cast him a wary glance while Samara answered for all of them, a militant glint in her eye as she regarded him from her perch. 'As Jyoti-Mom said, we're putting on a fashion show. These are the lights for the ramp.' She pointed to a long runner carpet on the floor directly below the ladder. 'That's the ramp.'

Instinctively, he put himself in a position where he would be at hand to rush forward and catch her in case she lost her balance. 'Why are you putting on a fashion show?'

Diya replied in an excited voice, 'To decide what we're going to wear on the big night! We all have multiple options and couldn't choose, so Samara suggested we try them all on and walk the ramp to see which one looks best. She also suggested we light up the ramp like a proper fashion show!'

Of course she did. He looked up at Samara. 'Why don't you come down and let Dhruv stick them? He's taller.'

'I'm just fine.' False cheer rang in her voice.

Diya smiled tentatively at Sharav. 'Will you join us?'

His wedding outfit, an embellished navy-blue sherwani, arrived yesterday, but he hadn't felt like trying it on. This was as good a time as any, he supposed. 'Sure.'

'Great!' Diya clapped her hands. 'I'll go get your sherwani!' She actually ran out of the room.

Jyoti bounced in her seat a little. 'This is so exciting! Just what we needed to get our minds off all the ruckus. The Kapoors have been lovely, of course, but at the end of the day, this is happening in *our* home.' She beamed up at Sharav and clapped her hands, just like Diya had. 'It's a dream come true! I finally get to see my son as a *bridegroom*!'

Without warning, Samara missed the spot she was stretching out to reach and wobbled, losing her balance with a loud squeak. Sharav dashed forward. The ladder bobbed and, as he'd dreaded, down she came. Just like she had at Kabir's wedding. This time, however, Sharav would be there to catch her.

Samara fell, with a whump, straight into his arms.

He tightened his hold, one hand under her knees and the other around her back. Hugging her to him. 'You were saying?' he murmured under his breath.

She huffed softly, her hands clutching his neck for support. 'I *was* fine until you came along.'

He smiled, feeling so much better with her body against his own. 'This is the second time you've fallen off a ladder in front of me.' A teasing note entered his soft murmur. He couldn't help it. She felt so good, fit him so perfectly. 'We can't keep meeting like this.'

A soft light entered her eyes, as if she couldn't help herself either. 'HDD to the rescue, huh? At least there's no death by flowers this time.' Then the light went out. 'Put me down.' She wiggled a little.

He held her tighter, his voice still a low rumble. 'Promise me you'll let Dhruv hang up the rest of the lights.'

She wiggled some more. 'I'll be more careful—'

'Please?'

She sighed and stilled. 'Fine.' She peeked at his face from dropped lashes and whispered, 'Put me down, Sharav.'

'Okay. Thank you.' He gently dropped her legs to the floor and used the arm around her back to balance her. Reluctantly, he let her go and turned away.

Only to find Diya motionless in the doorway, his sherwani in her hands. Behind him, Dhruv held a ball of tangled string lights uselessly, and Jyoti sat frozen, a cup of tea halfway to her lips.

They were all gawking, their eyes bouncing between Samara and him in shocked realisation.

Sharav cleared his throat. 'Should we try on clothes?'

No one answered. Then he heard, 'Son?' It was his mother, frowning up at him.

'Don't worry, Ma,' he said, trying to imitate Samara's fake smile. 'Shall I dress up as a bridegroom for you?' He strode over to Diya and took the sherwani from her, feeling like an actor in a bad play. A circus performer who'd lost control of his monkey and was attempting to entertain the audience with inane theatrics.

Then again, maybe he wasn't the performer.

Maybe he was the monkey.

CHAPTER 35

The theme for the night's decor was clearly 'Just Because It's an At-Home Wedding Doesn't Mean We Have to Hold Back.'

Courtesy of the Kapoors.

Samara sighed as she took photos of the theatrical columns, swathed in floral and light displays, which blocked the view of Jyoti's naturally flowered garden. A massive Moroccan-style marquee had been erected on top of it, covering the garden, most of the driveway, the light-wrapped facade of the Khanna house, and even some of the road beyond the gate. Traffic would be redirected to parallel streets for one night, a common practice in Delhi's gated communities.

Inside the tent, more flowers and lights hung in crystal chandeliers from draped brocades on the ceiling, while round tables adorned with elaborate centrepieces and a variety of sequinned, beaded, and sheer fabrics were distributed on the grass. In the driveway was a long table that would soon feature an elaborate buffet and a collection of counters with colourful signage that would host live food stations. There was a kebab-and-tandoor counter called 'Sharav's Favourites,' and another called 'Nonita's Lean Cuisine,' which would only serve healthy finger foods. A Cold Stone–style ice cream cart was set up nearby, and Samara had even spotted a mini taqueria, where guests would be able to build their own tacos from a generous selection of fillings. The Khannas were newly minted taco enthusiasts.

A fact that warmed the pieces of Samara's heart a little.

Behind her, guests milled around in their finery, most of the men congregating next to the bar that stood against the living room windows. Stressed-out bartenders bustled behind it, taking drink orders, mixing cocktails, and scurrying round the back for supplies. Festive instrumental music filled the air. It was ten o'clock at night, and most of the guests had only just arrived. The marriage ceremony itself would take place in the early hours of the morning, after most of the guests had left. A small floral gazebo had been placed in one corner of the garden for the ceremony—the exact spot where she would photograph Sharav marrying Nonita before whisking her off in a rented Bentley for a wedding night in the honeymoon suite of a luxury hotel.

A decision Samara had made in the throes of fury and was now thoroughly regretting.

Still, at least she'd be gone by the time the happy couple returned home tomorrow night. Her flight to New York left in the afternoon, and her bags were already packed. Tonight was her last night in Delhi, and she was going to spend it repaying the Khanna family by taking beautiful photos for them to cherish for a lifetime.

A small piece of herself she would leave behind for the people she loved.

'Samara!' Diya's frantic voice snapped her back into the present.

She turned towards Diya, who looked all kinds of fabulous in a black-and-silver lehenga, with diamonds in her ears and her hair in an artfully messy updo. Her expression, however, was anything but fabulous. 'What's happened?' asked Samara immediately.

'Did you pick up the house phone line at any point today? Take any messages?'

'No. Why?'

Diya shook her head. 'The caterer hasn't shown up yet, and most of the guests are already here. Mom and Amita Aunty are freaking out. There's no food!'

Samara had been so busy taking photos that she'd completely over-looked the fact that there were no waiters walking around, serving snacks. 'Don't worry,' she said in a calm voice. 'We'll sort it out. Let's go.'

Together, they rushed out of the tent to the rear of the driveway outside the kitchen, where the caterers had dropped off their cooking and prep equipment, crockery, and cutlery earlier in the day. A large generator, powering all the lights for the occasion, had been fitted into the garage, and laid out outside was an unruly web of extension outlets and cables running on the ground.

In the midst of it all, Samara saw Jyoti, Dhruv, and Biba facing off with Amita Kapoor and two of her domestic staff, a swaying older man who'd clearly been dipping into the bar stash and a rosy-cheeked young woman who looked like she'd just stepped off the train from a mountain village.

After stepping over cords and nudging past gas cylinders and prep tables, Samara reached them just in time to hear Jyoti declare in a hysterical voice, '*This* is what happens when you hire a cousin instead of a proper caterer! A hundred and fifty people, and no food!'

'He's my cousin-*in-law*,' Amita barked back, her usually obsequious tone soured by the situation. Taking a breath, as though to remind herself that she was speaking to her daughter's future in-laws, she continued in a milder voice, 'Besides, where else could I possibly find another caterer with three weeks' notice during wedding season, Jyoti? I had no choice!'

Biba muttered, 'Could have postponed the party.'

'Does *she* need to be here?' Amita bit out, pointing at Biba. 'This really isn't a discussion for servants.'

Rosy Cheeks behind her nodded vigorously. 'Yes, madam. You're right, madam. Can I make you some tea, madam?'

Biba bristled. 'Who're you calling a servant? I'll—'

'Okay!' interrupted Samara. 'Let's focus on the problem, shall we? I'm assuming someone has called the caterer?'

Jyoti looked relieved that Samara was there. 'Yes, child. He's not picking up his phone. Thank God Sharav arranged the bar service separately!'

'Thank God,' hiccuped the older man.

Amita threw him a slit-eyed glare before saying, 'I'm sure it's just a delay. Traffic problems.'

Jyoti waved at her watch. 'They were supposed to be here *hours* ago!'

'They're probably not coming,' came a sleepy voice from next to the generator. Samara turned to find a uniformed man sitting on a stool behind the garage door.

Samara frowned at him. 'Are you with the caterers?'

'No, I'm with the generator.'

'So then how do you know they're not coming?'

He shrugged at her. 'If they haven't come by now, it means something went wrong with the food.'

Jyoti's hands flew to her face. 'Like what?'

Generator Guy shrugged again. 'Maybe it fell off the truck. That happens if they don't close the door properly.'

'Oh no!' cried Jyoti. 'Our food might be all over the road right now!'

'With cars running over it,' added Dhruv, speaking for the first time.

Samara threw him a meaningful look before saying, 'Let's not start conjecturing. I'm sure there's a reasona—'

'Madam! Madam!' A heavyset man was running towards them from the other side of the tent. They watched as he darted past the guests, down the driveway, and into the back, stopping in front of the group and bending over to catch his breath. Then, instead of speaking, he fished a handkerchief out of his pocket and began moping his brow, gaping at them with fearful eyes. 'Madam,' he puffed, looking between Jyoti and Amita.

'What?' snapped Amita.

'I'm . . . Monty . . . catering manager,' he wheezed. 'The food . . . the trucks . . .'

'See?' remarked Generator Guy. 'Not coming.'

'What happened?' Amita shrieked at Monty.

Monty looked like a fox surrounded by a pack of hunting dogs. 'A train broke down on the road crossing between our kitchen and here. No vehicles can get through, madam!'

'But you were supposed to be here three hours ago!'

'Yes, madam. The train broke down four hours ago, and they're still trying to fix it. Our trucks, with the food and the chefs, are still at the crossing. Twenty-five chefs, madam. We added extra, just for you.' He smiled, like the idea of twenty-five missing chefs would somehow appease a furious Amita.

Samara frowned. 'Can't they just take a different route?'

Monty nodded with an apologetic smile. 'Yes, madam, but the problem is that traffic has been building up behind the trucks for the last three hours, and the road is completely jammed.'

'So get another truck—get twenty-five trucks!' shouted Amita, throwing her hands up in the air. 'Carry the food across the tracks and take taxis, for all I care! Just *get it here!*'

Cowering, Monty stammered, 'Y-yes, madam. So s-sorry, madam. You see . . . since it's late'—he cleared his throat—'everyone has left their vehicles on the road and gone for dinner. Including'—he cleared his throat again—'our drivers and chefs.'

'What?'

'Bastards,' muttered Drunk Old Man.

'Can't they just eat the wedding food?' asked Dhruv.

'Oh no,' exclaimed Monty. 'That's yours, sir. You've paid for it. Although'—he cast Amita another fearful glance—'the refrigerated truck only has about an hour's worth of fuel left and it's about an hour's drive to here, so . . .' He shrugged and gave a deep sigh, as though relinquishing himself of this responsibility. 'It's up to God now.'

'Won't make it,' stated Generator Guy.

'Shut up!' yelled at least three people.

'Oh God!' whimpered Jyoti. 'Oh God, oh God, oh God!'

'What do we do?' asked Diya.

Rosy Cheeks looked worriedly at Amita's panicked expression. 'Should I make you some milk tea, madam? It always makes you feel better.'

Dhruv spoke up. 'Should we send everyone home?'

Both Amita and Jyoti gasped. Jyoti shook her head. 'No! We can't do that, son. They're guests in our home. To send them away without feeding them is . . . is . . . sacrilegious!'

'Plus, it'll start *rumours*,' added Amita, as if the prospect of social ostracism was far worse than anything God could dish out in the afterlife.

Samara tapped her lips with a busy finger, thinking on her feet. She had to help save this situation, for Jyoti's sake. 'I think it's safe to assume that the truck isn't going to make it on time. How about we cut down the menu and order the food from a restaurant?'

'For a hundred and fifty people?' asked Diya with a sceptical frown.

'Worth a shot, right?'

Dhruv piped up. 'I can call the community clubhouse! They're within walking distance and have a large in-house restaurant.' He picked up his phone and, without waiting for confirmation, dialled a number.

Everyone edged a little closer to Dhruv, grasping at the metaphorical lifeline he was offering them. Amita said, 'Put it on speaker,' presumably because she didn't trust Dhruv to do the ordering.

Dhruv rolled his eyes and put his phone on speaker. It rang for a while. No one picked up.

'Bastards.' Drunk Old Man swayed back from the force of it. Dhruv dialled again. This time, a male voice answered: 'Panchsheel Park Club dining room. Manoj speaking.'

Amita was the first to speak. 'We want to place a home-delivery order!' she shouted, as if the phone wasn't right next to her face.

'Yes, madam. House number?'

'811!'

Dhruv reared back but kept quiet, probably afraid of what Amita might do if he told her to calm down.

'Okay. Order please,' droned Manoj from the club.

'They do good Indian food,' interjected Jyoti.

'And noodles,' added Diya.

'Yes, but noodles don't really go with Indian dishes.'

'Maybe if we also ordered Chinese food from somewhere else?' suggested Diya. 'Or asked the club to cook noodles with Indian flavours?'

'We're trying to cut down the menu, not complicate it!' muttered Dhruv.

'How complicated is it to add masala to noodles?' Biba shrugged with a superior air. 'I could do it in no time.'

Amita waved a shushing, rather frantic hand at them before rattling off a selection of dishes into the phone. 'Dal, butter chicken, butter paneer—'

'Slow down, madam,' interrupted Manoj from the club. 'Dal. How many orders of dal?'

'One hundred and fifty.'

There was a pause. 'What?'

Amita huffed. 'One hundred and fifty!' she shouted into the phone.

Which was when Manoj started laughing. 'Very funny.' Then he told Amita where she could put one hundred and fifty orders of dal before hanging up the phone.

For a shocked moment, everyone just stared at Amita's dumbfounded expression before turning away and biting down on their mirth with unconvincing coughs and snorts.

'I'll get some tea, madam!' cried Rosy Cheeks before taking off in a sprint.

'Stay out of the main house,' Biba yelled at her. 'I knew I should have locked up the good crockery,' she chided herself.

'Okay,' Samara managed to say once her shoulders shopped shaking. 'Let's stay calm. We have all the cooking equipment here. Maybe we can buy some basic ingredients and cook them.'

'Market's closed.' That was the ever-optimistic Generator Guy.

Drunk Old Man opened his mouth before Dhruv growled at him, 'If you say *bastards* again, I'm going to put you in the tandoor and switch it on.'

'What's going on here?'

Samara turned to find Sharav approaching them with his usual frown. She spun back around. Sharav looked devastatingly handsome tonight in his dark-blue sherwani, which showcased his tall, rugged frame. He was overwhelming to look at. Not to mention she might start weeping if he so much as smiled at her.

Jyoti and Diya quickly explained the situation to him, and Dhruv added in the part where Manoj had expletive-bombed Amita, probably just to see her react again.

Sharav turned to Monty, who'd been inching away from the gathering ever since dropping the news, probably in the hopes that he could slip away unnoticed. 'How many people do you have with you?' asked Sharav. 'Can you cook some food here with raw ingredients?'

Which was *exactly* what Samara had just suggested, but when Sharav said it, everyone started nodding like he'd stepped off a golden chariot to save the day.

'Sir,' replied Monty, 'it's just me, unfortunately. The food can be cooked here, but we will need ingredients.'

Sharav frowned impatiently. 'Do you have anything edible here with you?'

Monty shook his head. 'Only the special order, sir. Everything else is on the truck.'

'What's the special order?'

'Three hundred corn taco shells.'

Unthinkingly, Sharav looked at Samara just as she peeked upward. Their eyes met for a fleeting, explosive moment before darting away.

'We can't serve everyone empty taco shells!' Amita's voice was hysterical again.

Jyoti straightened her shoulders and cleared her throat. 'Biba.'

Biba turned towards Jyoti, her expression wary. 'What?'

'It's time.'

A gasp escaped Biba's lips. 'No!'

Jyoti nodded. 'Yes. I'm sorry, but there is no other way. We've exhausted every other option.'

For a few uneasy seconds, Biba seemed to struggle within herself under the confused scrutiny of the entire group. Finally, with a shaky lip, she sighed in resignation. 'Fine. Follow me.'

Everyone, including Generator Guy, followed Biba inside the house and behind a back door that led into her living quarters. Switching on a light in her bedroom, she led the way past her bed, dresser, and TV, and pulled open a curtain that concealed half the room.

Behind it were two very large deep freezers.

'If anyone ever mentions what they've seen in this room, I will curse you and your family. Don't think I won't. My grandfather was a tantric,' Biba stated in a matter-of-fact tone. Then she opened the freezers.

All the others in the room gasped. The freezers were full of frozen food. Half-fried samosas, fritters, spring rolls, paneer in different sizes and marinades in different freezer bags, and cutlets and croquettes of various types, from potatoes to vegetables to lentils. Marinated mutton and chicken, prawns and fish. Unidentifiable bags and boxes of pastes and pulps, batters, chutneys, and powders. All of it, prepped, labelled, and ready to cook at a moment's notice with the efficiency of a restaurant.

Crucially, it was enough for a hundred and fifty people.

Wide eyed at the sheer quantity of food, Samara exclaimed, 'Wow! This is amazing!' She peered at Biba's embarrassed face. 'Why do we have to keep it a secret?'

Biba glared at her. 'We are *Punjabis*. We only eat *fresh* food in this house. Got it?' Her tone brooked no argument.

Amita sniffed. '*We* only use *our* freezer for ice. My cook buys the freshest ingredients, straight from the market.' She waved towards Drunk Old Man, whose smile of acknowledgement was as pickled as some of the food in the freezer.

Biba raised an eyebrow at Samara. 'That's why we keep it a secret.'

Dhruv put his arm around Biba's shoulder and squeezed. 'I don't care what anyone says. Your food is legendary.'

'It absolutely is legendary. Right.' Samara gave Biba a nod and turned to face the others. 'Here's what we're going to do. Dhruv.'

'Yeah?'

'You're going to take those three hundred taco shells, put them in a bag, and beat them with your cricket bat until they're bite-size. Then you, the generator technician, and Mrs Kapoor's cook'—she cast a baleful glance at Drunk Old Man—'can serve them as chips to the guests.'

'Shouldn't my cook be cooking?' asked Amita.

'I think it's best to keep him away from an open flame right now,' replied Samara. To Dhruv, she said, 'Go!'

Dhruv immediately left with Generator Guy, pulling Drunk Old Man with him.

'The rest of us,' continued Samara, 'are going to unpack these freezers and start cooking the food under Monty's and Biba's supervision. Monty, go fire up the tandoor and burners. Sharav'—she focused her gaze on his collarbone—'you should probably go socialise with the guests. You're the groom. Jyoti Mom, you too.'

'Don't be silly,' replied Jyoti. 'I'll have you know I was quite the cook in my day. I'll stay and help. Sharav, you go out and keep everyone distracted until dinner is ready, son. We need someone on the outside.'

Amita would probably have been happy to leave the food preparation to Samara and the staff, but she couldn't possibly abscond once Jyoti had volunteered to stay, so she added with a pained expression, 'Don't tell Nonita about the caterers, though. Poor thing is so stressed. It's not easy being a bride, with everyone's eyes on you.'

Sharav looked torn for a minute, but then he muttered 'Fine' and walked out with Monty.

With him gone, Samara felt more in control of her senses. 'Diya, is Yash out there?'

Diya perked up. 'Yes! Should I call him to help?'

'No,' instructed Samara. 'Tell him to find the nearest open ice cream parlour and buy tubs of ice cream for the cart. Then come back and help.'

'Okay! How many tubs?'

'All of them.'

Diya ran out the door.

Samara scanned her eyes over Biba, Jyoti, and Amita and said, with the authority of an army general, 'Tuck in your tunics and roll up your sleeves, ladies. Let's show them how Punjabi women do.'

Biba smiled.

CHAPTER 36

'Dude, cheer up,' muttered Kabir as he surreptitiously nudged Sharav. 'You look like someone died.'

Sharav *felt* like someone died. Not only had the caterers not shown up, forcing his mother to sweat over a giant stove in the back, but seeing Samara this evening had been like getting hit by a truck. She wore a lehenga gifted by his mother, like his sister did, but whereas Diya's was black and sparkly, Samara's looked like an artist had taken a white canvas and just spattered on every floral colour in existence before embroidering birds on top of it all. She looked like nimbu pani in the garden on a bright and chirpy morning. Like optimism and exuberance.

Like Samara.

He gritted his teeth. Waxing poetic about his houseguest wasn't going to help the socially perilous situation they were in. He needed to focus. Distract the many people around him from the fact that they were only being served smashed tacos for at least another hour.

'Sharav!' called Nonita from a few paces away. 'Come, meet the Chopra family!'

Automatically, Sharav walked towards her, pasting a smile on his face. Nonita looked like a million bucks tonight, decked out in a sparkling royal-blue lehenga that matched his sherwani, with a bustier top that left her neck and shoulders bare for a diamond bib necklace the size of a small country. She blazed like a star at the centre of it all.

Which was exactly the point.

He reached the group in time to hear Mrs Chopra, a small woman in her fifties, tell Nonita, 'When you were young, Amita and I had hoped that you and my son, Virat, would make a match of it. But then he went off to America and got a girlfriend! He's a VP now, so very much in demand.' She tittered and shook her head indulgently. 'These boys will have their fun, but now I want him to settle down, so I convinced him to come home for a few weeks. He's parking the car.'

Nonita nodded as if she agreed, but Sharav suspected she wasn't really listening. She laid a proprietary hand on his sleeve and looked at Mrs Chopra. 'This is Sharav.'

'Hello, Sharav!' greeted Mrs Chopra. 'I've heard so much about you from Amita. Congratulations on catching our beautiful Nonita! We've had our eye on her for years!' She laughed. Then a man about the same age as him came up behind her and tapped her shoulder. Mrs Chopra turned and exclaimed, 'Virat! We were *just* talking about you. This is Nonita and Sharav, the happy couple!'

Virat Chopra, who looked like he'd just stepped off a *GQ* cover, gave them a smirk that had probably won him more than just one girlfriend. 'Hi. Don't believe a word my mother said about me.'

Sharav laughed politely at the somewhat campy opener, but Nonita seemed charmed. 'Your mother is bride-hunting for you this season, you know,' she teased Virat in a playful tone that Sharav had yet to hear directed at him.

Virat lowered his chin and pointed the full force of his stare at Nonita, his smirk still in place. 'Well, if she's as breathtaking as you, I might end up married soon too!'

Nonita giggled. Actually giggled.

A thump on his back, accompanied by 'Sharav, my boy!' interrupted Sharav's incredulity.

He circled around to find Yash's father, Mr Malhotra, beaming up at him with a boozy grin. 'Hello, Uncle.'

'Our facilitations, dear chap,' slurred Mr Malhotra. Some people became weepy or aggressive when they were drunk. Mr Malhotra apparently became British.

'Thanks.'

Fortuitously, Dhruv wandered over to them with two bowls of what looked like taco-shell dust and offered it up with, 'Appetiser?'

Mr Malhotra looked inside one bowl with a dubious expression. 'What is it?'

'Crumbed reduction of masa harina.'

Sharav snorted and quickly covered it with a cough. He cast a glance around and asked Dhruv, 'Where're the other . . . servers?'

Dhruv shrugged and muttered, 'One of them passed out in the room where the booze is being stored.' He smiled. 'The other one is drawing on him with a permanent marker.'

They shared a chuckle.

Mr Malhotra, however, shook his head. 'Can't trust the help these days. Off their trolleys, the lot of them!'

His brother cast him a curious look, but before they could excuse themselves, Mr Malhotra grasped Sharav by the shoulder and exclaimed loudly, 'So, marriage! The old ball and chain! How're you holding up, dear boy?'

Horribly. As though he were standing in the eye of a cyclone, the world around him spinning out of control. He wanted to scream, run. Hide. 'I'm fine, Uncle.'

'Well, then, you're a better man than most!' guffawed Mr Malhotra. 'I was belly-up at my wedding, I tell you. Ah, but the honeymoon . . .' He winked. 'That more than made up for it.'

Dhruv shifted on his feet, looking ready to bolt, but Sharav gave him the Eye. If he had to suffer through this, then his brother would suffer with him.

'Your aunty and I,' continued Mr Malhotra, 'were quite the pair back in the day. Went to Goa for our honeymoon, we did. The Splendour Hotel, and by God, was it splendorous!

We didn't step out of the hotel room for four days!' He nudged Sharav with an overzealous elbow. Twice. 'Nine months later, there was Yash!'

This is it, the extent of my forbearance, thought Sharav. Any second now, he was going to make a run for it. Head for the hills.

'You should take your bride to Goa too! Perhaps the good luck will *rub off* on you. *Penetrate* your endeavours, eh? What do you say?' He winked again, his mouth hanging open.

Forget the hills. Maybe he could wedge himself under his mother's bed. It was closer. 'Thank you, but I think Samara has other plans for the honeymoon.'

For a moment, both Mr Malhotra and Dhruv were silent, with twin expressions of surprise. Then Dhruv said, 'Nonita.'

Sharav frowned. 'What?'

'*Nonita* has other plans for the honeymoon. You said *Samara*.'

'I did?'

Dhruv nodded. Mr Malhotra blinked rapidly in confusion.

'I did,' stated Sharav, a hand coming up to clutch his head. He'd said *Samara*. Suddenly, the spinning vortex around him came to a standstill. The music, the lights, the tent, the people who surrounded him—it all fell away. The ground beneath his feet fell away too.

What was he doing?

In his mind's eye, he saw Samara: Samara in the garden, laughing as she bullied him into posing for photos. In his bedroom, dressed in only a towel and a smile. In the TV room, shrinking into his shoulder and spilling popcorn on his lap over a horror movie. In the garage, helping Dhruv and his band prep for a performance. In the kitchen, plotting to bring Diya and Yash together. In the driveway, dressing him down while dressed to kill in that shirt. In the car, as she waited for him to kiss her with closed eyes and bated breath. In her room, her lips and body moving against his, all softness and drugging, desperate heat. In the living room, hanging up lights while fighting back tears. In the back, just minutes ago, a multicoloured Valkyrie commanding her troops as she saved the day.

Samara, who had occupied every inch of his house and breathed life back into it.

Samara, who had conquered the hearts, and problems, of his family. Samara, who challenged him, intrigued him, confounded him, and excited him. Who haunted his dreams and his thoughts, even while standing in the middle of his own wedding party.

Samara, who was in love with him.

Do you want me to stay?

You never asked me to stay!

It could have been us.

'Oh my God,' he whispered. 'What am I doing?'

He loved her. He loved Samara. She had wanted to stay, for him, and he . . . he'd been the coward she called him.

A pigheaded coward!

No more. He had to bring this farce of a wedding to a close. He had to tell Samara! Ask her—no, *beg* her—to stay. She could go traipsing all over the world, taking photos if she wanted. As long as she came home to him.

'Dhruv.' His voice was raw.

His brother was immediately on full alert. 'What?'

'I need to talk to Nonita privately. Hold the fort.'

Nodding, Dhruv replied, 'Got it. Don't worry.' He put the edge of a bowl to Mr Malhotra's back and gently prodded him towards the bar with a jovial 'Let's get you another drink, sir. You know, I love Goa too. Where exactly is the Splendour Hotel?'

Sharav made his way to Nonita, who was chatting with a new group of people. He murmured near her ear, 'Nonita, can I talk to you for a minute?'

She didn't seem to register the words. Her face was frozen in a requisite bride-smile, suitable both for greeting guests and modestly receiving their compliments. 'Sharav, come and meet my parents' frie—'

'I *need* to talk to you.'

Nonita's smile faltered. 'Now?'

'Now. Please.'

Eyes narrowing, she flashed her bride-smile at the group and chimed 'Excuse me, I'll be right back' before following him to the back area, outside the tent. Farther away, on the other side of a sea of wires and extension outlets, were Monty, Samara, Biba, Diya, and the two mothers, cooking up a storm. Nonita cast them a confused glance but clearly didn't comprehend the entirety of the situation because she gave Sharav a scowl of distaste and asked, 'What are we doing over here?'

There was no gentle way of doing this, nothing he could say that would lighten the blow. So Sharav took a deep breath and said, 'I'm so sorry. I can't marry you.'

Nonita sucked in a breath and held it for a shocked second. Then she wheezed out an unnatural laugh. 'Very funny!'

'I'm not joking.'

'Of course you are!' She shook her head, still laughing. 'This is just your idea of a silly joke.' She looked around, like there might be a hidden camera or a punch line she was missing.

'This is not a joke, Nonita,' murmured Sharav. 'I'm so very, very sorry. I let things get out of hand, proceed too far. But I have to stop this wedding. I can't marry you.'

Nonita's eyes glittered in anger, all traces of forced mirth gone. 'You can't back out now, Sharav Khanna. We've got a hundred and fifty of our family and friends out there! It's done! We're as good as married already!'

'We're *not* married, though,' replied Sharav with a contrite sigh. 'And I can't get married to you, not now and not in the future. I . . . I haven't been honest about my feelings.' He braced himself for the explosion he knew would follow his next words. 'I'm in love with someone else.'

Nonita's reaction was unexpected, to say the least. 'I don't *care*!' she hissed. 'You made a commitment to marry me, and you *will marry me*!'

'But I love someone else! And'—Sharav cleared his throat—'if I'm being completely honest, I kissed her too. I'm so sorry. It was unforgivable. I should have ended things between us before I took any steps in that direction. There's nothing I can say except that I hope you'll—'

'I don't care what you did with that meddling harpy!' interrupted Nonita, her voice rising to the point that their family members stopped cooking and started staring at them. 'You will *not* ditch me at my own wedding, Sharav Khanna. Do you hear me? I won't let you!'

Sharav could feel Samara's stare, but he kept his gaze on Nonita's furious face. 'I'm sorry.'

'No! *Mummy!*' Nonita twisted around and vaulted over the wires to where Jyoti was standing, frozen, with a ladle in her hand. 'Mummy, tell him he has to marry me!'

His mother looked speechless. 'Um . . .'

'Tell him!'

'Keep it down. The guests can hear you,' remarked Generator Guy, who'd just walked out of the house, presumably after he'd finished doodling on the cook.

Nonita blinked. 'Who're *you*?'

'I'm with the generator.'

Nonita cast him a baffled frown before turning back to Jyoti. 'Mummy, he's your son. *Do* something! He'll listen to you!'

Jyoti's expression, when she realised what was happening, was solemn. 'I'm so sorry, child.'

'*No!* You can't do this! I did *everything* right!' shouted Nonita into her face. 'Touched your feet, complimented your garden, made you tea, gave advice to your fat daughter, put up with that rude college brat and that kitchen hag! Ate her *disgusting* food!'

Biba bristled. 'Some people eat more than just leaves, shrew.'

'Shut up!' shrieked Nonita, her voice turning hysterical.

Next to her, Amita Kapoor stood stunned and wide eyed. She blinked at her raging daughter and gasped. 'This *cannot* be happening to me.'

Sharav tried to interject. 'Nonita, Aunty—'

'And *you*!' Nonita wheeled around to point a finger at Samara. 'This is *all your fault*! With your clown clothes, waltzing into this house as if you own it. Poking your nose into things that are none of your business! If it hadn't been for you, we wouldn't have had to bribe Panditji to bring the date forward. *None* of this would have happened! I would have had a *proper* wedding,' she screamed, 'at a *proper* place, with a *proper* number of people. Not this scrap heap of a party, with an *off-the-rack* lehenga!'

'You bribed Panditji?' asked Sharav.

Biba shook her head. 'I knew it.'

'Madam!' Without warning, Rosy Cheeks came dashing out of the kitchen door, a large tea tray in her hands. 'I'm so sorry for the delay, madam! I couldn't find the cardamom!'

As those gathered watched in horror, Amita's maid tripped over a wire and fell, launching the tea tray into the air. Diya screamed and Jyoti shouted *'My Wedgwood!'* as Rosy Cheeks tumbled down, and teacups and saucers shattered on the ground. The large teapot with pink flowers smashed, too, spraying scalding-hot tea into the plugholes of numerous extension outlets. There was a spark, then a sizzle, and finally a series of bangs, pops, and flashes as electrical connections short-circuited and fuses blew out. The generator succumbed with another, louder bang, and the entire wedding party was plunged into pitch blackness.

Everyone stood stock still, as though petrified by the dark.

'Bastards!' came a muffled shout from inside the house.

CHAPTER 37

'Guys, I don't mean to interrupt,' called Yash from farther up the now-murky driveway. 'But I have forty-five tubs of ice cream in my car.'

Samara expelled a giggle. She couldn't help it. The wedding guests were standing in the dark, there was no food and no groom. Meanwhile, Biba lamented the loss of her frozen stash by muttering to herself, Rosy Cheeks was apologising profusely while crunching what was left of the tea set under her shoes, and Nonita had started to growl dangerously.

The sheer outrageousness of the situation was . . .

Another giggle escaped her. Then the air she'd been holding in her lungs, along with all the anguish over Sharav and the stress of the evening, whooshed out in hysterical laughter. Loud and uninhibited.

After a silent moment, she heard Sharav chuckle and then break out into laughter too. A swell of happiness mended Samara's wounded spirit. *He's not going to marry her!* it squealed as it skipped over meadows filled with sun-warmed wildflowers and danced with rabbits, who played lyres as they hopped around a maypole.

Next, Diya joined in, and before Samara knew it, everyone except Nonita and her mother was laughing. There was nothing more to be done. The evening was officially over. Now they just had to tell everyone.

'Seriously? *Seriously?*'

And deal with the Kapoors, of course.

Sharav was the first to recover. 'Nonita,' he said, 'I'm so sorry it had to end like this. Obviously, we'll take care of all the expenses . . .'

'Hello?' said a voice walking towards them from inside the tent. By now, Samara's eyes had adjusted to the dark, and she could just make out a tall man in a suit. 'I heard a commotion back here,' he said. 'Can I help with the electricals? I'm an engineer.'

Amita, who'd been mostly silent until now, whispered frantically to her daughter, 'Nonita, start crying. *Now!*'

Nonita burst into tears.

'Oh, Virat,' exclaimed Amita. 'Thank God you're here!' She caught hold of Nonita and shoved her towards Virat none too gently. 'Nonita here needs to be taken home,' she whisper-shouted. 'Immediately!'

'What happened?' Virat's voice was full of concern.

A small flashlight came on in the corner before Amita could reply. Generator Guy was holding it and watching the proceedings with interest, chin in hand. 'Go on.' He waved for them to continue.

Now that they could see each other better, Samara did a double take as she beheld Virat, who looked like he should be on the cover of a romance novel about a billionaire and his secretary. She watched as he beheld Nonita quietly sobbing into her hand and put an arm around her shoulders.

'The wedding is off!' declared Amita. 'She cannot marry Sharav.'

Virat frowned at Sharav. 'Why?'

Amita sniffed. 'The groom has just informed us that he is impotent.'

A sound like a clogged blender erupted from Diya, but Yash, who was now conveniently standing right next to her, pressed his lips together and thumped her on the back. Sharav rolled his eyes and Jyoti huffed, but no one said anything. If this was how the Kapoors wanted to save face, then the onus was on the Khannas to accept it.

Preserving Nonita's reputation was obviously important to her mother, and if Sharav had to declare impotence to do that, then she knew he'd suck it up. He owed it to Nonita.

'It's a blessing my daughter found out now rather than on the wedding night! Can you *imagine*?' continued Amita. 'Anyway, *I* have decided to call off this wedding, for Nonita's sake. Yes, people will talk, but Nonita's happiness—her *future*—is more important! Don't you agree, Virat?'

'Yes, absolutely,' replied Virat. He glared at Sharav. 'I should punch you for waiting until now to inflict this ordeal upon her, but'—he glanced down at Sharav's crotch—'I'd say that's punishment enough.' He squeezed Nonita's shoulder. 'Come, I'll take you home,' he murmured.

Nonita cast Sharav a look of pure hatred from under Virat's chin but said, 'I loved you. I loved your family. I would have done *anything* for you, moved heaven and earth to make you happy. But this—to never have children of my own, to never know the joys of a happy marriage? I can't! I'm so sorry, Sharav. I can't marry you. I hope you'll forgive me someday.' She buried her face in Virat's chest, weeping delicately. It was an Oscar-worthy performance. Her mother even looked a little proud.

Virat held her to him. 'You're doing the right thing. He doesn't deserve you. Come with me.' He led Nonita away, towards the road beyond the tent.

'Take the Bentley!' called Amita after them. Once they were gone, she turned around with a contemptuous look and addressed Jyoti. 'I'm taking my guests and leaving. I'll send you the bills for everything in the morning, and we're keeping the jewellery you gifted her.' She marched back into the tent, Rosy Cheeks jogging behind her.

'You won't get the deposit back for the generator either,' Generator Guy said, sighing. He stood and returned to the garage now that the excitement was over, generously leaving the flashlight behind.

Sharav, Samara, Jyoti, Diya, Yash and Biba stood around the sea of fizzled extensions, the smell of burning hovering around them. Inside the tent, the crowd began to get restless and noisy, given that the lights hadn't come back on after a polite interval. There was work to be done—electricity to be restored, ice cream to be rescued, and excuses to be made. Yet they all just stood there.

'Well,' said Jyoti, with an air of finality.

'I'm so sorry, Ma,' said Sharav.

His mother shook her head. 'Don't be. Marriages are things of destiny, son. Besides'—she gave him a rueful smile—'despite all this, I can't help feeling a little relieved that girl isn't going to be living with us.'

'Oh God, me too!' exclaimed Diya. 'What a royal—'

'Okay, that's enough,' interjected Sharav. He gave Samara a look. 'We need to talk later, but first, I have to go wrap up this fiasco of an evening. Dhruv is in there all alone.' He strode off into the tent.

Jyoti came up to Samara, cupped her cheek in one hand, and squeezed gently. Then she went into the tent, too, followed by Diya and Yash, who ran off to unload forty-five tubs of melting ice cream from his car. Biba began to recook the food, salvaging whatever she hadn't defrosted to put back into the freezers and plating up the rest. They were going to go from no food to a feast for the ages and then leftovers for days.

'Go sit down somewhere, girl,' instructed Biba as she stirred something in a huge pan. 'Think about what you want to do next.'

Samara looked at the bubbling curry in the pan. 'I could help you,' she offered.

'No, I meant with your life.' Biba looked up and gave her a rare smile. 'You've got some decisions to make.'

Her heart began pumping faster. 'Do you think so?'

'Yes. Go sit in your room and think.'

'It's dark inside.'

'All the better for thinking,' replied Biba before returning to her cooking.

Samara stared at her for a few seconds and then slowly groped her way upstairs to her room.

Which was where she sat for hours, even after all the guests had left and the activity below her window had died down. At some point, her bedroom lights had come back on, and Samara had leapt up to turn them off again. Darkness was her friend now. She sat with it on her bed, still decked out in the gorgeous lehenga that Jyoti had insisted on buying for her, along with multicoloured navratna earrings that must have cost a fortune. In fact, Jyoti had wanted to buy the matching necklace too, before Samara convinced her that she'd have no occasion to wear such lavish jewellery in New York.

New York.

She was supposed to be leaving for the airport in a few hours. But that was before, when Sharav was getting married. Now he was single. Did she still want to go, knowing that she would be leaving the man she loved behind? Choose to live without him even while knowing they could be together?

Admittedly, she had her career to consider. The dream she'd shared with Maya about sharing an apartment in New York and getting a job there. But that dream had been borne out of her love for her best friend. Realistically, she could take on photography assignments from anywhere. She could still cover Paris Fashion Week for *Vanity Fair* with Delhi as her base. Maybe even apply to photograph other fashion weeks once she had a track record. And, truthfully, she kind of loved wedding photography, taking photos that meant the world to the people in them. It was a job she both excelled at and enjoyed.

And what about the Khannas? Could she leave them? This family, this house that she loved?

The only place she'd ever lived that felt like it loved her back?

She gasped at the realisation. Prior to her arriving in the Khanna household, Samara's entire life had been a series of transitions. Every place she'd lived in a transit terminal, just a gateway to the next. Here, for the first time, she'd felt settled. Right up until the moment she'd been forced to make a decision.

Samara had felt like she belonged.

A feeling she'd never experienced, not even with her own father.

Could she give that up?

A soft knock sounded on her door before it opened. Sharav stood silhouetted in the light of the hallway, looking exhausted and apprehensive.

The answer screamed at her from every fibre of her being. No, she couldn't give it up. Couldn't give *him* up.

She was staying. With Sharav.

Well, if he wanted her.

'Come in.'

Sharav stepped inside, shut the door, and switched on a lamp. Soft, warm light cast a glow on his skin. 'Can we talk?'

'Sure.' She didn't move.

He came and sat down on the bed in front of her. Without preamble, he said, 'Don't go.'

'Why?'

'Because I'm in love with you,' he replied, catching her eye and holding it with the intensity of his gaze. 'Because you're in love with me. Because we belong together. Because if you go now, I'll have to follow you to New York and leave behind my family and my business, and I really can't afford to do that. But I will if I have to.'

He raised his hand and pushed a tendril of hair behind her ear. 'I love you, Samara Mansingh. I'm asking you to stay. I know what you'll be giving up, but I promise to do everything in my power to make you happy and support your dreams. As long as they include me.'

The poor man had been through a lot today, including being declared impotent, so Samara decided to put him out of his misery quickly. She lifted the heavy skirt of her lehenga and moved closer, planting herself on his lap with her arms around his neck. 'Yes, my Hot Designated Driver,' she whispered before kissing him. 'I'll stay.'

His arms reached around, locking her in his embrace.

She was home.

EPILOGUE

Their hands laced together on his chest as Samara burrowed her face into that sweet spot where his shoulder dipped into his collarbone, creating a perfect nook to rest her weary head after some spirited lovemaking. As sleep tugged her eyelids closed, she remembered something. 'Damn it.'

'Now what?' asked Sharav in a gravelly voice, his limbs heavy as he lay on his back, one arm hugging her body to him.

'I forgot to pack the rain cover for my camera.'

Sharav shifted a little, sinking deeper into their bed. 'Pack it in the morning.' He slid his fingers up and down her naked back.

'I'll forget,' she replied, ignoring the goose bumps he was activating all over her body. She pushed his arm away and got out of bed.

He groaned, trying to pull her back, but she dodged his grabbing hand and padded over to the trunk where she stored her camera equipment. After pulling off the vibrant throw that covered it, she riffled through the trunk's contents. Over the course of the last year, ever since their marriage, Samara had slowly introduced her own decorating touches to Sharav's old room, hanging dream catchers and photographs on the walls and adding colourful cushions and bedding. Sharav always resisted anything new to begin with but then slowly began to love it even more than Samara did.

Their wedding had been a rushed affair, given that the bride was already residing with her in-laws and the groom was supposedly impotent. A handful of people had given Samara sympathetic glances at their ceremony, but overall, it was the wedding of her dreams. The garden had been adorned with nothing but fairy lights, and the attendees, only fifty of them, had gorged on Biba's homemade specialties. Her father and Maya had flown in, too, a thought that still brought a smile to Samara's face. At Jyoti's adamant insistence, Dilip Mansingh had stayed a *whole month* and even brushed off a tear during the kanyadaan ceremony, where he had to symbolically 'give her away' to Sharav. Maya, on the other hand, had shown up with her new roommate, who also happened to be her new boyfriend and, judging from the way he'd kissed her left palm when Sharav and Samara were declared wed by the priest, was on track to becoming her new husband.

All in all, it had worked out better than Samara could have planned.

Even for Diya and Yash, who were getting married later this year. They'd be hosting nine hundred people at their wedding reception and had categorically refused to let Samara photograph it, despite the fact that she was now a well-established photographer.

In fact, soon after her marriage, Samara had photographed a feature story for *Vanity Fair* during Paris Fashion Week. That had led to offers to cover fashion weeks in Milan, Miami, Copenhagen, and New York, where she'd stayed with Maya and they'd lived out their old dream for a few days before Samara returned home. She'd also continued photographing weddings. Come four o'clock tomorrow morning, she was flying off to shoot a destination wedding in rainy Mauritius, and once the shoot was over, Sharav would be joining her for a few days of diving.

Not to mention lovemaking without the need to be quiet because your in-laws slept just a few doors down from you.

Samara planned to moan her beach villa down. Get it out of her system before they flew back home.

After finding the rain cover, she quickly balled it up and stuffed it into her suitcase, prompting Sharav to groan again. 'Fold it properly, or it'll get crushed,' he said.

'Relax.' She climbed back into bed, shivering a little before cuddling up to her husband's sturdy warmth. 'I'll pack it again, just the way you like, in the morning.'

He kissed the top of her head. 'No, you won't,' he grumbled.

Samara smiled. 'No, I won't.' She closed her eyes and drifted off to sleep.

Acknowledgements

I find writing acknowledgements far more difficult than writing the actual book. Funny how even the most verbose people can get tongue-tied when trying to express their own feelings. So I'm going to keep this section short, as I always do, and hope that my peeps know that brevity doesn't translate into lack of appreciation in my case.

If anything, it's the opposite.

First and foremost, a HUGE shout-out to my readers, old and new. Thank you so much for your messages, reviews, and comments over the years. Thank you for buying and reading and sharing and recommending. Your support and encouragement have meant the world to me, and I have never, not once, taken them for granted. Also, if you're still reading, chances are you liked Samara and Sharav's story and might want to know about my previous or upcoming books. You can follow me on Instagram @ trishadas or email me at trishadasauthor@gmail.com for regular updates.

To my longtime friend and agent Jayapriya—a bear hug and shared shimmy. From day one, twelve years ago, you have believed in me. Your maturity, tenacity, and foresight are so very appreciated. Smita, Helen, Radhika, and Pari at Jacaranda, thank you for everything you do.

My editor, Selena—you are the best rudder, anchor, mainsail, and helm a dinghy like myself could wish for, and your thinking cap makes for a truly outstanding navigator! This book has been a departure for me in many ways, and with you, I have felt buoyed and on course (okay, now I'm done with the boat analogy). Thank you for being so kind and generous with me.

Speaking of generous—Krista, your flags during our edits were like sips of nimbu pani on a hot summer's day. Thank you for your insightful notes and for your enthusiasm and humour.

To Gabi, a full bow for giving me the opportunity to share my writing with a new readership. I lay on the floor of my study for a good ten minutes when Jay told me you loved my writing voice. My family thought I was having a seizure. Thank you.

To the team at Amazon Publishing—production editors Lauren Grange and Kellie Osborne, copyeditors Rachel Norfleet and Iris Winslow, proofreader Bill Siever, art director Jarrod Taylor, marketing manager Rachael Clark, author relations manager Sarah Shaw, PR representative Paige Hazzan, and Alex Levenberg—you've been every author's dream come true. Thank you for making this book your own.

To my editor in India, Sivapriya—you totally bowled over my anxious, little writer-heart when you compared my writing to Georgette Heyer's. Thank you for believing in this novel and for being so open, warm and inclusive in all our conversations.

To the team at Bloomsbury Publishing in India—thank you for taking on this book and flying with it.

To Miel—thank you for taking the initiative to illustrate this amazing cover for the Indian edition. You are very talented and I wish you so much success.

To my tribe of friends and family, who drag me out of my cave and make me live in the sunlight, my deepest affection and gratitude. To Rajiv Mehrotra, my eternal thanks for kicking off both my film and writing careers.

To Ma and Naniji, my mother and grandmother, to whom this book is dedicated, my undying devotion. Ma, you continue to shape my life every day, despite the distance. Naniji, I miss you. A lot.

Pops, Vir, R, and J—my astrology chart says I'm a good-luck charm for all the men in my life. You're welcome!

Deeps—soulmate, teammate, best friend, and every other corny cliché in the book—I think your frown line is sexy too.

b . . . my gratitude, as always.

Finally, I must mention the late Georgette Heyer, whose books have left an indelible mark on my writing. I grew up reading Heyer's romances, and this novel is a humble homage to her unforgettable characters and flawless comedic timing.

About the Author

Trisha Das is the author of *Ms Draupadi Kuru: After the Pandavas* and its sequel, *The Misters Kuru: A Return to Mahabharata*; *Kama's Last Sutra*; *The Mahabharata Re-imagined*; and *How to Write a Documentary Script*. Her work has appeared in *Cosmopolitan*, *Harper's Bazaar*, *Grazia India*, *Hindustan Times*, and the anthology *Magical Women*, among others. Trisha has also written and directed more than forty documentaries, is the winner of the Indian National Film Award, and was named University of Georgia's International Artist of the Year. Her films have been screened at international film festivals and on the Discovery Channel, the Star Network, and NDTV and have helped propel funding for grassroots social change across India. You can find Trisha on Instagram @trishadas or email her at trishadasauthor@gmail.com.